VARIETAL
TENDENCIES

Book I of the Crush Chronicles

by
Michael J. Caldwell

with recipes by Shawna Caldwell

Tannin Ink Press

ISBN: 0-9661486-0-6

Published by Tannin Ink Press
2375 Montello, Hood River, Or 97031
email: tannin@linkport.com

Cover design and layout by Shawna Caldwell
Cover Art Copyright © 1997 Shawna Caldwell

First Edition

Manufactured in the U.S.A.

For Shawna

Acknowledgments

Many thanks to the incredible staff at Tannin Ink Press, especially my editor, Travis Neal, who hates it when I enclose people in commas   thanks man.   And Jeff Lesselyoung for giving color, depth, and life to Be There Bennett.   And Mom, for teaching me to love books. When I was little she used to read to me with a diaper on her lap to keep away my younger brother Matt, who didn't like having his pants changed too much (love you, bro). And my dad, for throwing me pop-flies until dark in his suit after an hour commute from work, very cool.   Many thanks to the Flerchinger Family, especially Don. You've taught me a lot and we've barely scratched the surface.   Here's to many good crushes in the future.   Joe, it's your year to come in late at night and punch down the grapes. The village of Hood River Valley.   All of our grape growers.   All my coaches and teachers including Hukari (thanks for Ken Follett, Phil), Sawyer, Bassham, Greenough, Graves, Einarsson, Price, Burton, Elliott, Level, Moore, Wolff, Masters, Bohlmann, Kallok, and many more   nice work, people.   Most of all, my beautiful wife Shawna, I still can't believe we actually met. Thank you for your patience and encouragement through all of this. And thank you for that darn fish and wine bottle lithograph on the cover that got this whole thing started. "Wow, that's cool," I said, over two years ago. "That'd make a great book cover. . . ."

AUTHOR'S NOTE

This is a work of fiction. Honest. There is no evil empire known as the Washington Wine Guild; I made it up. The flashbacks to World War II and Vietnam War era are meant to entertain and remind, not educate. Millions and millions of people died in those wars and there's certainly nothing funny about that.

I got my start in the wine industry just after graduating from high school. I was hired as the "banquet set up kid" at the Columbia Gorge Hotel in the Hood River Valley. As luck would have it, the wine cellar was next to the ballroom. The Maitre 'd was swamped (as they all are) with inventory, a new summer staff to train, and a new computer system. To my surprise, he asked me to help build new wine racks and computerize the 1200 or so bin numbers for the cellar. As I cataloged the various wines, I became intrigued by the diversity of grapes, regions, and prices. Without knowing it (as I read book after book late into the night about wine for the fun of it) I was learning about one of the most interesting topics in the world.

My favorite author often discloses the meaning of his books in the preface. Or at least he tries to convince himself that it was worth writing in the first place. And so I ramble, too. Because, for some strange reason, I used up countless kilowatts and trees to say this . . . There is no better time than now to be in love and enjoy good food and wine. That's it. That's the whole point. Oh, one other thing, "Varietal" is a term used to describe a characteristic found in a glass of wine, NOT a type of plant or a type of wine. "Tendencies" are habitual patterns of behavior that approach compulsive . . . never mind, if you get it, you get it. Nuff said. If you're legally old enough to enjoy a bottle of wine while reading this, do so. It can't hurt.

                                                        -M.C.

VARIETAL
TENDENCIES

1

This was only the first of seven courses and Jack Miller was already having trouble staying awake. He'd spent the entire day training a new pruning crew and barely had enough time to shower before tonight's dinner. He looked at the bubbles climbing inside his glass and smiled, thinking about the oversized bed waiting in his hotel room   free cable and golf, completing the package. He reached for the glass of sparkling wine and despaired as a small roll of winter fat vaulted over his belt and landed softly in the hammock of his shirt. This was just the third in a long series of winemaker's dinners for the year and Jack had already gained seven pounds. Oh well, he thought, rubbing the lazy pouch; it's still winter - for another week.

He'd agreed to the lengthy series of appearances at the urging of his distributor. The hotel chain had bid very generously for 1,200 cases of a poorly-rated vintage that was just months away from gourmet vinegar. The fact that they charged him for the upgrade to a hot tub room made it very clear to Jack that they knew they were doing him a favor. Quid pro quo. The hotel's wine buyer, having an experienced palate, suggested the catering department could sell the wine during the upcoming wedding season before the slight onion smell developed into full-blown rotten eggs.

At least a couple of the hotels were nearby and he could drive home in the morning. And, Jack had to admit, the hotel guests were definitely upscale and well worth cultivating. How better to promote your label than over pan-seared rack of lamb and pinot noir at someone else's expense? Besides, he thought, dinners like this could sell hundreds of cases of wine in the futures market alone; so what if a 60-year-old widow in sequins kept rubbing his leg.

The first few minutes of the evening were always the toughest on Jack. People at wine dinners always wanted to know about his Grandfather Henry, but thought it might be too rude to ask. This led to several inane questions about Jack's winery when no one was really paying attention to what he said. They were just being polite. Henry Mueller was still an icon in the California wine industry, despite his 85 years, and everyone wanted to know what being his grandson was like. Jack had learned from watching his dad to alleviate the discomfort by offering an update on Henry without being asked.

"On behalf of the Eugene Little League Association, I want to thank you all for your generous contributions. The new uniforms and equipment will make this summer a lot nicer for a lot of kids," he said, looking around the large table.

"I know how curious you all are about Henry and Rose Mueller, as well as my dad. As the night progresses, don't be shy about asking questions. But feel free to ask about my winery anytime, too. Let me just start by saying that Henry and Rose are healthy and their business is doing great   for you stockholders in the room." Jack smiled and continued. "Their production this year will exceed 3.5 million cases of premium table wines. That's roughly 8 million gallons of wine, and over twenty thousand acres of grapes. Three times the total produced here in the Beaver State. A little perspective: I'll make just a hair over nine thousand cases if all goes well. Dad will bottle about sixty thousand cases and that's one of the larger by Oregon standards."

The guests pondered the numbers for a moment with wide eyes and confusion, still somewhat intimidated by the legacy the 28-year-old winemaker regarded so casually. How could a kid come to such a gala event wearing a shirt that said "Oregon Wine   It's The Acid"?

A flock of waiters, dressed as penguins, filled the room and removed the caviar. The pinot gris was poured and the fresh,

[2]

floral aromas filled the air. "I hope you enjoyed the sparkling wine. That creamy yeast texture and deep mid-palate is what got my dad to move to Oregon in the first place," Jack said, referring to his dad's bubbly blend of chardonnay and pinot noir grapes. Another fluid sweep by the wait staff produced a strange-looking plate of wafer thin smoked duck and wild grains. Jack savored the contrast of the smoky meat with the crisp, melon flavors of the wine. This chef knows his stuff, he thought, observing a room filled with blank stares.

The duck was cleared without a flaw and Jack relaxed into his chair. He could feel the farmer falling asleep as the winemaker slowly took over his body. He reached for the heavy fish knife and gently tapped his glass.

The mood during a winemakers dinner always takes a positive turn at the seafood course. The wine has flowed freely for about an hour by then, and the lifelong, two-hour friendships between strangers have formed. The lighting appears softer and the questions less awkward. The stress of the world is washed away by the only thing they have in common. Jack had seen it a hundred times before; even he wasn't immune to the narcotic effect that prosperity had on people.

A dinner like this celebrated much more than grape and food. It celebrated success. And that was only fair as far as he was concerned. Most of these people didn't care about the sugar level at harvest, or the pH after primary fermentation. They wanted to meet someone who did, and share their appreciation for their own good fortune with people who felt the same. The seafood offering was just a dividend to most of these people, an actual course after suffering through two attempts at Picasso cuisine. The overwhelming joy of food they recognized, paired with a wine they could pronounce, inevitably lead to admiration for their host. The proverbial salmon and chardonnay was served and all was well with the world.

Looking around the large room, Jack saw the familiar glow in the faces of his guests and, feeling the time was right, slowly rose from his velvet chair and nodded to everyone at the table while tapping his glass. He had watched his grandfather, and then father, do the same thing in the same lavish style of dining room for many years. Even some of the guests were aware that it was a family tradition to lead off the descriptive portion of the dinner with an insult for the chef, foregoing the usual blather about their amazing "gift" or "ability," to find the essence of the wine through their subtle use of spices. It started long ago in Napa with Grandpa Henry roasting Grandma Rose during the annual crush celebrations. It was now a ritual anticipated by almost everyone seated at a table with the Millers.

"Ladies and gentlemen," he said calmly. "Thank you for your kind comments about tonight's wines. I hope that some of you still have room for the entree." His sarcasm was greeted with a few nervous chuckles that grew into genuine laughter when some of the husbands realized he was making fun of the portions to the dismay of some of the more refined ladies in attendance, especially the chef's wife. "Apparently, the chef wants to leave as much room as possible for the wine."

Jack smiled at the group, enjoying the shock value for a moment. Then, sensing the awkward tension, proposed a toast to further break the ice as well as the chef's back.

"Just kidding, folks," he said, speaking with the sudden sincerity of a Catholic at confession. "Here's to the wonderful presentation of cuisine so far, and two ounce portion of lamb in the future . . . including the bone."

The chain-smoking Cadillac dealer seated to Jack's right, wearing a large pinky ring that resembled the car company's famous hood emblem, slowly coughed his way to laughter and slapped the widow's thigh in satisfaction while snorting amens to the table, obviously agreeing with Jack about the chef's apparent lack of generosity thus far.

Oregon manners were long gone at this point. The guests, consisting of members of Eugene's more prominent business community, were well into their adolescent phase for the evening and Jack was assured another moment or two of brilliance while coasting through the final three courses. The formal behavior that usually strangled an evening like this could now only be found among the wait staff. All were careful to serve from the left and avoid the widow in sequins except one, who caught Jack's eye and made him forget his Grandpa's joke about which spoon to use next.

The wait staff had conspired, as usual, to avoid certain hazards that a night like this presents well in advance. The widow, seated in between the car dealer and Jack, had become their "white elephant" for the night. The pleasure of serving her was passed down the seniority train, course by course, until the newest male member of the banquet staff was stuck for the rest of the night changing ashtrays and getting checked for a hernia each time he refilled her wine glass. The cruelty of such a thing was too much for Maria to handle. The young waitress volunteered to serve the widow from the sorbet on. The other waiters merely bowed in thanks as she proceeded towards the danger zone with an air of confidence and nonchalance. "Gee, Maria, you're really too kind," the maitre d' quipped, knowing full well that she wanted to use this opportunity to meet the handsome grandson of Henry Mueller.

Jack had regained his tempo at this point and was ready to continue his presentation when he caught a whiff of Maria's hair as she cleared the widow's salmon. She was unable to clear from the right, because the car dealer was whispering something to the widow about a condo in Sunriver and a casino on the way. She quietly excused herself as she brushed gently against Jack's arm, careful to extract the plate of food and not interrupt the flow of the meal. The damage, however, was done. BANG! Jack recognized the scent rainforest, intelligence, wit, and charm. It had it all. Like a $55 bottle of Bordeaux, her hair possessed qualities that poets dream about. He was lost. Luckily, the chef's wife recovered the momentum by asking the typical idiotic question about the use of sulfites in his wines.

"Yeah, uh, sulfites . . . good question," Jack responded. He was still taken with the scent of Maria's hair that was quickly losing a battle with the widow's Pall Malls. "The wine industry as a whole owes a great deal of thanks to the ancient Greeks for their discovery of sulfur and its use in the fermentation sciences." He wasn't quite sure where the answer came from, but he was happy with it nonetheless.

"Exactly how did the 'ancient Greeks' know to use sulfur in wine?" she replied, somewhat displeased that his answer was less than an answer.

"Well," Jack said, "the way I heard it, they observed the gases that escaped from volcanic vents and noticed the large number of insects that died as they passed through the vapors. The gas was comprised mostly of sulfur and the rest, as they say, is history."

The widow looked up at Jack and, as soon as she regained focus in her left eye, blurted "It's the damn sulfuric acids that give me a headache, isn't it?"

Before Jack could answer, her gaze had drifted to the city lights twinkling fifteen stories below the restaurant. Any response on his behalf would only complicate things. At least the proceeds are going to charity, he thought, shaking his head in disbelief.

"Does anyone else have any questions?"

"Is it t–true that you're named after J–J–Jack Kerouac?" a young man stammered from across the room.

"Uh, yes, I guess I am," Jack cringed. "My mom and dad were pretty close to all those guys, as some of you probably know. The whole hippie, Berkeley thing was going on right in their backyard, and they just jumped right in with both feet. I think I came out okay though, considering they named my brother Skye and my sister Sunflower."

The table had to pause for another round of laughter from the Cadillac man while a cherry sorbet was served in frozen glasses with fresh mint as a garnish. Maria began to pour an ounce of sparkling wine over the flavored ice in front of Jack and, as she twisted the bottle to finish the pour, smiled in the usual 'excuse me' way that servers do. Jack blushed from the unintentional gesture, taking a moment to create a scenario where he was the object of her uncontrollable lust.

"Is there an ideal temperature to store wine at my house?" a lady seated to his left asked.

"It depends on a lot of things," he replied, still groggy from his intimate encounter with the sorbet goddess. "If you buy a young red and want it to last for ten years, then I recommend 56 degrees. If you buy something that is three or four years old and you're going to drink it in a few months, then room temp is fine."

"Do you grow your own grapes?" she asked quickly.

"Most of the grapes I use are from the old family vineyards near Salem. My dad hogs the best fruit that comes from the Dundee vineyards, but there are a lot of good grape growers around the Eugene area who will sell a few tons here and there. I have about 200 acres here in Eugene that are in their fourth season and I'm looking forward to using them for the first time in this year's crush."

"What does your shirt mean?"

Jack smiled at the logo on the breast of his denim shirt. "It's an old family joke. I had it made to tease my mom and dad about their quest for titratable acidity. They were drawn to the cooler temperatures of Oregon for winemaking, hoping that if the grapes ripened from sun and season length instead of outright heat, they would retain their natural balance of sugar and acid. They were right. But it goes a little further than that, you know, the hippie stuff; their vision quest on LSD which, by the way, was legal at the time - results in the discovery of tartaric acid and so on. It's kind of complicated, but funny."

"Funny on dope," said the widow. "Beatnik farmers on drugs is more like it, huh?" Her tone was strangely seductive, almost intelligent, perhaps even enlightened.

"Hardly," said Jack, sharing a moment of eye contact with the widow. She held his stare and smiled, telling him to relax and continue without a word. She meant no harm, just having a little fun. "Actually, Dad wasn't anything close to being a hippie. It's his kids we have to worry about. He's always been very committed to growing grapes and making the best wines possible. I had the shirt made just to give them a hard time. Oregon has always been perceived as a refuge for hippies and Dad hates that image. They came here to raise grapes and a family. Mom studied law at Willamette University."

The waiters circled the table and, at an overly dramatic nod from the maitre d', gently presented a beautiful rack of lamb to the ladies on their right. The Dijon crust was slightly cracked and the translucent flesh of the animal was shining through the openings. Sprigs of tarragon and rosemary balanced slices of mandarin orange in the cradle of bones at the top of the plate. The aroma was dazzling. A second wave of servers repeated the performance for the gentlemen at the table, all of whom, for a brief moment, savored the feeling of royalty. Jack was impressed by the widow's sudden attentiveness to the task at hand as she somehow managed to hold a cigarette and lamb bone in her right hand while her left hand continued to rest on his thigh.

"I've had a little fun tonight at the chef's expense, and I want to make sure that everyone knows that it's customary in my family to keep the kitchen humble and on their toes. When you see, smell, and taste an offering of this magnitude, you understand the little jabs we 'shoe-makers' take at the their egos. Any attempt to give sincere praise is futile. Ya' just end up sounding stupid. So we have always shown respect and adoration through the jibe. A farmer's most honest form of thanks." He raised his glass again, and looking at everyone in a slow, deliberate stare, simply said, "Let's eat this goat."

"Here, here," chortled the Cadillac man.

The young lady on his left slowly tasted the wine that had just been poured from large, black bottles bearing no label. She paused and then, experiencing something completely foreign to

[8]

her memory, nearly choked at the sensation. The wine secreted passion, warmth, and comfort to her body. She joked to herself for a second that this must be what heroin is like. Her delight forced a childish giggle to escape. Afraid that it would be misunderstood, she glanced at her husband to explain; the look in his eyes mirrored her feelings exactly. They smiled at each other for the first time in weeks. Literally short of breath and slightly confused, she asked Jack to describe the wine.

"It's like smelling a bowl of crushed herbs, isn't it?" he said, swirling the glass under his nose. "This is the '94 Reserve Pinot Noir, not too bad at all. Tons of dill and raspberry on the nose. The chef set this wine up perfectly with a little anisette in the demiglace. Look at that color!" He saw the euphoria on the diners' faces and continued thoughtfully. "The pinot noir is capable of such greatness. Layer upon layer of complexity: aroma, depth, color, and texture   this damn grape has it all. Nothing comes close when it's this good. It's too bad it's so hard to make large quantities of it."

"What makes it so hard?" the woman asked, still somewhat giddy.

"Well, Mother Nature for one. Remember, it's farming first, then it's winemaking. And farming is a very risky business, especially with grapes in Oregon." He smiled, looking at his wine glass. "But it's worth it most of the time. We get a lot lower yields per acre than most of California, so that makes it more expensive. And pinot noir by its nature is a very delicate grape, so it requires a lot of extra care during processing. It took forty people over eight hours just to sort these grapes for the crusher. That type of handling doesn't pencil out for every vintage. It's a gamble in Oregon. Grandpa has it made; he hasn't had a bad year in two decades. Can you imagine that?"

"Do you or your dad talk to Henry very much?"

Jack laughed. "Both of us, all the time. He's always ragging us about moving back to California and making some real wine, when he's not telling his war stories."

[9]

"D-d-does he like your w-wines?"

"He'd never admit it if he did. He thinks that pinot noir is for little girls. Even the great ones from Burgundy. Sunflower said he tried some of the pinot gris and was pretty impressed, though. But she could get him to try anything."

"Do you have a 'varietal totem' too?"

"Uh oh, someone's read Henry's biography," Jack replied with a big smile. "Yes, I do. It's cabernet sauvignon. When I was little I called it 'shabernet caucasian.' Henry thought that was the funniest thing he'd ever heard. He couldn't resist pinning me with it for the rest of my life. The bastard. My dad thinks he did it just to make me unhappy in Oregon. They still fight about it. Nothing serious, you know; they just bicker over it all the time."

"Excuse me, what's a varietal totem?"

"Well, when they're a kid, everyone in the family is nicknamed for a certain grape. No big deal, you know, just a nickname. Grandpa Henry chooses it, and for some strange reason it's been really accurate. It's kind of spooky how grapes and people share the same characteristics. My dad's, for instance, is pinot noir. He's always been extremely shy and meticulous. He doesn't like contact sports and he has a very cool temperament. Some people would call him a sissy, but in the right environment he's a genius, capable of anything. It's the same with pinot noir. It can be the richest, most complicated wine on earth. Get it?"

"Do ya' think Henry would like this wine?" Cadillac man asked, cramming his huge gin blossom nose into his wine glass.

"In a blind tasting, he'd spit it out and kick my dogs for trying to trick him. It's more than liking the wine to Henry; it's the whole California against the world thing. When you produce three and a half million cases of wine a year, everyone is your competitor."

"Do you like California wines?"

"Most consistent wines on the planet. Really. I joke with Henry that I'm a California wine man stuck in an Oregonian's body. He loves that. He says that's what I get for studying psychology instead of enology." Jack paused, smiling at the thought of his Grandpa.

"You didn't go the wine school?" the widow asked loudly.

"Shhh! Don't tell the grapes! Just kidding. I grew up in a kind of wine school. My dad spent most of his inheritance on research and development. We had test vineyards and fermenters going everywhere all the time. It was crazy."

"What other wines d–d–do you like?"

"The blended wines from Washington are easily the best value on the market right now. The cab/merlots and sem/chards have BIG fruit and good flavor. I shouldn't say it, but they have a very good future in the high-end wine market, too. There's already a thief or two up there making a fortune on each bottle."

"D–do you have any l–l–land up there?"

"No, not yet. My aunt has some massive orchards in the Yakima area, but nothing in the way of grapes yet."

"Is that the one that gave everything to the Rajneeshpuram?"

"Oh yeah, that's the one! She tried to give everyone's stuff away. I guess the Bhagwan needed some apples or something. What a drama that was. Fifty-five attorneys for ten people. It's still a mess. There were long-term leases issued and lawsuits filed left and right. We're still not sure who owns what. That was the only time I ever saw my dad lose his temper."

"What's your aunt's totem pole?" hacked the widow.

Jack smiled at her politely, looking around the room for help. "Cherise, according to Henry, is blessed with all the characteristics of the petite sirah. As a child her hair was black as coal and her eyes were big and brown. She was a brat until after lunch and always had to have her way. The multiple personality thing didn't come until much later but it makes a lot of sense now; there's a jumble of shiraz, syrah, petite sirah, Durif, and Rhones, so it's hard to keep up with it all. Maybe she couldn't either. We always called her Syrah, so maybe that didn't help matters."

[11]

The young waitress made sure to keep her hair out of Jack's face as she cleared his plate. The other waiters were teasing her because the maitre d' was obviously jealous that Jack couldn't keep his eyes off of her. She knew her attraction to Jack would fade, as usual, and decided her little flirtations could only do more harm than good. The last thing she needed was to get phased early or loose some shifts because of a hurt ego. Darn Geminis' she joked to herself, great friends but moody managers.

Maria's caution didn't make any difference to Jack. He was captivated. He watched her walk to the kitchen while he thought about how to get an introduction. The wait staff gathered at the pass-through and watched with joy as the maitre d' tried to attract Jack's attention with a secretive whisper about the next course. She failed twice to break Jack's stare, then with her feelings crushed, she finally tapped him on the shoulder to gain his ear. The table was silent. With a full stomach and pink face, the Cadillac man winked at Jack and asked him what he wanted for dessert.

"Chocolate, cheese, cognac, cigar," he said, and walked towards the bar, his eyes firmly locked on the place where Maria had disappeared.

🍇 🍇 🍇

2

Private Henry Mueller watched the French countryside roll by from the front seat of the jeep. It was the nicest military vehicle he'd ever seen, perfect in every detail. Even the driver was impeccably dressed. In two years of active duty, Henry had never been escorted anywhere. He was still dirty and tired from fighting when his orders for transfer came through. The jeep had arrived just a few minutes later so he'd barely had time to pack.

The Axis stronghold in southern France had been weakened just a few days prior. The addition of American troops in the area had further diminished Italy's fondness for Hitler and Mussolini. Germany had problems of their own with fronts to the north, east, and west. The Allied forces had stepped up their presence in the region, so conflict did not appear likely. The liberation of Southeastern France was imminent; the campaign moved into a phase of recovery.

General Nelson T. Bennett was a fifth generation commander from the great state of Virginia. His ancestry included several ambassadors, three senators and one governor, all of whom were graduates from the Virginia Academy of Military Science, including himself. His great grandfather had dined, on many occasions, with Thomas Jefferson at the famous vineyards of Monticello. In the classic tradition of the military elite, General Bennett had consumed volumes of literature about the arts, science, and history. He was considered by his superiors to be the brightest man stationed in Europe. His ability to mobilize thousands of men and tons of supplies with equal efficiency had earned him the nickname of "Be There Bennett."

The only thing Bennett enjoyed more in life than conversation about military strategy was wine. His passion for the grape, its growers, and masters was perhaps his only flaw. He became absorbed by the world of wine after his first taste of Clos Vougeot in 1912, understanding instantly the diplomatic lengths that Thomas Jefferson had gone to secure a stable relationship with France well-over a century before.

As the jeep approached the general's tent, Henry saw stacks of wooden boxes he recognized instantly. They didn't contain guns or ammunition as one would expect at a military installation. They were full of wine. His heart raced at the thought. After

[13]

three attempts at talking to the driver with no response, Henry eagerly waited for the jeep to stop at the entrance to the quarters.

He was greeted warmly by a man he'd only seen in the papers. It was Be There Bennett. Shocked at the general's pleasant demeanor, Henry saluted and relaxed without waiting for the customary "at ease, Private," which came fast enough anyway. The general was holding two glasses of wine that, to the unknowing eye, appeared brown and lifeless. He smiled at Henry as he looked him over from head to toe.

"You been enjoying yourself up north, Mueller?"

"Sir, yes sir. Fighting the Germans, sir!"

"Don't bull shit me, Mueller. Here, try this," Bennett said calmly. He handed Henry a glass and gestured for the young man to give it a try.

Henry held it up to the light and gave it a very sophisticated swirl. The quick motion created a torrent in the glass that continued as he brought it to his nose. He repeated both steps before tasting the wine. General Bennett was delighted by the performance of his newest reconnaissance man. Henry gazed thoughtfully at the wine as a flood of childhood memories drowned his senses. His brother Merle was throwing warm clusters of fermenting grapes at him; their father was laughing as he watched his two boys walk through the enormous vats up to their waists in wine.

"Strange, sir," Henry said, still thinking of Napa.

"What do you mean, Mueller?" asked Bennett.

Henry hesitated. "Eighty-five miles from Italy, in the heart of French vineyards, surrounded by the greatest wines of the world, and you serve me a ten-year-old Inglenook from Napa?"

General Bennett couldn't hold back his pleasure. "I'll be damned; those snobs in England were right! I just wanted you to feel at home, Mueller. Come on. Step inside and let me fill you in on your new assignment. I think you're really going to like it."

🍇 🍇 🍇

3

Blake Stewart looked at himself in the mirror and almost cried. His face, despite his bedtime prayers, was still badly contorted towards the left ear. The muscle spasms from the palsy would go away, according to his doctor; he would just have to cope with the goofy smile for a few long months. His newly-acquired stutter, however, was a complete mystery. Ten thousand dollars' worth of diagnostic testing and C.A.T. scans had turned up nothing. He thought he had handled the stress of the bar exams without a hitch. Apparently, he was wrong. His speech, face, and career were a mess.

The hangover from last night's wine dinner was just starting to come on. The three glasses of water and three aspirin he remembered to take before bed had done little to protect him from the Cadillac man and Jack Miller. Drinking one's way through the alphabet was something new to Blake, especially after five glasses of wine.

The phone rang louder than ever before and Blake turned to pick it up.

"Hello, Mr. Stewart."

"Uh . . . yes, t–t–this is Mr. Stewart."

"Good morning! This is your 8 a.m. wake up call. It's currently 48 degrees and raining. Have a nice day!"

He hung up the phone and laughed at the thought of coming to Eugene for some good weather and golf. It's not that much different than Seattle, he thought. The sky was gray and the wind was blowing very hard. He sat on the bed and contemplated suicide and eggs. He chose the eggs. As he reached for the phone to call room service, it rang again.

"Hello?"

"Stewart!"

"Yeah, Spalding, it's m-me."

"How did the dinner go?"

"Uh, fine. It was great. He makes some d-damn good wine. The f-food was incredible."

"Are you kidding me? Do you think I care about the food?"

"Oh . . . yeah, sorry. I'm a little out of it."

"Does he know about the land?" asked Spalding.

"Yes. He said it w-was his aunt's, though. He said that the Bhagwan m-m-must of liked his apples."

"Apples?" Spalding West laughed in a mocking voice. "It's even better than I thought. How many acres does he know about?"

"He used the phrase 'm-massive orchards'."

"Hmmm. Are you meeting him today?"

"I'm not sure," Blake replied timidly.

"What do you mean, 'you're not sure'?" Spalding shouted.

"I'm not sure."

"You drunk bastard. You don't remember!"

The voice was screechy and abrasive. Blake rolled his eyes as Spalding continued to spew threats into the phone. I used to beat up guys like this all the time, he thought to himself.

"Okay, Spalding . . . yeah, no problem. T-talk to ya later."

Blake had to call Jack Miller and confirm his appointment for today. He was pretty sure they had talked about it last night between the Kamikaze and Long Island Iced Tea.

Spalding had made it very clear to Blake: get Jack to renew the lease on the land in Yakima or find a new job.

"Damn stutter," Blake said, looking at his crooked face in the mirror. "If I could talk I'd be in a courtroom making a hundred grand a year, n-not kissing some idiot's butt in probate."

4

"Mai Tai, Nelson's Blood, Old-Fashioned, Presbyterian. . . ." Jack groaned as he tried to remember what came after 'P' in the cocktail alphabet. The whole evening was nothing but a haze. His eyes were closed and he was still in bed. How many of those things did he really drink and how many did he pour into that car dealer's glass? That guy was amazing. He had three Zombies and a glass of Port before calling it quits. The guy with the funny face was drooling on himself after the Fuzzy Navel. How on earth could the maitre d' keep serving us that long?

The sun was definitely up but there was little chance of it shining through the usual dung that hovered above Eugene in the spring. That, coupled with the pounding in his head, made it easy for Jack to lay in bed for a few more hours of cartoons. The hot tub looked great, but it was twelve feet away.

He usually kept his consumption to a minimum when he was at a dinner like this. It was much more professional to exhibit moderation and respect for alcohol. That's all he'd heard growing up. He had watched his dad Anthony spit wine out at several functions in the past. When would he ever learn?

Last night he had gone to the bar hoping to meet the waitress after her shift. The introduction the maitre d' had promised never came. A deluge of free cocktails did, however, as did an endless supply of crude jokes courtesy of the Cadillac man.

Jack couldn't stop saying her name as he lay there motionless, the words escaping through a mouthful of soiled kitty litter in a long, slow, mumbling sound. "Mmmaariiiaaa."

The perfect cure for Jack's hangover was only a few short

hours a way. A bowl of Sunday night chili with Mom and Dad was too good to be true. He could feel the cumin and cayenne ripping the formaldehyde from his liver as he fell asleep. Maria's face faded into darkness. He would live to drink another day.

5

The interior of General Bennett's supply tent was simply massive. The first forty or fifty feet contained nothing but paintings stacked on top of each other. A small aisle led past mounds of candlesticks, vases, and picture frames. Several clerks were cataloging the stolen treasures into a ledger. Most of the items were already tagged or labeled in some fashion.

As they walked into an adjoining room, Henry was stirred by a familiar aroma. The general walked over to a box and carefully opened the lid. He retrieved two very large cigars and smiled at Henry. He put down his wine glass and offered him a cigar. Henry was startled when the general proceeded to light it for him.

"Thank you, sir," Henry said absently. His attention was focused on the pallets of boxes identical to the one the general had just opened. "Excuse me, General, but are all those boxes full?"

"Son, what you see behind me," Bennett said, turning to look at the thousands of boxes, "is one of the most powerful tools of diplomacy in all of Europe. Do you have any idea what that wind-bag Churchill would trade for just one box of these Cubans?"

"I'm sorry, General, but isn't he on our side?"

"Oh, Mueller, we're wrapping this thing up," Bennett said, referring to the war. "You've seen what's left nothing. Now it's a matter of finding what's gone across the borders and returning it to its rightful owners. Minus a small commission, of course. That's where we come in."

"We, sir?"

"Well, you. My reputation is on the line, Mueller. I sent four men to recover sixty cases of grand cru that turned out to be grand pew. I was the laughing stock of the Quebec Hearings for that fiasco. It's your primary responsibility to field test and approve every cache of alcohol you discover. You've been around wine all your life. You know the difference between swill and thrill. You leave for Italy in the morning. Understood?"

"Yes, sir," Henry said, smiling from ear to ear.

"Millions of cases have crossed the borders, Mueller. Your job is to find the good ones and get them back where they belong. And don't waste my time with any garbage. Sample everything."

6

The two-hour drive from Eugene to Salem requires about two minutes of concentration including the on and off ramps. The straight shot north through the heart of the Willamette Valley was still a challenge for Jack; his body was numb from dehydration. Traffic was moving a little fast for his current state of mind. He clung safely to the right-hand lane, unaware his turn signal was flashing. The rain had transformed a normally pleasant Sunday drive into a white-knuckled hell. His mind wandered back and forth from Maria to the aquatic gauntlet ahead, thinking of his mom's chili as he avoided the waves of water thrown his way by the tractor-trailers.

The Willamette Valley features some of the world's most fertile soil. Tucked between the soggy coastal range and the volcanic Cascades, it produces an amazing array of agricultural products. The moderate winters and long, warm summers provide an ideal climate for almost anything you stick in the ground. The massive valley is also home to several universities, large cities, and one freeway. Commercial grapes arrived here about a hundred years after the first settlers completed the Oregon Trail. A new industry was born. The sun, soil, and affordable land gave hope to a new generation of winemakers. All of whom were anxious to make a living and enjoy life while pursuing one of the world's most frustrating yet rewarding occupations.

Anthony Miller is considered by many to be as much a pioneer as those who arrived in Oregon by covered wagon. His innovative vineyard practices and mail-order distribution legitimized the bottom line for many Northwest wineries. As a son of California wine, he reluctantly became a father of pinot noir, combining science, hard work, and marketing to create demand for an unknown commodity. Always aware of the business side but more concerned with quality, Anthony made wines that people enjoyed, and generated profit. In a region where grass seed was king, the elusive wine of kings from Burgundy flourished, turning heads around the world towards a little place called Oregon.

His decision to grow pinot noir in Oregon was no fluke. He and his young wife Lisa had tasted the wine in France while studying the production of Champagne during a business trip for Henry. They had tried their hand at pinot noir in California with little success, producing wonderful wines that were thick and chewy, but lacking the ultimate feature of varietal character   the nose. The wines they enjoyed in Burgundy were unlike anything they had ever tasted   they were elegant and bold with the incredible aromas of earth, smoke, and leather. They were also hypnotic and affordable. A person could, after a little practice, taste the soil and smell the air in which the grapes were grown. More than once on a Sunday drive, the car stopped suddenly and Lisa or Anthony shouted "This is it! These are the vines. There, do you smell it?" They would immediately throw down a blanket and consume a bottle or two in the wine's 'terroir' (or point of origin), smiling as they smelled their glasses and then the air. Jack's younger sister Sunflower was the happy result of a terroir tour.

After drinking their way through Burgundy (now a generic term for bad wine thanks to California), the only common characteristic they found in pinot noir was its inconsistency. Anthony marveled at the diversity of flavors he found in a single village. After talking with numerous growers, he found that very little technical information was available about this phenomenon. The seed was planted. Anthony's quest for varietal perfection had begun.

Unfortunately, Henry and Rose rarely served French wines at home and if they did, it was only Bordeaux   a silly imperfection of Henry's that would cause great strife for a remarkable family. Anthony's and Lisa's love for pinot noir produced in its proper environment led them to Oregon.   And Rose would never completely forgive them for moving, nor would she forgive Henry for calling Anthony his little Pinot as a child. A harmless jab that Henry said referred to Anthony's frequent colds and allergic reactions, and the fact that the other kids routinely beat him up like a neutered cat. But Rose always knew better and so did Anthony. He would eventually prove that being called Pinot Noir was no insult.

Jack pulled off the highway and headed for his mom and dad's house. Thanks for the rainstorm, he thought to himself. His fatigue (not to mention his bad breath and anemic appearance) from last night could now be explained by the concentration required to stay on the road.

🍇 🍇 🍇

7

Henry took a bath for the first time in several months. It was an elegant latrine, to say the least. Enjoying hot water from a tap and privacy, he was in heaven. His second cigar of the evening burned slowly on the edge of the tub, a glass of rare cognac in his hand. If only his old sergeant could get a look at him now, he thought, as the layers of dirt melted from his skin.

Bennett had shown him a lamb rotating on a spit as they walked to his tent. As they passed it, the general had smiled and asked Henry to select an appropriate wine from his cellar for dinner. Henry gasped when he saw the collection assembled before him. All of the regions, styles, and textures he could imagine were at his command. The choice however, was simple 1934 Pétrus. The relatively unknown Merlot was from the Pomerol district of Bordeaux. In a fifteen year span of poor vintages, the '34 stood out as superior. Henry had enjoyed other '34 Bordeauxs, but not the Pétrus.

His anticipation of the wine and the aroma of the lamb made it hard to relax despite his surroundings. Bennett had given him a

[22]

map of the Alps to study. His first contact was an Italian vintner just a few hours away. He was doing his best to smoke his cigar, drink his Cognac, and read the map without getting them wet   a task he enjoyed immensely. It was hard for him to believe that death and despair existed anywhere on earth. He shook off the guilt that had snuck into his bath, dreaming of large barns full of Champagne and Italian farm girls. His glass of Cognac slipped under the water as he fell asleep, and the map of the Alps gently came to rest on top of his cigar.

8

As Jack turned his car into the winery's entrance, he slowed down to look at a new mural on the side of a building.   An enormous cluster of grapes was curled around an equally large salmon. The two shapes clearly formed the symbol of opposites known as yin and yang.   The detail of the painting was incredible. The dark purple grapes were ready to explode   the fish looked alive. Jack laughed as he stopped the car and got out for a closer look at Sunflower's latest masterpiece.

The sun was setting behind him, adding a touch of pink to the scene.   Hidden inside each grape was the face of a family member. It showed a family cluster with Henry and Rose on top, then Anthony and Lisa in the middle with their brothers and sisters alongside.   The faces of Sunflower, Jack, and Skye were spread out in the lower rows with empty grapes all around. The scales of the fish were laced with metal flakes that glimmered in the sun. Jack pondered the notion that it's a good thing this place isn't open to the public, since people might think there's something in the wine other than grape juice.

Sunflower was the youngest of Anthony and Lisa's children. Her varietal totem, according to Henry (with Anthony's blessing), was pinot gris. It fit her beautifully. She had thick blonde hair with hints of copper and straw. A pleasant demeanor and charming smile made her a favorite with the valley's growers, pickers, and winemakers. Her ability to argue in Spanish with the most stubborn of workers was legendary. As an Agriculture major at OSU, she assumed control of all vineyard operations at the age of 23.

Working with Anthony to find the wine through the land, Sunflower's understanding of terroir and its role in the Willamette Valley were Zen. It was how she saw the wine that made her so special. It didn't exist as a beverage in a bottle to her. It was sunlight, soil, and energy an elegant elixir of nature's life force. She could smell a glass of wine for hours, and often did. She wrote journals about her various observations, then compared her notes with Anthony about which specific row of vines he'd captured in the glass. He was constantly amazed at her accuracy.

The type of yeast, the method and length of fermentation, the temperature at harvest, and the slope of the vineyard are all apparent to the well-trained nose. After several years, Anthony and his children shared a language that was unique and sophisticated, using terms like "cat-piss," "plummy-cake," and "balanced acid" with equal clarity. If a slightly off flavor was detected in a grape, it would later be found in the wine. Their ability to communicate these sensory findings with each other led to the practice of fermenting the vineyards, row by row, in 200 gallon tanks. Insanely expensive, messy, and time consuming, this exploration of terroir made Anthony Miller famous.

Jack stopped at the winery to see if anyone was there before going to the house. The multi-level building sat on a hill, looking more like a computer software plant than a winery. A lack of

[24]

windows added to the already mysterious nature of the architecture. Inspired by eastern religion and peyote, the building combined Frank Lloyd Wright with The Jetsons. Jack used his key and entered through a side door.

Anthony was 61 feet away, standing sideways and staring at Jack. The barrels behind him were stacked eight high, forming a massive wall as wide as the winery. The look in his dad's eye was pure evil. His mouth appeared to be full of vomit. The anger on his face was matched only by the intensity of his stead. Jack held his stare for a moment and then slowly walked to the office and retrieved the stick. They come in many sizes. This one was custom made by Jack. It was a 36-inch, wine-stained beauty a veteran of six crushes and still going strong. Used for centuries to break up the cap (or chapeau) of yeast and grapes that forms on the top of fermenting red wine, it was also perfect for battle.

Dressed in his usual rubber boots, apron and beret, his chubby dad stood motionless while Jack returned to his place. Anthony's bushy grey hair just barely touched the back of his old black shirt. His fuzzy beard and moustache also had a touch of grey that softened the effect of his bad mood, whether he liked it or not.

Jack looked behind his dad at the upper loft of tanks, above which stood yet another loft of fermenters. The interior of the winery was one gigantic room featuring five levels. Jack slowly shook his head in a display of remorse. His face showed signs of regret as he slowly began to swing the stick and speak. "Let's go, Bear show me what you got" he said, pointing the stick at his dad.

Anthony raised his front leg as his back one dipped a little. His huge hands separated and he quickly lunged forward, throwing a ball made of shipping tape. It took no time at all for the rock-hard wad to travel across the cellar. Jack stood firm as it came directly at his face. Trying hard to see the ball's rotation, he tilted back on his heels just as the tape ball suddenly dropped away and tore the imaginary strike zone to shreds. Adding insult to injury, the ball bounced off the wall and returned to Anthony's feet before Jack could even turn around. His dad finally smiled. "So, I guess you had a little to drink last night, huh?"

"Wow . . . uh, yeah, I'm a little slow, but that pitch was awesome. One knuckle or two?" Jack inquired.

"That was a two-knuckle drop curve" Anthony said, as he picked up the ball and went into his wind-up. This time he paused for two seconds at the top of his leg kick, then finished his delivery side arm. The pitch was a low-riser. Jack watched it and waited as long as he could. He still swung early and pulled it foul into the tanks on the far left side of the next loft. The system of lofts in the winery incorporate the use of gravity in the racking of wine from one container to another. Because it's so sensitive, avoiding the use of pumps is fundamental in the production of premium pinot noir. However, the lofts also make terrific scoring targets in home run derby.

"That's a double, baby!" Jack said, knowing full well it was a foul ball.

"Oh, don't start that shit. It was on the other side of the post and you know it."

"Come on, D.Q., serve me something sweet," Jack said, conceding the foul ball and asking for another pitch.

"Your mom's got dinner waiting. She told me not to play with you until after we ate," Anthony said, walking towards his son. "Hey, what did you think of Sunflower's new painting?"

"I don't know about you guys. Too much philosophy for me, man. What is that, a wang fung kind of thing?" Jack said, teasing his dad.

9

Henry dreamed only of mud as he slept in the bath. The trenches, artillery, and endless rains had decimated their positions. Mud was everywhere. An intricate system of boards and planks connected everything   including enemies. Henry saw his wounded comrades falling one by one from the walkways into the muck. He was unable to reach them as their faces slowly went under, hands reaching for help.

He awoke to flames and screamed, disoriented by the smoke and a bathtub full of black water. The map of the Alps was burning beside him, sitting on top of a half-burned cigar that was smiling in the ashtray. Henry slapped the water and cursed the war. "This place is driving me crazy," he said, and then he remembered the Pétrus and rotating lamb and relaxed.

He tried to think of the last time he ate meat, salivating as he climbed from the bath. He'd had venison a few months ago at a little cafe up north. The owner had vineyards and a small wine press. Henry had drawn him a diagram of a better way to graft the new rootstock he was receiving from America after the war. That night, they'd dined for hours with several members of the French Resistance. The cafe owner had converted his attic into an underground print shop during the height of the German occupation. They printed thousands of forbidden transcripts of British radio programs, and the speeches of Charles de Gaulle and other French leaders. The villagers had risked their lives circulating the flyers. The success of the D-Day invasion and the welcome presence of the Americans assured a steady flow of red wine and whatever else the owner could spare, including venison in a raspberry-Roquefort sauce.

A new uniform was sitting on Henry's bed. A clean undershirt and even a pair of new socks were next to his new shoes. He thought about Napa and the vineyards as he dressed. His older brother Merle was working the vines with their father, just like Henry should be doing. They were more than capable of finding buyers for their grapes without him, but he was ready to go home and be with his family anyway. He had fought for his country and lived.

A Private knocked at the door, signaling that the time for dinner was at hand. Henry felt better than he had in weeks. He walked to the general's tent, smoking the bottom third of his waterlogged cigar on the way.

"Well, look at you, Mueller!" the general said. He was standing at a buffet table surrounded by a small group of well-dressed men.

"Hot water and shaving cream will do it every time, sir. Thank you for the fresh change of clothes, especially the socks."

The general bowed at the hors d' oeuvres, gesturing for Henry to help himself. "Have you had much caviar lately, Henry?" he asked mockingly.

"Just Beluga, sir," Henry smiled.

"Oh, I do enjoy the company of an educated fighting man," said Bennett.

The table was set with beautiful china and exquisite wine glasses. Four bottles of the Pétrus were breathing at the center of the table. The lamb that had been outside was resting on a platter, no longer rotating. Henry still had trouble relaxing, though. A glass of Champagne was offered and he gladly accepted, hoping the bubbles would make him more comfortable.

"Gentlemen, please let's be seated, shall we?" Bennett said. "I'd like to propose a toast to the newest member of our team." He continued as everyone was seated. "To Henry Mueller, California grape grower and eonophile. May you taste great wines always, especially this month." They all laughed as the general sat down, holding up their glasses and smiling at an embarrassed Henry.

The general waved to a server and the first course was presented. A bouillabaisse with enormous pieces of crab, lobster, and fish was served. The wine was a fragrant, young Sancerre. Finished semi-dry, the sauvignon blanc was crisp and assertive, mixing beautifully with the seafood oils and fresh herbs.

"So, Henry, I bet you're a little curious about how you ended up here?"

"Yes, sir. The thought has crossed my mind" he said, tasting fresh lobster for the first time in nearly two years.

"General Morton is a good friend of mine. He was bragging about you last year." Bennett was referring to Henry's previous commander in England. "He kept saying how much you knew about grapes and wine, so I did a little research into your family. That's when I was putting this team you see here together. How many acres do you have in production now?"

Henry thought about it for a moment. "Well, we're still trying to recover from phylloxera and Prohibition . . . but probably somewhere around ten thousand acres in three counties. The varietals took a big hit, though. Nobody cared about quality in the bulk market or home winemaking for a long time, sir."

One of the guests muttered something in French about the poor quality of bulk wines, obviously very upset. The general thought that now was an appropriate time for introductions. Henry had been uncomfortable with the long delay in meeting everyone but felt it was the host's responsibility as far as he was concerned.

"Henry, these gentlemen own and operate some of the more famous chateaus and trading houses in the world. As you can probably imagine, they're a little concerned about the current location of their inventories. Apparently, the Fascists enjoy good wine, too. These men have hired us to return those items taken across the borders. Are you willing to be a part this program?"

Henry was surprised by the sincere tone of the general's question. "Do I have a choice?" he responded.

"Oh, yes. There's a wonderful little place in the South Pacific that I'm sure you'd enjoy very much. Why . . . some would even call it the tropics." The general paused, waiting for the group of Frenchmen to stop laughing and then continued. "You have a chance to save and sample some of the world's finest creations. I know how much respect you have for wine. In fact, let's try a little of this gentleman's now."

Bennett grabbed a bottle of the Pétrus and began pouring it to the chateau's current manager. The moment was very powerful for Henry. Bennett was right; he did love wine. His family had been growing grapes and making wine for over 60 years. His grandfather, Fritz Mueller, was a pioneer of the riesling varietal. He was lucky to even be considered for such a team. Besides, he thought, the Japanese were still putting up one hell of a fight. He recalled the barn full of Champagne and Italian farm girls from his memory. "Sir. . . . Gentlemen, it will be an honor to reunite you with your inventories. I can think of nothing I'd rather do." Henry smiled and held out his glass for the general to fill.

Bennett did so eagerly, thinking of the thousands of dollars in commissions he was so close to earning. The lamb was carved and succulent pieces were served with a truffle demiglace. The Pétrus was wonderful. It had the familiar aroma of currants and plums and a soft, velvety texture. The lack of tannin allowed loads of fresh fruit from the wine to mix with the demiglace.

"Did you study the area circled on your map?" the general asked, his mouth full of food and proud of it.

Henry blushed before he could answer, knowing full well he couldn't bull shit Bennett. "It slipped under the water when I fell asleep, sir. I meant to ask for another one."

Smiling at Henry, the Frenchman who spoke earlier said something to the rest of the table about Henry being able to hold his alcohol; no insult was intended, that much was obvious. The gentlemen all raised their glasses and the general remarked that they would find out about Henry's tolerance for drinking tonight.

Bennett paused while raising his glass and smiling at his

[30]

guests. "Here's to a safe journey for all of us. Even Mueller, if he can keep his map dry. The way I see it, gentlemen . . . if we only deprive those Fascist bastards of one more case of wine, we've done our job."

🍇 🍇 🍇

10

Sunflower and Lisa were talking on the porch as the boys walked towards the house. Anthony was holding the tape ball. His first two fingernails were dug deeply into its surface as his wrist moved back and forth in slow motion, repeating the delivery of his elusive new pitch. Jack was listening carefully, his eyes following the movements of his dad's hand. The sun had set, but twilight was all they needed to get from the winery to the house. The path was several inches deep from many years of use.

Lisa watched them approach and smiled at Jack as he looked up to receive Sunflower's hello. It was different now that he had started his own business. The moments she took for granted were lost. She missed cheering in the upper loft of the winery and shagging the home run balls that made it into the fermenters before they sank. Silly games in the cellar had become some of the best memories of her life. Proud of his accomplishments and yet saddened by his independence, she loved it when Jack came for dinner. Lisa looked at her tall, young son. His thick brown hair, like his father's, was in dire need of cutting. His friendly smile was shining through the darkness as they moved closer.

Jack couldn't hold back his laughter despite his dad's warning. "My goodness, Sunflower. What's that wang fung thing on the side of the barn, anyway?"

"You know you like it, Jack," Sunflower snapped. "Yin and yang are what make wine possible and don't you forget it."

[31]

"Yin and yang!" Jack said. "I thought it was yeast."

"Did you see the faces?"

"Yeah, I saw the faces. Why the heck aren't there any empty grapes around me? You trying to tell me something?"

Sunflower smiled and laughed at Jack. "You noticed that, huh? You'll never get married, Shabby. But if you do, I promise to paint her (or him) in there somewhere."

"Oh, that's some good stuff, Petal. Really, funny stuff," Jack said to his sister.

"Okay kids, dinner is ready," Lisa said. The jabs and greetings continued as they entered the house. Jack felt a twinge in his eyes from the sauteed onions and spices. The place smelled wonderful. The large living and dining rooms were connected by dark hardwood floors and intricate Asian rugs provided warmth. Across the room, a table for twelve had four place mats at one end.

"Where's Skye?" Jack asked.

"He canceled," his mom said from the stove. "He had to work all weekend."

"What a wimp. I'd like him to wear my shoes for a week," Jack said.

"Pew, Jack. I'm trying to eat," Sunflower said, gasping as she plugged her nose.

Anthony and Lisa spoke quietly in the kitchen before joining them at the table. Their moods had become sullen, and they wore fake smiles as they carried the chili and cornbread into the room. Sunflower saw their faces and immediately got scared. Jack lunged for the cornbread and butter, spreading with reckless abandon. Normally intuitive, his senses were still a bit dull from last night's bender. His sister was petrified. She grabbed Jack's hand while looking at her parents. His mouth was full when he looked up and saw the serious faces surrounding him.

Anthony looked at everyone with a faint smile, trying to be strong. "You guys, they found your Aunt Cherise dead yesterday. She apparently stockpiled her medication . . . and took it all at once before going to bed. She never woke up."

"God, Mom, we played all those games of backgammon today and you didn't say a word? I thought she was doing so much better." Sunflower trailed off.

"We all did, Petal," Anthony said. "She was really positive the last time I talked to her. She and Henry had spoke, and Mom said everything sounded great. But, all in all, it's not a real big surprise to anyone, is it?" He continued softly. "Those demons had been with her for a long time. A lot of bad things had happened to her and she wouldn't let anyone help. Your mom and I were going to wait until after dinner to tell you but it just didn't feel right to wait anymore. I'm sorry. I loved her a lot. I know you guys did, too. She was wacko but always in a fun kind of way!"

"That's not nice, Bear!" his wife scolded.

Jack was silent. He had spent a lot time in the vineyards with Crazy Cherise. She had shown him how all the varietals were so different: the buds, leaves, clusters, and resulting wine. Her insight and love for the plant was contagious. When they were young and their parents were building their home in Oregon, the kids spent many weeks with her, touring the other great wineries of Napa with V.I.P. treatment all the way. Cherise "entertained" a lot of winemakers when they were growing up and Jack got to hear everything about the latest trends in the world of wine through her frequent dates with local vintners. She always joked that cabernet and petite sirah went well together, referring to their totems. Perhaps that was why they always got along so well, he thought.

"I'm sorry, Jack. I know she wrote to you a lot when you were younger. Anything lately?" Anthony asked.

"No, Dad. I haven't heard from her in years. It's strange, you know; I called and never got a response. I stopped trying after awhile. Now she's gone? How could she have been hurting that bad?"

"I don't know, Jack. Cherise was pretty messed up. You

remember. It was just one thing after another. The marriages, the twins, the drugs, and then that damned Bhagwan."

The air in the room was hot and uncomfortable. They ate slowly without talking. Sunflower thought about the mural and cried. Cherise had been so pretty in the photo she had used to paint her likeness. Jack downed his sixth glass of iced tea and thought about how to ask Petal about pruning the grapes in Eugene without sounding too insensitive.

"This may sound strange," said Anthony, "but Cherise's ashes arrive here on Thursday. Your mom and I would like to spread them in the vineyard, if it's all right with you guys."

"That would be nice, Dad. Thanks," Jack said.

Sunflower nodded her approval, tears streaming down her cheeks.

"I know it's tough, you guys," Lisa said. "Cherise just got confused - that's all. Try to think about the good stuff for a little while. She loved you kids like her own."

After another long silence, they managed to eat their dinners and talk about work. There was a lot to get done in the cellar as well as the vineyards: racking, bottling, and pruning. Everything seemed slow, but there really weren't enough hours in the day to get it all done. Jack's head was pounding even more, despite the three bowls of therapeutic chili.

"Hey, Petal, do you have a crew coming down to Eugene tomorrow?" he asked.

"Yeah, you've got Lupé and his crew all week. How bad is the mud down there?"

"They shouldn't hurt anything. The drainage has been pretty good so far. Thanks for sending Lupé's crew. His team works really well with the guys I have down there right now."

"Lupé likes your vineyard, Jack. Besides, you're paying them mileage and a per diem," Sunflower said, winking at their dad.

"Oh, come on, Bear," Jack whined. "We share all that fruit

anyway. Man, I need some new tanks and I donated all that money to the new Little League field yesterday. Karma right? You're the ones who keep preaching all that stuff. I don't have ten grand to prune all those acres. That's it. I'm selling to Queen's Estate. I can't take this crap anymore."

Anthony and Sunflower burst into laughter for the first time since the bad news about Cherise. The oppressive air in the room was blown away. Jack slammed the table with an open hand, more for effect than anger. He didn't like being on the receiving end of one of their set-ups, preferring the role of conspirator rather than victim. Jack put his face in his hands, concealing his embarrassment. "You guys have been waiting to spring that one on me for awhile, haven't you?" he said, the words muffled by his hands. "I need some yin, Sunflower. I'm all alone down there and baseball doesn't start for another week."

Jack tried to make up with both of them at once for his little tantrum, his psychology degree paying off again. The Tao reference never failed with Sunflower and mentioning a baseball "jones" to Anthony was like telling him you had brain cancer. They immediately assured him that his vines were well cared for and so was he. He didn't need to sell the farm just yet.

"Hey, I've got a great book on the life cycle of the fruit fly. It's written from the fly's point of view. You'd love it," Sunflower said. "You know the fly carries the yeast around in his belly over the winter so we can make a living in the spring, that type of thing. You need some good ju-ju, Jack. Remember, look to the east. The most enlightened vines grow on the eastern slope. When was the last time you read a book?"

His eyes rolled back in his head and he almost groaned out loud. Luckily, he hadn't removed his hands from his face so the act was still effective. Anthony patiently waited his turn to offer inspirational commentary on the upcoming baseball season.

"Jack . . . son, two words - wild card." He smiled at Jack as if he'd discovered a good California riesling. To Anthony, the greatest thing to happen in human evolution lately was the addition of another weekend of playoffs in Major League Baseball.

Lisa sat back and enjoyed the familiar dialogue, happy to have everyone here again. She waited for a moment and dropped the bomb. "All of the Napa clan will be here Saturday for the wake."

Jack slowly removed his hands from his face and looked at his mom. "Everyone?" he asked, blinking his eyes in shock. "Even Henry?"

"Everyone," she said. "Even Henry."

🍇 🍇 🍇

11

The morning light was barely shining as the jeep pulled away from General Bennett's quarters. Henry had proved that he could hold his liquor the night before and he was feeling surprisingly well. The morning air was crisp and full of excitement, stinging his face as he drove. He was off to Italy to recover stolen wine, brandy, and Champagne. The butterflies in his stomach were very active in spite of the early hour. This was the type of adventure he had dreamed of when he'd enlisted in Uncle Sam's war. Working the airfields in England and hobnobbing with the true connoisseurs of French wines was nothing compared to the excitement of this job. Bennett had provided him with cash, cigars, several fake IDs, and a map. He was to play the role of a black-market buyer. Not unusual in a time of war and not too far from the truth, either.

The evils of war continued in the wake of liberation. Germany and most of northern Italy were still Hitler's. Refugees were starving by the millions as celebrations broke out in the streets of Paris, London, and New York. The value of money was still secondary to many people. Food rations in the form of powdered eggs, canned meat, and jerky were worth more than gold. Henry was prepared to deal in any form of trade with the support of Be There Bennett. An order for cash, food, clothes, or water by Henry would be filled in less than 24 hours by Bennett's supply sergeants.

It was nothing to be proud of as far as Henry was concerned. Taking advantage of an already desperate situation wasn't his idea of helping the war effort. Bennett had made an excellent argument late last night, though; these things were happening with or without him and Henry was now in a position to provide relief to people by using the barter system in exchange for helpful information. There was no way to offer help to the millions who needed it. Even Bennett didn't have those connections. But some good could be accomplished and yes, some money made, if things were returned to their rightful owners.

The route was highlighted on his new map in black ink. Henry stole glances at it as he negotiated the gravel road and drank his coffee. A prominent, Italian winemaker with sympathetic ties to the French underground had a winery just a few hours across the border. Henry hadn't heard of him but his name was written on the map: Antonio Vessini. The trip to his facility would take about six hours according to the notes written on the map. The Allied Forces were moving north through Italy and the Germans were taking everything they could as they fled. It was risky to go in now but the railroads made efficient carriers of stolen wine and artifacts, as well as prisoners. If they waited, the leads that Vessini provided would be useless.

[37]

VARIETAL TENDENCIES

According to Bennett, the Italian countryside was a nightmare for the Germans to patrol. The mountains, hills, lakes, and rivers required enormous manpower to cover. Henry would be safe as long as he followed the route on his map. His Italian was more than adequate and, thanks to Bennett, he had the resources to bribe an entire army. He was still afraid of any contact with the German Wehrmacht. The rumors of mass killings and atrocities against humanity had been confirmed in recent months and Henry had no desire to experience this brutality firsthand. If captured, he hoped his Aryan appearance would provide him some clemency. Actually, a small part of him had grown ashamed of his German ancestry in the last few years. However, four generations in the United States was enough for Uncle Sam. Henry Mueller was an American farm boy from Napa, California.

The thick morning fog had burned off, revealing a beautiful summer day that reminded Henry of Napa. He saw old rundown barns and sheds as he drove through the country. Like twenty years ago at home, the most common piece of farm equipment in Italy was the mule and wagon. He couldn't even count the number of carts he'd seen being pulled by an old horse, mule, or ox, most of them containing everything the family owned. He was surprised to see that the people were waving at him, apparently happy to see some sign of the war's end.

He looked at the map to confirm his location, thinking that Vessini's winery should be just ahead. When he'd left Bennett's camp, he was told to find Antonio and give him a box of cigars. They were in an antique, hand-carved humidor that was exquisite in every detail. Henry had asked for one like it and Bennett had laughed at him, saying it was worth more than his jeep. After a little more inspection, Henry saw the initials "W.C." carved on the lid. He didn't need to ask if they were real. After two days with Be There Bennett, authenticity would never be an issue. He knew anything could be in one of the general's tents, even the Crown Jewels. Henry had simply gulped and carefully placed the humidor under the front seat of the jeep as the general wished him luck.

Henry saw the winery and stopped to confirm his location. The building looked deserted. He drove up to the main door and stopped again, looking for signs of life. He extinguished his fourth cigar of the day, got out of the jeep, and walked towards the door. The afternoon sun was bright, and the dust kicked up from the jeep tires still hung in the air as he approached the building. The enormous structure had a small front door that was partially open. He knocked softly and said "bonjour." After panicking for a moment and looking around, he wisely tried Italian. He slowly pushed the door open and looked inside.

The office was full of papers and the usual business items. It made Henry homesick to be inside a winery again. He could smell the wine despite its many barriers and great distance. His head reeled at the intensity of the fruit and wood mingling in the air. There is nothing like it in the world, he thought. The smell was brand new again. He had stopped smelling it in Napa after being around it all the time. It is a beautiful but short-lived aroma that visitors always mention but workers cease to notice, in time, as the brain grows tired and moves on to other matters.

He walked through another doorway and saw a familiar object approaching his face. It was definitely a bottle of red wine, and it was definitely going to hit him very hard in the forehead before he could do anything about it. He saw a young, delicate hand holding the bottle. It was connected to an angel with strange, grey eyes and gorgeous black hair. Her face was grimacing as she flexed and put all her effort into the swing. He tried to reach up as the bottle struck his head. BANG! His knees buckled as the wine splashed around him, the aromas of cherry and tar filling his nose. The room filled with darkness as he crashed to the floor.

🍇 🍇 🍇

12

Jack played back the extremely long weekend in his mind as he drove home to Eugene. The monotonous trip south offered little more distraction than a day at the Department of Motor Vehicles. Thankfully, he was headed against the early morning traffic on its way to the state's capital. The alphabet soup of cocktails from Saturday night was now a horrible memory; mom's chili had come to the rescue once again. His synapses were firing with alarming clarity from the three cups of coffee he'd enjoyed with Sunflower during their morning walk. He was currently in the passing lane, overtaking cars with little thought. The old pick-up truck was still king of the road when Jack was sober.

They had stopped to look at the new mural on the side of the barn earlier that morning. It was strange to have a corpse in the family cluster all of a sudden. Jack had made a poor joke about the onset of mildew as he gazed at the painting through the steam rising from his coffee; he said that he hoped that Cherise's suicide was an isolated case of spoilage, curable by the upcoming application of some ash on the vines. Sunflower was disgusted by his lack of compassion. She detected sadness on another level however, and decided to let the sarcasm go for awhile. People handle stress and pain differently, she thought.

They stared at the mural for a long time without talking after his rude comments. Jack reminded his sister about their aunt's endless search for the answers in life. She had traveled throughout Asia and India without finding the source of happiness, then came home and told Jack, "God gave us the truth and the devil organized it." He was unaware at the time that she was referring to religion. Cherise had had nothing but bad luck when it came to fulfillment. Her various husbands and religions had provided nothing but confusion, sweat, and pain. Unfortunately, the same would be true of her two children.

Cherise moved to Washington's Columbia Valley on a whim after her divorce. She was going to be a farmer and grow apples and cherries on a 1000 acres of eastern Washington's finest land. A new crop and climate seemed to be the perfect answer.

The disco scene was raging hard and the thumping bass and free cocaine were too attractive in the Bay area. "Get away from the city and spend some time with the Nouveau Twins," Henry had suggested. Her babies had been born several weeks premature. They spent many months in the I.C.U. while Cherise battled for custody and danced all night. Their early arrival and identical features made the selection of their varietal totem extremely easy for Henry.

Everyone knew he wanted a set of twins in the family to represent the Gamay grapes from Beaujolais, France. The annual nouveau festivals revolve around the consumption of the fresh, young, red wine that has little hope of aging. As the twins slept in their incubators with their thin, pale skin exposing all their veins, Henry had said "Look . . . carbonic maceration." This was hilarious to everyone except Cherise and Rose, superstition and intuition getting the best of the two mothers.

A few years after Cherise's arrival in Yakima, the twins developed leukemia and died. She was alone and furious at everyone in the family, especially her father. The nouveau totem was weak and inappropriate and no one should have accepted it. "The wines are wimpy and usually saved for blush. They never live past the age of five," she had yelled during a fight at a crush dinner.

She immediately severed all connections to anyone related to Henry. Another void was created in her life in the absence of her family and there are people out there who can smell vulnerability. Like a fine glass of wine, a broken soul with money has a very distinct aroma. Her introduction into the Rajneeshpuram came six months after the deaths of her children.

Exiled from India, the Bhagwan had found a home for his followers just a few hours south of Yakima. The small community of Antelope, Oregon became the religious center of the universe for the Rajneesh movement. The spiritually blessed and well-educated flock of worshipers took over the town in a short period of time. Composed of lawyers, doctors, architects, and scholars, the movement had little trouble negotiating and financing the construction of Utopia in central Oregon. The lavish expenditures for the Bhagwan's material desires were covered by every media organization on the planet.

Cherise saw the happy faces of the members on TV as they watched their Bhagwan ride by in one of his ninety Rolls Royces. BANG! the hole in her heart was suddenly filled. Her enormous wealth and need for unconditional love made her an easy target for the cult's more persuasive recruiters. After her first visit to the commune, she leased her land in Yakima to the Washington Wine Guild and signed over the papers to the Bhagwan.

No one in the family knew she had planted over 1200 acres of Bordeaux grape varieties in the Columbia Valley. Not even her brother Anthony, who had encouraged it in the first place. The grapes were currently being processed under some of the state's more famous corporate labels, whose owners had no desire to relinquish such lucrative contracts. When the Bhagwan was asked to leave Oregon and the higher members in the order were arrested for attempted murder, Cherise broke down and ended up in an institution. Again, she denied herself the help of her family and crawled into a web of drugs and dependency.

Her land in Yakima kept her well-cared for, however. Her doctors at the institution shared attorneys, tee times, and country clubs with the C.E.O. of the Washington Wine Guild. Because Cherise was a complete basket case, she trusted her attorneys, giving them proxy and power of attorney for her holdings,

[42]

confident that they had her best interests in mind, of course. In a good year, her vineyards could gross nearly $15 million dollars for the Washington Wine Guild. Her daily regimen at the care facility included a steady flow of pharmaceutical joy. The time-release lobotomy assured **THE GUILD** of an annual harvest, while her caring doctors and lawyers drank very good wine and never waited for a tee time or table at the country club.

Sunflower had assured Jack that the pruning crew would be at the vineyard before he arrived. She was true to her word. Jack saw their trucks as he pulled into his place. The vineyard was an ugly forest of naked little vines, their scrawny skeletal arms reaching for the sky and earth. Jack hated the sight of dormant, winter canes. There was absolutely nothing to like about their dead appearance. It was hard to imagine six-foot shoots growing out of those things. In four months' time, though, he would be cursing the vigorous growth they enjoy so much in the rich, volcanic soil.

His dogs, Pino and Vino, heard his truck and tore around the corner of the winery in excitement. They were brother and sister. The comical pair of Australian Blue Healers did an excellent job of chasing birds during crush. Short in stature but full of piss and vinegar, the dogs were relentless in their pursuit of the vineyard's winged enemies. Looking like mutated hyenas, only uglier, the pair of dogs had but two good eyes between them; the other two had been kicked out by cows during their previous employment. A medley of howling and barking broke out as Jack sat behind the wheel of the truck and laughed at the dogs.

They circled the vehicle in a frenzy, nipping at each other and calling Jack to come out and play. He carefully inserted the cassette of Gaelic music that always makes them cry, watching their faces change as it started to play. When he turned up the volume, they stopped dead in their tracks, sat side by side, and began to sing into the air, performing an eerie ballad dedicated to lost sheep and dead masters. The strange duet could be heard for miles, giving the toughest of farmers goosebumps and shivers. This was at least their four hundredth performance, and the tribute still made Jack laugh to the point of tears.

He got out of the truck and tackled both dogs as their wailing continued. He hadn't seen them in nearly two days. The three of them walked into the vineyard to check on the pruning crew. It was a sunny morning and he could see the first row of cane-pruned vines in the distance. The long rows of pinot noir sloped down to the west, where a small tributary to the Willamette river ran through his property at the bottom of the vineyard. He saw Felix a few hundred yards away and waved to him. Felix had been the vineyard foreman for as long as Jack could remember. He had a wonderful family and was very religious. His Spanish accent was still thick, despite his forty years in America. They walked towards each other, greeted with a sincere handshake, and exchanged hellos in the other's native tongue.

"No freeze, Jack?" Felix inquired.

"No worries, Felix, nada. You guys go ahead and work. What's the temperature in the low spot over there?" Jack pointed to a trough in the hill that was susceptible to frost in the spring.

"Forty-tree. It's okay, yes?"

"Yeah, go ahead, no problem. Let's get this stuff cut," Jack said. "Hey, how's Lupé's crew doing?"

"Too young, Jack. They're very fast. They make us look bad with all of our smoking breaks."

They both laughed as Pino and Vino bolted down the slope in a rage, barking madly. Jack watched them run and felt sorry for the rabbit that must have accidentally wandered into their turf. He turned to Felix while still watching his dogs. "Do you guys want lunch in the winery or out here?"

Felix smiled and said that his wife would make sure that Jack got some tacos when she came by later on that day. Jack couldn't hide his true intentions about lunch. He wanted to know where it was, so he would be there. An authentic pork taco with fresh lime and radishes was the highlight of Jack's day. Sometimes he poured a little pinot gris for the crew when they treated him to tacos. They were shocked that they tasted so good together, always being polite and smiling but quietly preferring cervesa. "It's the citrus," Jack would say, as he gulped down the spicy pork creations.

A humorous cry for help could barely be heard in the distance. Jack strained his neck a little to the right and heard it again. Scattered in between the endless yapping of the dogs was a woman's voice. "Somebody . . . hello? Please help me!"

Jack said goodbye to Felix and started walking down the hill towards the voice. He started to run when he realized that the dogs had someone cornered in the creek. As he approached the scene, he couldn't believe his eyes. There, crouched down in a foot of water shivering from head to toe, was Maria. She was holding a bag partially full of water and what appeared to be frogs. Her clothes were soaking wet. They looked at each other for a second as the dogs continued to curdle milk with their growls.

"Pino! Vino! Shut up!" Jack yelled. The dogs looked at Jack and decided he was nuts, shaking their heads as they returned to the vineyard, surprised that he was so ungrateful for their discovery.

"I swear to God. I didn't know this was your property," Maria said, tugging at her clinging flannel shirt. She was mortified when she saw Jack approaching. She wanted to meet him again but not doing something stupid like this.

"Yeah, sure," he said, savoring the view as well as the moment. "So, why are you sitting in my creek . . . holding a bag of frogs?"

"I'm researching the Northwest tree frog."

"You're what? A roadie for the Tree Frogs?"

"Don't be a smartass," she snapped. "I'm doing my thesis on the tree frogs here in the Willamette Valley."

Jack went limp at the thought of a girl as beautiful as Maria

[45]

with a Masters. There was nothing wrong with her when she was a waitress, either, he thought. But she was now something to definitely avoid.   The last thing he needed was a girl who understood chemistry complicating his life. She was exactly what he had dreamed about: an intelligent woman with all the trappings. He watched her walk from the creek in a pair of faded wet jeans, his life flashing before his eyes.

She saw the little kid in his eye and knew exactly what he was thinking. She slowly turned to face him as she climbed to the bank, her breasts revealing the water temperature to be a cool 43 degrees.

"Yep, all that and brains too," Jack thought to himself. "You are in trouble."

🍇 🍇 🍇

13

Henry felt a wet cloth blotting his face as he rested with his eyes closed. It felt so good that he was afraid it would stop if he opened them. He tried to remember what had happened as he lay there. He thought about Bennett and saw the humidor. He remembered the refugees and their wagons lining the sides of the streets on his way to . . . Vessini's. He slowly opened his eyes and faked a helpless groan. He was hushed by a beautiful woman and told to relax in a soft, angelic voice.

"Is he awake?" Antonio asked in a concerned tone.

"Yes, but he is very weak."

Henry looked around the room. He saw a dark-skinned man with a huge smile that was barely visible through a heavy, black moustache. The man was very eager to hear Henry speak. His hands were tightly clasped around the humidor.

"You are American, yes?" Antonio asked.

Henry nodded. "My name is Henry Mueller. I'm from California. You Vessini?"

"Yes. I'm Antonio Vessini. This is my wife, Corrina. And you've met my little Nebbiolo Rose. She thought you were Gestapo. We are very very sorry that she hit you so hard. She is very strong, yes?"

Henry saw her face and managed a little grin. Nebbiolo, he thought, how appropriate. "Yes, she is very strong. How did you know I'm American?"

"Your teeth," Antonio replied. "They are too nice for English."

"How long was I out?"

"All day," Rose replied. "You mostly just slept and groaned. We didn't want to wake you." Her grey eyes were blank and her face showed no emotion. She was diligent in wiping the sweat from his face. He could see a little piece of the bandage that covered his forehead.

"You speak English very well," Henry said, his mouth extremely dry.

"We were all educated in England," Antonio said proudly.

"My radio?" asked Henry.

"It's still in the jeep. Can you get some medicine from your army?" asked Rose.

"Yes, I can get anything you need. I need my radio. . . ." He tried to get up and Rose pushed him back down, smiling for the first time. His stomach turned a somersault at the sight of her face. Her skin was like porcelain. Never before in his life had he seen anything so beautiful.

"You need to eat something first," she said.

Corrina brought Henry a bowl of stew and loaf of bread, and Rose placed pillows behind his back as he sat up to eat.

"Let the man have some room to breathe, you two," Antonio

[47]

said gruffly. "You're suffocating him, my goodness."

"It's fine, really," Henry said. "I feel very good." He looked at Rose and smiled. "Thank you for not killing me. I'm sorry I scared you. Are there still Germans around here?"

Antonio looked at his wife and daughter. "Not so many, no. They made sweeps for Italian officers and soldiers a few weeks ago. They are still taking as many prisoners as they can up to Germany to work in the factories. They took my sons. Goddamn Fascists. That is why Rose hit you. You look very German. You know that, though, don't you?"

"Yes," he said, rubbing his head humorously to tease Rose, her face showing signs of embarrassment.

"I'm sorry about your sons," Henry said.

"They'll be okay They're very strong, too. Like my little Nebbiolo who welcomed you to our home. Those fucking Nazis can't hurt the Vessinis." He paused for a moment and then lifted the humidor. "Is this for me?"

Henry could see the pain in everyone's faces over the abduction of their boys. Antonio was looking for a diversion by talking about the humidor, and Henry obliged. "Yes it is. That belonged to the cigar-smoking diplomat himself. We appreciate your help, Antonio. My employers wish to remain anonymous, however; I'm sure you understand."

"Yes, yes, of course," Antonio said. "It is very beautiful. Eat your lunch and get some rest. I have some good news for you and your employers." He looked at his wife and nodded towards the door. She left and Antonio walked out behind her. "I'll let my daughter apologize in private," he said, smiling at Rose as he left the room.

"Nebbiolo, huh?" Henry said.

"Since I was a little girl he has called me that. My hair and eyes, you know - the color, like the wine and the fog?"

Henry melted at the tone of her voice and how she described the nickname.

"What kind of wine is that?" he asked, even though he knew

[48]

the answer.

"The Barolo, of course, well, around here anyway. Other places grow nebbiolo, too. Have you had it before? It's very good. I'll bring you some later. What's America like?"

"Big. America is very big. One gigantic garden. You haven't been there? I'm surprised, you sound like you're from New York."

"Is that a compliment?"

"Yes, it is. Can I ask you a personal question?" Henry asked, starting to flirt.

"Maybe," Rose said, flirting back.

"How old are you?"

"How old do you think I am?"

"I asked you first," he said, avoiding the dangerous situation.

"Twenty."

"Really. I thought you were much older," he said, knowing to always say older if a woman is under twenty-three.

"You're just saying that. Where in America did you say you live?"

"California. It's on the west coast. We grow a lot of grapes, too."

"Do you work in the vineyards?"

"You could say that," Henry said, smiling at the harmless deception.

"Isn't it wonderful? My family has always made wine."

"Making wine is the most wonderful thing in the world. We make a little bit for ourselves in Napa."

"Do you think the war is almost over?" Rose asked.

"Definitely the Russians are very determined. They're moving into Germany from the east and we control the west. Hitler is surrounded and he knows it. That's why the trains are running so often. They need everything they can get to protect the heart of their so-called Fatherland. Berlin will make a nice tomb for those bastards."

Rose's thoughts were with her brothers. She stared at the

window as her mind wandered along the railroad tracks that had carried them to Germany. She'd heard the reports about the death camps being found in Poland and feared for her brothers' safety. The Nazi war machine had depleted most of Europe's natural resources as well as its share of young men. Henry saw her sadness and reassured her that they would be home soon.

"If your brothers hit half as hard as you do, Rose, those Germans don't stand a chance. Your father knows how strong they are. Does he call them a wine, too?"

"Not wine — grape, silly. Yes, Mario was . . . is Sangiovese and Luigi is Barbera. All our lives we hear these names and now I hope I get to hear my father call them again. I'm sorry I hit you so hard . . . If I had known you were an American. . . ."

"It's okay, Rose. It'll be all right. I'm going to be fine and so will your brothers."

Antonio and his wife entered the room with a bottle of wine and some cheese.

"Do you like the goat cheese, Henry?" Antonio asked.

"It's my favorite. Nothing makes wine taste better than fresh goat cheese."

Corrina handed him a platter with a knife, bread, and cheese. Antonio opened the wine and easily poured the entire bottle into four large glasses. They were each the size of a small bird bath. Vessini held up a glass to the light overhead, examining the wine's color through the bottom of the glass, swirling and then smelling the wine as he handed it to Henry. His smile was so proud that the guessing game wasn't going to be much of a challenge for his guest.

Henry repeated the formalities of wine tasting for his audience. A careful look, thoughtful smell, and then a taste . . . the wine was incredible. It had a huge and robust palate with at least 14% alcohol. The waves of fruit came through the back of his nose as he swallowed. The ripe tannins stripped away the goat cheese and the finish of coffee and tar lingered for several seconds as Henry cataloged the experience. He recognized the aromas of cherry and tar on his shirt from a few hours earlier.

"I think Rose already shared a bottle of this with me," Henry said, looking at the wine and his blushing nurse. "Very hot summer; good sugars and a lot of tannin. I didn't think you could get this kind of alcohol in these hills. The acid level is consistent with Barolo but the mouth is so big. These must have been fairly young vines when this nebbiolo was harvested; it's very concentrated and balanced and wonderful, but the overall depth isn't quite there, is it?"

"Now I know why they sent you," Antonio said, very impressed by Henry's observations. "The vines were five years old during that harvest. How old do you think that wine is?"

"Twelve or thirteen?" Henry guessed casually.

"Twelve," Vessini frowned. "Where in California did you say you're from?"

"Napa."

"I knew it! As soon as you smelled your glass I knew you were from wine. Does your family make the wine?"

"We mostly grow grapes for other people."

"Who?"

"Almost everyone," Henry said.

"Mueller . . . from Napa, eh? Do you sell your rootstock?"

"Yeah, most of the new stock around here is ours."

"Including mine," Antonio smiled. "I bought these from Napa. Mueller Vineyards, that's you?"

"Yep, small world, huh?" Henry said, raising his glass to Antonio.

"How did you make out with that Prohibition thing?" Vessini asked.

"We've been fighting the Nazis for over twenty years in America. We came out okay, though. Consumption actually went up during that time."

"Oh, yes, I know," Antonio smiled. "We Catholics do like our sacramental wine, don't we?"

🍇🍇🍇

[51]

14

Maria was shivering in the chilly spring air as the two exchanged a moment of exhilaration from the strange circumstance they suddenly enjoyed. Jack was searching for things to say that wouldn't appear to be too flirtatious. He battled the overwhelming temptation to look at her breasts, clearly a violation of the flirting rule. He quickly considered several options that would test her salt before he fell head over heels in love with her. As he offered her a change of clothes from the winery, he deliberately cracked his knuckles and opened a five-month-old pouch of chewing tobacco, inserting a small wad of dried leaves into his cheek. In an instant, this bold move had revealed his two worst habits. The cards were on the table. He watched her face for some sign of irritation.

"So, you have clothes that will fit me, huh?" Maria asked, unscathed by the test of vices. Her smile was warm and sincere as she looked him directly in the eye.

Oh no, he thought; she's a keeper. "Yeah, my sister has all sorts of work clothes and stuff up there," he said, as they walked up the slope to the winery. Jack was chewing the tobacco like a stick of gum. "So, what ever happened to you the other night at the dinner? You just disappeared."

Maria gave Jack a look that said he knew what had happened to her. "I got phased because you were flirting with me. Roberta was furious. She wanted you all to herself. But you just kept staring and smiling at me even though everybody knew what was going on. The staff wouldn't stop teasing me."

[52]

"Really . . . everybody saw that? I thought I was being pretty sneaky. She wasn't really mad at you, was she?"

"Not really, no. She's a great gal. I had asked to be cut early so I could go home and study for mid-terms, but that was before I saw you." She turned and smiled at Jack. "Roberta had to remind me about going home to study. I left during the dessert. She wasn't that unhappy to have me go, though. She was pretty jealous. She said a wealthy Gemini was supposed to play a significant role in her chart this month. I think she was hoping it would be you."

Jack faked an attack of the willies at the thought of Roberta being jealous over him. "That girl's a trip. She really, actually, asked me what my sign was. I couldn't believe it. She wanted to know if we consulted the stars about when to crush."

Maria laughed out loud as Pino and Vino ran towards them, their tongues dangling from their mouths from fatigue. Unfortunately for Jack, the dogs' playfulness had a sobering effect on his morality. He looked at the dogs and felt like a Boy Scout. Any impure thoughts inspired by Maria's wet clothing were wiped clean by the two glaring eyes of Pino and Vino; dogs seem to have a way of reducing people to their most honest level.

He unlocked the winery door and they all walked inside the old warehouse. Pino and Vino immediately hid under the labeling table. The building was filled with barrels, tanks, and cases of wine. Maria stopped just inside the door and took a deep breath while raising her nose into the air. "Oh, that's incredible," she said, as she exhaled loudly and took another deep breath.

"What's that?" Jack said, with his back facing her.

"That smell. How can you possibly get anything done?"

"Well, unfortunately, your brain doesn't let you smell it after awhile. I never even notice it anymore."

"That's too bad. It's wonderful." She walked around the large room, looking up at the high ceiling and the many rows of barrels. "Do you mind if I ask you a question?"

"Not at all," he said, throwing her a pair of Sunflower's pants

[53]

and an old sweatshirt. "There's a bathroom around that corner and I've got some socks and boots upstairs in the office. Did you want a bowl or something for those frogs?"

"No, they're fine. The other night at the dinner you said something about a varietal totem or something. What was that about?"

"Oh, that's just one of those silly things that gets all blown out of whack by people. It started out as just a nickname, you know, really nothing to it. Grandpa always called Grandma Rose his little Nebbiolo, that kind of thing. Then, when my Uncle Richard was a kid, grandpa called him Zinny, for zinfandel, because he was as big as an ox and really tough   like the grape. Same thing for my two aunts - one was Char and the other one was Syrah. My dad was Pinot and so on; silly crap like that. It was no big deal until the Wine Inflator wrote it up as some sort of prophecy shaman crap after my dad gave an interview during his medicine-man phase."

"Medicine-man phase, huh?" she said, looking around the winery. "What does Henry call you?"

"Shabby. I called it shabernet caucasian when I was a little kid instead of cabernet sauvignon."

"And your sister?" Maria said, in love with the whole idea.

"Sunflower is Peanut for pinot gris; because you'd have to nuts to grow anything with the word pinot in it. And my brother Skye is Franky, for cabernet franc   which I have to admit is perfect because he's so damn mellow. He just goes with the flow and gets along with everyone. The whole thing was really silly and fun, but it's been kind of a bad scene sometimes lately, too. Anyway, go get changed before you freeze to death."

Jack tried to remain calm as he watched her walk into the bathroom. His head was still spinning from his dad's bag of "crush" tobacco. Jack and his dad averaged about ten chews a year, all during the month of October. He thought about asking Maria out for lunch but he didn't want to miss out on the tacos. Just relax, he said to himself, going crazy with curiosity about her sudden appearance in the creek. Walking upstairs for the boots he talked to himself out loud: "Frogs? What's that all about? I can't be polluting the river. Sunflower would never hurt anything. She's got to be here to see me, right? She's making that up."

"Hey, Jack, what are those for?" Maria asked from downstairs, pointing at a large stack of conveyers and bins.

"Uh, that's the set-up for sorting grapes as they come in from the vineyards. It's about thirty feet long and people stand on both sides and throw out the clusters with any type of deviation in color or signs of rot. I'm welding the broken rollers and sanding the splinters off. Crush is only seven months away,'' he said, rolling his eyes to emphasize the farmers' workload. "Hey, I need to do some lab work. How much chemistry did you take?" he asked.

"It was my minor, well . . . organic chemistry was, anyway. What kind of test?"

"Just basic titrations, checking the free sulfur and the pH and some other stuff. It's pretty boring but kind of interesting. If I have somebody to talk to when I do it, I'm usually a lot more accurate." He lied.

"Like talking to yourself, only with somebody there, right?" she said, letting him know she had heard him talking about her frogs.

"Yeah," he smiled. He knew he had just been busted. "Go get changed, you bum."

He did a quick loop around the barrels and tanks, looking for any sign of trouble. Sometimes a bung or valve will mysteriously pop off or open by itself. He saw the row of plastic fermenters and winced at the thought of Henry seeing them. Old Henry would never allow anything but stainless steel and wood in one of his buildings. "That poly crap is for shoemakers,'' is what Henry would always tell anyone who tried to convince him otherwise. Jack hoped for a brief second that Henry and Rose would be too busy to come down to Eugene and see his little operation this

[55]

weekend. Maybe Sunflower can play activities director and send them into Portland to see one of Skye's, he thought.

He put on his apron and grabbed the sampling tray from the lab. The scanner was the only new feature in this process for the last thousand years. Similar to a grocery store scanner, this hand held device read the bar codes on all the barrels, tanks, and carboys. The thief and glasses on the tray were still the most important, however; a set of lab tests can reveal a wine's components, but only tasting can determine its true value. He set the tray on the cart and plugged the scanner into the laptop computer that was hidden in the first drawer next to the pH meter.

"Wow, look at you. Winemaker man all of a sudden," Maria said, returning from the bathroom. "Pretty hi-tech stuff you've got there. Are you sure you don't need some help with that?"

"There's an apron in the lab and a towel for your hair," he said, climbing a step ladder to the top row of barrels. He scanned the universal stripe on the first barrel and the computer screen automatically turned on. The top row of the spreadsheet showed vintage, grape, clone, vineyard, block, soil, slope direction and degrees of slope, spraying schedule and applications, trellis, irrigation, total degree days per block, temperature at harvest, total acidity of the grapes, pH, free and total sulfur, brix, cluster weight and average number per vine, Petal's notes, vigor, rainfall, wind speed, estimated hours of sunlight, tonnage per block, gallons per ton, fermentation, and tasting notes.

Maria walked back to the cart and looked at the screen without saying a word. Jack was using the thief to draw a sample of wine from the dark oak barrel. He placed it deep into the wine with his thumb over the top hole. Then he lifted his thumb to allow the wine to flow into the thief from the center of the barrel. He trapped the wine inside the glass tube by placing his thumb back over the breathing hole at the top, like a child trapping soda in a plastic straw. He carefully removed the thief and let the wine flow into a beaker by removing his thumb from the hole, like a child pouring soda in your lap. He replaced the bung on the barrel and handed Maria the beaker as he climbed down the stairs.

"You use a pH meter a lot for your water samples, don't you?" Jack said.

"Yeah, I was just wondering if that was the same type of thing or what. What does the pH have to do with wine?"

"Everything. It's probably one of the most important things we track throughout the year."

"Really, how much does it vary?"

"Well, water is about 7.0, right? And your palate begins to register flavors around 4.0 or so, usually. So, anything above that is flat or dull to the tongue. Well, some of the rieslings around here are from 2.9 to 3.3, and the pinots are anywhere from 3.3 to 3.6. Go ahead and measure this, please," he said, as he climbed the ladder and retrieved another sample, this time pouring it into a beautiful wine glass.

Maria turned on the meter and placed the wand in the beaker. She had measured hundreds of samples at school and this was absolutely the first time she ever wanted to taste what she was testing. She couldn't hide her smile as the numbers on the digital display rapidly adjusted from the buffer solution to the wine. It took a few seconds for the meter to stop and adjust for temperature and atmosphere. A tone similar to an answering machine beep signaled that the reading was complete.

"3.55," she said.

"Excellent," Jack said. "Malo is history."

"What's that mean?"

"The secondary fermentation is probably complete. I'll do a chromo just to make sure after we're through with these samples. Malo stands for malic acid. In Oregon especially, we want to convert all of the malic acid to lactic acid. That's what we call a malo-lactic fermentation."

"What's the difference?"

"Lactic is a little smoother, softer, and rounder in the mouth.

It can help capture that buttery aroma that people talk about, too. It's better for our peace of mind if we know the wine has already converted before we bottle it. It can be a real drag if it happens after bottling, obviously."

"How does the pH tell you that?" Maria asked.

"Well, it doesn't exactly but it helps. An increase in pH means a reduction in acid. Acid is really important in wine making. The balance between the acid, sugar, and pH in the grapes are the three things we follow the most." Jack gave her another beaker to sample as he tasted the wine from the first barrel.

"Like your shirt from the other night, right? 'Oregon Wine It's the acid' I get it now."

"Select pH on the screen and enter 3.55 and today's date, please," he smiled.

Using the trackball, Maria moved the cursor to the pH column. When she double-clicked on the red button, the screen changed to barrel #1 and all of the previous categories disappeared. She was surprised by the speed of the small machine as the history of barrel #1 unfolded before her eyes:

1995 pinot noir (108)-Salem, south block#6, eastern slope@10 degrees

Planted '77 Date last sampled-1-3-97	Previous samples F1, Menu F2
Barrel#1-Racked 10-2-95, 1-15-96, 7-15-96, 10ppm. per	
Spray-21 day S.O.2, Lupé,	Degree days-1953
Crush temp.-71, 9-21-95	Must temp-68
T.A.-8.1	pH-3.27
Volatile-.04	R.S.-.11
Amino-2600.0 @ 28	Soil-R-28
Alcohol-13.1	Fining- none
S.O.2-46 free, 77 total	Brix-23.7
Clusters-16, 8.6#	Wind-Average
Irrigation-35 gal. per	Protien-Stable
Rain-2.3 inches, July-crush.	Sun-approx. 1100 hrs.
Yield-2.6 tons per acre	Gallons-390
Cooperage-Limousin	Toast-Heavy
Vigor-Too much, four feet +	Trellis-Vertical
Canes-2	Botrytis-No

Petal's notes-okay, seeds 80% brown, small, clean clusters, no mildew.
Fermentation-F7/password. Racked to barrels #1-6 on 10-2-95.

Tasting notes-Still gritty and somewhat veggy. Color very good. Massive nose and tannin. There's that eastern undertone of aromatics that Petals' been looking for. They could be right.

Maria found the pH and date and changed both entries. She read the list in awe as Jack tasted the wine in his glass. He filled another beaker and suggested they trade places. She managed to squeeze by him and climb on top of the barrels as he took the pH of the new sample. She placed her forefinger through the handle on the thief and placed it into the barrel, pouring the wine into her glass just like a professional. She was smiling from ear to ear. Jack got a kick out of watching her work so diligently at the mundane task.

"What's your last name, Maria?"

"Taylor. What's yours?"

"How embarrassing. Hi, I'm Jack Miller," he said, his empty stomach filling up with wine. "Sometimes I'm a little too busy thinking about other things   sorry."

"I know what your name is, silly. How else could I have found your vineyards?"

Jack thought about it for a moment and then smiled like he had been duped. "Very impressive. So are you really working on your Masters?"

"Yes, at U of O. I'm only a few months away from finishing. And yes, frogs are in my thesis."

They continued to check the barrels and make entries into the laptop. The tasting glasses were being filled a little more with each sample. A paper napkin inside of the dump bucket was still bone dry. Jack was trying to plan the next bottling run and keep the entries somewhat organized, a major accomplishment considering the early hour and quantity of tasting.

"Do you taste all these?" Maria asked. Her face was beginning to glow. She was stirring the wine with the pH meter like it was a stalk of celery in a Bloody Mary.

Jack saw what she was doing and thought now was maybe a good time for a break. "Lets go over to the house and grab a bite to eat. Sound good?"

"Perfect. Got anymore chaw?" she asked.

Jack was stunned by the question. "That's probably not a good idea right now. Do you really chew that stuff?"

"Not really, but it sounded kind of good for some reason. My dad's a high school baseball coach. He chews all the time."

"Baseball, huh?" Jack said, trying to conceal his excitement.

"Yeah," said Maria, "he's got a game tonight. Wanna go?"

15

Henry saw the look in Rose's eyes as her father thanked him for the work his family had done for winemaking; many of the new varieties and pest-resistant stock were being developed in America. The rogue, new world of greed and wealth had actually contributed to the lifestyle Antonio's family cherished so much. He wanted to know more about the farming in California and Henry was eager to share, smiling at Rose as she changed the bandage on his forehead.

"How much land do you farm?" Vessini asked, still excited.

"The land is very different in California, Antonio. We don't have to climb the mountains and terrace the hillsides with a few vines here and there. There's a lot of land and a lot of water for irrigation, but the air is very warm and the sun is hot. Everything grows   everywhere. So . . . it's not the same."

Antonio smiled, sensing the scope of Henry's operation. "How much land do you own, Henry?"

"Ten thousand acres," he said shyly. "But remember, it's not the same. We have over one hundred tractors and thirty trucks with trailers, not mules and baskets. There is so much land, Antonio. Huge, rolling hills and rivers and we have the nebbia, too, just like here. It rolls in slowly and is very thick   the fog is so thick that we have accidents in the vineyards."

"Ah, the nebbia," Vessini said. "We have accidents from that, too. I call Rose my little Nebbiolo because of the grapes, but her eyes are like the nebbia. They are very beautiful, don't you think?"

She blushed as Henry looked into them. "Oh yes, Antonio, they are very beautiful." Rose pushed a little harder on the dressing than necessary, giving Henry a silent but painful warning to stop flirting in front of her parents. Her warm smile indicated that she liked what Henry had said, though.

"My brother's name is Merle," Henry said, thinking of home.

"For the grape, or the bird? That's French isn't it?" Antonio asked.

"Yes. I think he's named for both. The blackbird eats the merlot first at home and Merle was the first born."

Antonio smiled and turned to his daughter. "Rose, go and help your mama with the dinner. I need to talk to Henry alone for a few minutes." She tucked the bandage tightly and smiled at him as she got up to leave.

Henry watched her go and felt a horrible pain in his stomach as she left the room. There was no doubt in his mind that she would be his wife. He turned to Antonio who was smiling like a man who's just won the lottery. "She is very strong and smart, Henry. She is much smarter than her brothers. I have been teaching her the winemaking for many years   she is even better in the winery than she is in the kitchen, but she is very good in

[61]

there, too. Rose would be a wonderful wife to a California grape man," he said in a sly voice.

"You want your daughter to leave Italy, Antonio?"

"This can no longer be the home of my family. The Fascists know that we supported the French. It is no longer safe for any of them to be here. That is why they took my sons, Henry. Even though they lost the war they will still make their enemies pay. It's just a matter of time before something bad happens to many of us around here."

"I thought you said you had some good news for my employers. How can that be if you're worried for your family's safety?"

"We will be fine for awhile. We need the money to get to America. There is a man who operates the trains for the area and he knows where a lot of Cognac and other boxes are too. He has told me the location and I'm familiar with it. We have gone fishing and hunting there for many years."

"Did he know the quality or age?" Henry asked.

"No, he said that the guard had traded a bottle to his brother for an American wristwatch. No label or anything, but he said that it was extremely smooth and very good. Each bottle had its own box. So that's a good sign, yes?"

"Yes, that's a very good sign. Can I find it alone?"

"No, so many roads. I can't leave Corrina alone, either. Rose will go with you and you can spend some time together. She needs to not think about her brothers for a little while."

"Why isn't Rose married, Antonio?"

"The men are all gone. The war and emigration have destroyed her chances for a good husband. And she is too stubborn and picky; many callers have tried for her hand, Henry. But she likes you, I can tell. You might have a chance because you love the grapes, too."

The air was saturated with the smell of garlic and roasting meats. It was intoxicating. Henry's appetite was raging from the cheese and Barolo. It had been a very long day. His earlier daydream of

Italian farm girls and Champagne was a nightmare compared to meeting the Vessinis. He thought about Rose and a wave of adrenalin rushed through his body. He could see her grey eyes when he blinked. Both men succumbed to the smells emanating from the kitchen, their conversation fading to a dead silence.

"Do you know what that smell is?" Antonio asked in an obvious daze.

"Garlic . . . and anchovies?"

"Those are always in the air. Come on, what else?"

"It's musky, but wonderful. I'm not sure what it is," Henry shrugged.

"You must be a very special guest, Mr. Mueller. Those are the last of the white truffles until the new season. I'm glad you're here. I haven't had any in weeks. Now you will know what a Barolo is supposed to taste like."

16

Maria placed her left forefinger and thumb at the base of her chin and quickly pushed her head to the right. The eruption of calcium deposits in her neck built up from mid-term stress sounded like a car wreck. She looked at Jack and apologized for the disgusting maneuver. "Oh, I'm sorry but that felt incredible. That was the best one in days. I guess the wine made me relax a little bit, huh?"

Jack was absolutely enchanted by her casual behavior. "Yeah, it has a way of doing that. Let's go get that lunch before I pass out from hunger." Her dad's a baseball coach and she cracks her bones, he thought as he turned to leave. What am I getting myself into?

He checked the lab notes on the computer and sent a printout to the house. The sulfur tests could wait until later; nothing was going to spoil in the next hour. Maria's hair was dry now and the scent was overpowering his senses. His ability to identify the wine's various aromas had been compromised by the sexy new smell in the winery anyway.

"How come you're not in class?" he asked, still distracted by her long, auburn hair.

"I only go on Tuesdays and Thursdays."

"How long have you been waiting tables at the hotel? asked Jack."

"Three years. But I don't wait tables   I just work in the catering department on the weekends. It pays very good for part time," she said, following him out the door.

"Yeah, my Aunt Char has a few restaurants in San Francisco. Her newest server has been there six years. Those guys make big bucks and they only work four days a week."

They both blinked their eyes as they walked out of the winery into the bright afternoon sun. Pino and Vino ran over to the house without any encouragement from Jack. Maria laughed at the two dogs jumping over each other as they headed across the lawn, waiting for Jack to fill their bowls when they reached the porch. The dogs would jump off the steps and run towards them, stop, turn around and run back up the steps, and then turn around and jump off again, barking madly as they circled.

"How long does this go on?" she asked, still laughing.

"All day if we just stand here   they're amazing. Wait till you see them chase birds during crush," he said, suddenly aware of what he had just implied. He tried to back-pedal out of it softly before she got the wrong idea. "I mean . . . you should see them. They won't stop. I have to catch them and put 'em on a leash or they'll run themselves to death. It's really something."

Maria blushed and smiled, letting Jack know that she hoped to

[64]

be here during crush to watch the dogs, too. His rubber boots were a little too big for her so her stride was somewhat awkward; the combination of her clumsy walk, baggy sweatshirt, and wine-stained teeth was so cute it made Jack laugh out loud. He quickly looked at the dogs to conceal the source of his amusement. Maria faked a smile, suspicious of the origin of Jack's laughter.

As they walked up to the front porch, a car that Jack didn't recognize pulled into the driveway. He watched the man get out of the car and walk towards the house. As he got closer to Jack and Maria, the man's face went into a spasm and pulled to the left side. Blake quietly cursed under his breath at the involuntary reflex.

"Hey, you made it out alive, after all. I didn't think you stood a chance once you passed out on the bar. I'm sorry, I forgot your name," Jack said.

"Blake. Blake Stewart," he said. "I'm surprised you remember me, J–Jack. That gal poured us a lot of drinks the other night."

"Yes, she did. This is Maria, Blake. What can I do for you?"

"Hi Maria," Blake said, shaking their hands. He recognized her from the hotel immediately but didn't say so. Seeing the two of them together came as no surprise to Blake. He chuckled to himself as Maria looked at the ground, his palsy relaxing somewhat. "Jack, I don't know if you remember, but I had some stuff to t-t-talk to you about regarding your aunt from Yakima."

"I don't remember a whole lot, Blake. I'm sorry. I don't usually drink like that. Come on inside and join us for lunch."

Jack opened the door to the house and offered everyone a drink. The house was very old and the repairs he had planned three years ago when he bought it still weren't done. A big-screen TV sat alone in a corner. Overflowing bookshelves lined the other two walls. The heat had been left on all weekend and the air in the room was stale and hot.

"Sorry about the heat," Jack said. "Go ahead and have a seat on the porch and I'll get us some snacks."

Blake followed Jack to the kitchen while Maria threw a dirty

[65]

tennis ball at the dogs; this was a move she'd regret in five minutes. They insisted on playing fetch until dark if the game was initiated by a human.

"Jack, I'm sorry about your aunt. I just found out yesterday. The farmers I represent lease the land she owned in the Columbia Valley."

"Pretty strange stuff up there, Blake. I liked my aunt a lot. We were really close when I was a kid."

"I know, Jack," said Blake. "She t-told me."

"She told you? Why do you guys need to talk to me, anyway?"

"She had signed over all power of attorney to you just a f-few days before she   uh, died. She was trying to leave the care facility and didn't want to be responsible for all those d-d-decisions anymore. The group that employs my firm has invested millions of dollars developing and maintaining a lot of land that apparently . . . you now own."

Jack wasn't sure what he had just heard. He was watching Maria throw the ball further and further each time, a classic trick that only makes your arm sore and the dogs more excited.

"What?" he said.

"Jack, you'll be contacted by v-various attorneys with similar interests. Your aunt's estate was considerable, and now it's all yours."

"Why would she leave it to me?"

"I don't know. The actual estate is being handled by another f-firm. My clients are anxious to renew their lease, Jack. They've been working that land for over ten years. They're prepared to offer you five hundred thousand dollars a year for the n-next twenty years."

"How many acres of apples are there?" he said, stunned.

"Almost twelve hundred currently under contract; the pumps, out buildings, and cold storage have all been constructed at t-their expense. They had a very good relationship with Cherise. They want it to continue with you, Jack."

Juanita's truck pulled into the driveway and the familiar horn

[66]

sounded. Jack began to salivate just from the sound, thinking only of tacos as he walked past Blake to the door.

"Blake, you ever tasted heaven? Get ready, buddy." He walked out the door and told the dogs to "go lay down." Maria said thanks and slumped down on the porch, completely exhausted from the friendly game.

"Hola, Juanita!" he said. "I have guests today. I need twenty, please."

She gave Jack a motherly smile as she looked over his shoulder at the beautiful, young girl sitting on the steps. "Senor, Jack, you have girlfriend?" she teased.

"Shhh, she might hear you," he looked back at Maria and then gave Juanita a childish smirk. "I hope so. She's very nice. What kind of goodies did you bring us today? Cat?"

Juanita slapped him for his little joke and he grabbed his arm to comfort the pain from her harmless jab. This routine had been played out a hundred times before and they both enjoyed it more each time. She pulled a box out of the front seat of the truck and counted twenty foil-wrapped tacos into a bag that Jack held. He counted each one out loud as she did so but he always tried to cheat, deliberately saying the wrong number to confuse her. When she finished, he kissed her on the cheek and gave her a twenty-dollar bill.

"I think there's only eighteen in here, amiga."

"You're a flirt. I'm telling Felix you kissed me," she blushed.

"Isn't that old man finished with those vines yet?"

"You no give him any breaks, Jack. He's tired. He needs new cutters, too," Juanita said, spinning her familiar yarn, teasing Jack about the abuse of field labor.

"Ya, ya, ya, ya," he said, walking back to the house, his nose sticking into the bag.

He set the tacos next to Maria and went inside for the beer. Maria slowly peered into the sack with a look of uncertainty, surprised by the wonderful smell. Blake was sitting quietly at the table behind her on the porch when Jack returned with green salsa, lime, and a six pack of homebrew. They joined Blake at the table and the tacos were passed out.

"Do you think you got enough?" Maria asked sarcastically.

"I'm expecting my sister any minute," Jack said.

An old man was slowly walking towards the house with a small group of pigeons following him. He turned and waved at the birds, trying to make them go away, but they were very content where they were. Maria saw him and turned to Jack as she ate her taco. "Hey, Jack, you have a visitor," she said.

"Oh, it's Cornelius. He's on his daily walk to the tavern. Nice old guy. He used to own the whole county a long time ago. Now he has Alzheimer's, I think. He used to be as sharp as a tack and really into talking about farming. He hasn't said much in a few years, though. It's really sad. Wave to Cornelius, you guys. Hey Cornelius, how ya doing? Is that a new coat?"

Cornelius stopped at the same spot he always did and waved at Jack with an empty stare. The wave was similar to the one used by the Queen of England. It was more of an empty reflex than a deliberate gesture. He almost said something, but then turned and headed towards the bar, patting the bulge in his pockets and waving a wrinkled hand at the birds as he passed them.

"What's with the birds?" Maria asked.

"He always fills his pockets with croutons at the salad bar on his way to the tavern. And, sometimes he feeds the birds and sometimes he doesn't. They always smell him, though."

They shared a strange silence at the thought of the old man. Jack was consuming his third taco faster than the first two, applying salsa and fresh lime on every bite. He tried, without any luck, to get his mind off of Cherise; he couldn't stop thinking about the twelve hundred acres in the Columbia Valley.

"Hey, Jack?" Blake said.

"Yeah," he said, through a mouthful of carnitas.

"Was that true about the ancient Greeks, the other night at dinner you know, the sulfur and the bugs?" he said, without a

[68]

hint of a stutter.

Jack flinched at the question. For him, talking about sulfites was like getting a rectal exam. He wanted to scream that on average, a restaurant salad bar contained more sulfites than a case of wine, but you never saw a government warning on the sneeze guard. "I'm not sure. I think so, though. Hey, look, there's Petal."

Sunflower's jeep pulled up and she jumped out quickly, anxious for a taco. She ran to the porch and said hello to everyone as she stuck her hand into the bag like a bear grabbing a salmon. Despite her love of animals and firm belief in yin, yang and Karma, Sunflower ate Juanita's pork tacos as fast as Jack.

"Petal, this . . . is Maria . . . and this . . . is Blake," Jack said very slowly, implying that she was being rude by eating so fast.

She got the hint and stopped chewing. "Hi, you guys. Sorry, I'm starving. It's nice to meet you both."

"It's nice to meet you, too. I've heard a lot about you," Maria said.

Blake hadn't taken a breath since she jumped from the jeep. His bowels had turned to water and he felt queasy; Sunflower was the most beautiful girl he'd ever seen. BANG! Her eyes were on him and her smile was piercing his heart. As he started to say hello, the left side of his face yanked like he was a fish being pulled from a river. His heart sank at the palsy reflex. The stutter returned and captured his words and breath like a steel trap. After several painful convulsions, they managed to escape through his contorted mouth in the form of a salty, viscous spit bubble. He wanted to cry.

"That's cute," Sunflower giggled, chomping into her taco. Her warm smile never left her face. Jack looked at the two of them and Maria, and decided that spring must be in full bloom. Something is definitely in the air, he thought, squeezing more lime on his carnitas.

🌾 🌾 🌾

17

Henry got up from bed and walked to his radio. His head still ached and his stomach was growling. The smell of the bagna cauda was everywhere. It was so thick, he thought he could actually taste the hot dip of garlic and anchovies as he tried to radio one of Bennett's men stationed in the village. After several unsuccessful attempts, he decided to try again after dinner. Maybe the hills are getting in the way, he thought. He walked through the winery towards the kitchen, letting his nose lead the way. Thanks to his appetite and Corrina's skill, finding the dining room was easy for Henry.

The magnificent room was like the inside of an opera house or theatre. The wood paneling and long, red tapestries created the perfect atmosphere for a feast. A table big enough for twelve was covered with platters of cheese, bread, and vegetables. The crostinis were still warm and Henry couldn't resist spreading the paste over the top of the small circles of toasted bread. Several ornate chandeliers provided a soft glow from above. Bottles of wine dominated the center of the table.

The clang of pots, pans, and voices could be heard through the kitchen door. The voices were audible but the language was rapid-fire Italian. Antonio and Corrina were fighting about something and Antonio was definitely on the defense. Henry walked away from the door to allow them a degree of privacy, circling the table to admire a large, antique buffet. The craftsmanship of the piece was extraordinary. Hand-carved gargoyles and numerous family crests garnished the vertical posts that separated several mirrors. Dozens of drawers lined its bottom, running almost the entire length of the massive room.

Each handle was made from an ancient grape vine. The gnarled, old wood appeared soft and splinter-free, sanded through the years from thousands of hands carefully opening the drawers. A chafing dish on top was stacked with egg-battered perch and sprigs of fresh sage. A delicate sauce of lemon, mustard, and herbs was in a bowl nearby.

Henry's stomach was growling again. He went for the bagna cauda and savored the truffles as he poured a generous glass of Vessini's Barolo. Rose entered the room and grabbed a slice of bell pepper, dipping it in the paste with a smile on her face. She asked Henry to pour her a glass of wine.

"Did you talk to your friends?" she asked.

"No, I think the mountains make it a little too hard to get through."

"How do you like the truffles?" she asked, flirting again.

"Amazing, I've only had the black ones from France. These are much better. Where are they from?" Henry asked, obsessed with the food for the moment and unaware of her intentions.

"They grow in the roots of the oaks we use for the wine barrels. They are very beautiful trees, surrounded by the willows and beech trees. We use dogs to find the truffles, not pigs; sometimes they are five or six inches underground. We gather them in the fall and winter, but only at night so no one will see where they are. You can dry them and keep them in olive oil, but they're much better fresh. Do you have them in California?"

"Nothing even close," he said, still blending the wine and warm paste in his mouth. The combination created aromas in the back of his nose that were completely new to his experience as the bold flavors of tar and cherry mixed with the pungent tones of the fungus. The anchovies provided salt and the lemon came through with just the right amount of citrus. It was a strange medley, achieving balance and harmony throughout his palate as it developed.

Antonio and his wife entered from the kitchen with yet more food. They carried plates of fresh trout and roasted pheasant, their smiles indicating some form of truce had been reached in their earlier dispute. Henry was relieved to see the happy face of Antonio come through the door in a rush of excitement. Vessini found a place on the table for the birds and quickly poured two glasses of wine for he and his wife. Henry could see from their faces that preparing a meal for guests was a treasured moment in their lives. A toast was offered and everyone was seated.

"May God look out for our sons, and may Hitler swallow a bomb for dinner tonight. Mein Kampf my ass!" sang Antonio.

"Amen," they said in unison. The platters of food were passed around, and heaping portions piled up. The wine flowed freely as Corrina described every dish to an attentive Henry, his head swimming from the combinations. Rose made him blush throughout the meal, gently touching his hand as she passed him the platters. Her warm glances were shy and yet inviting. Antonio watched quietly as Henry fell in love with his daughter. It was the first time that Antonio Vessini had been truly happy in a long, long time.

"How long have you been in Europe, Henry?" Antonio asked.

"I came over in '43. I was stationed in London, supplying the airfields for the bombing runs."

"So have you seen the V-1's?" Antonio inquired.

"Yes, just recently they're terrifying. And now they have the V-2; they are not bombs, but rockets that are much faster with better range. Fortunately, it looks like we now hold most of the launch sites in France that they needed to reach London. You can hear them flying through the air, though, buzzing like hornets. Our planes and artillery still get most of them, but when they get through it's devastating. The noise is so frightening for everyone."

The smile had gone from Rose's face, and Henry felt bad for his poor lack of judgment. He tried to recover the good mood at the table by recapping the success of the D-Day invasion.

"We cleaned up those bastards in the north, though. It's just a matter of time before Hitler gets killed by one of his own

[72]

generals. He blew it in Africa and Russia   and last winter cost him all of his supply lines through the Balkans," he said, looking at Corrina who wasn't eating. "What kind of harvest do you expect, Antonio?"

Vessini smiled at Henry's question; a new topic was wise. "Everything is growing very fast and the canopy is very thick. If it gets a little hotter, we should have a wonderful year."

"I saw the fermenters out back. Who stirs the grapes? Those things are huge," Henry said.

"That is Rose's favorite thing to do," Antonio said proudly. "She hangs from the planks across the top and stirs with her legs. She is purple through the new year," he laughed. "But that is why her skin is so beautiful, like her mother's."

Corrina smiled fondly at her husband and offered more perch to Henry. He grabbed a large fork and eagerly served himself two more filets, smothering them with the mixture of fresh sage and butter. Antonio was so inspired by Henry's appetite, he poured another bottle of wine to everyone and tore the leg from a pheasant in a classic display of hedonism.

Henry laughed and tried the gnocchi and almost fainted. They were layered in a baking dish with Fontina cheese and butter. The sausage shaped balls of potato and flour were Corrina's specialty. She saw Henry's face relishing her cooking, and looked to Antonio to signal her approval. If the way to a man's heart is through his stomach, there must also be a path to the chef's through his or her ego.

"Henry Mueller from Napa, California," Antonio said, raising his glass. "It is a true pleasure to have met and dined with you. May your quest for plundered eau-de-vie be successful, and may you experience many good harvests in your future."

Antonio looked at Rose and continued. "Henry needs a guide to get to the lake, Rose. Do you want to go with him? I need to stay here with your mother in case your brothers try to reach us. I've discussed it with your mother, and Henry. You know the way, and the Germans are gone from that portion of the northwest. It would good for you to get away and enjoy yourself."

Rose tried to remain calm and hide her excitement. She did a very poor job. A weekend with the young American, away from her parents, was something she hadn't imagined. A smile emerged as she looked at her father. It was strange to have his blessing and for a moment, she struggled to find out why something must be wrong, she thought. She looked at her mother and sensed that she was worried for her safety, but not for going with Henry. She was afraid to have her stay. Corrina looked away from Rose and went to the kitchen.

"What's wrong, Papa?"

"Nothing, Rose. Mama is only worried to have you away from her, that's all."

Henry sat quietly, watching Antonio comfort Rose as she realized their family was no longer safe in the small village she called home. Her grey eyes began to water as she listened to her father lie about their safety. He walked to her side and put his arms around her in a fatherly embrace.

"Don't cry, Rose. Why are you crying? There is nothing wrong," Antonio said. He looked at Henry and smiled. "It must be the vino," he said, unconvincingly.

Corrina returned from the kitchen with a tray full of custards and puddings. The zabaglione was served warm, providing instant levity to a desperate situation. Corrina saw the tears on Rose's cheeks and immediately served her a glass of her favorite dessert. Rose was pouting as she took her first bite, her lower lip protruding. A smile slowly formed at the corners of her mouth as she ate. Henry fell hopelessly in love, watching her smile bloom as the pudding disappeared.

"I've had better meals in Poland," Antonio said, burping and clearing his throat at the same time. "You're losing your touch in your old age, woman."

Corrina blushed and then winked, smiling at her appreciative husband. Rose laughed out loud, forgetting her worries for the moment and enjoying Henry's look of dismay and horror.

The dishes were cleared and Antonio invited a confused Henry to the roof for a cigar. Henry thanked Corrina for an incredible meal, and exchanged smiles with Rose as he followed Vessini up the stairs.

The ancient stairwell was dark, steep and narrow. A long day, and numerous glasses of wine, turned the short climb into an arduous journey. The fresh air coming down the stairs provided inspiration however, and a victorious Henry emerged on the roof, relieved to be at the top.

The humidor was waiting on a small table. Vessini was smiling, obviously aware of Henry's fatigue. Their view of the small village and mountains was spectacular from the little patio. The terraced hillsides, vineyards, and plats were barely visible in the moonlight. The surrounding stone houses were stacked like oranges in the produce market, their ceramic roofs reflecting the soft light. A flame ignited as Vessini presented a cigar to Henry.

"You have had a very long day, my friend," Antonio said.

Henry drew on the cigar several times. Their shadows pulsed in a staccato rhythm of light with each breath as the flame grew larger and then disappeared into the cigar. After a moment, a large cherry of burning tobacco formed on the tip. The Havana was smooth and satisfying. Henry rubbed the bruise on his head and paused, thinking about the day.

"This has been a very wonderful day, Antonio. You are a very fortunate man."

Antonio reached into the small cabinet between them and pulled out a decanter of dark liquid. "Do you like Port, Henry?" he asked, rhetorically.

Henry smiled, not at all surprised by the appearance of the rare nectar. "Well, I don't know, Antonio. How old is it?"

"Oh, it's very young. You may not like it," he said. "It's from this century." There was a sincere hint of disappointment in his

[75]

voice. The small, crystal glasses were filled and Vessini casually pointed for Henry to help himself.

After a long pull on his cigar, Henry tasted the Port. "It's barely from this century, Antonio. Thank you. It's perfect." He looked at the village and relaxed deeply into his chair.

"The '04 is still a little young, but . . . war is hell," Antonio said, smiling at the night. "You will take good care of my little Nebbiolo, won't you, Henry?"

"I will protect her for the rest of my life, Antonio. I promise."

"I know. I saw you fall in love with her. I look at her mother the same way." Vessini paused, admiring the smoke from his cigar. He placed his hand on the humidor and caressed the initials, his thoughts drifting many miles away to his sons.

"What have I done, Henry?" he asked, not looking for an answer. "The Fascists and Monarchy were morons, but they let the farmers own and work their land. It was the Communists, I feared. That's why I supported the West; I had many friends in the wine business over there." He looked at the humidor and took a deep breath. "I had no idea how many Communists were around here waiting for their turn. So much finger pointing now, the next few years will be hell on everyone. Remember, Henry, always remember, family is all that matters. It is everything."

Henry waited several minutes for Antonio to continue speaking. The two men sat comfortably in the warm night air, listening to the crickets. "If you need a sponsor to get to America, Antonio, my family can help. Between the vineyards and the connections of my employer, we can obtain any documents necessary for your departure. We shouldn't wait too long, though."

Antonio snored softly as Henry continued to talk about immigration. He went on to describe his family's operations, talking about the size and quality of their yields, and how they commanded the highest prices every year with little or no complaining from their buyers   thanks to him, of course; how his brother, Merle, was designing their own winery so they could begin large scale processing of their best grapes; and how he was eager to return home and tap new markets back east for their fruit, using the new highway systems that were now under construction. He described the new roads and highways, and the large trucks being developed.

"America is the land of opportunity, Antonio. My family is living the dream," he said, finishing his speech in a triumphant crescendo. He looked at Vessini and smiled. Antonio was sleeping, his loud rhythmic snoring revealing his love for good wine and his wife's cooking.

🍇 🍇 🍇

18

"So, what's with the frogs?" Sunflower asked. Her forefinger was deep in her mouth, extracting a piece of caramelized pork from her back molars.

"They're mine," Maria said casually. "I'm collecting samples from all over the valley for my thesis."

"What's your thesis?" Sunflower asked, immediately concerned about any negative impact her vineyards might have on the little froggies.

"Easy, Petal," Jack said.

"That the genetic deviations are part of a normal pattern in a corrective cycle to compensate for global warming and reduced habitat," Maria explained.

"Cool," Sunflower said, remaining calm and turning to Jack. "So, did you hear what Grandpa sent up to Mom and Dad's?"

"What?" Jack said, afraid of the answer.

"Five cases of wine, via one day air. Henry can be a real butt sometimes."

"What did Dad do?"

"Believe it or not, he just smiled. I was pretty impressed. Mom almost sent them back, but Dad said there might be some really old Bordeauxs, so we should just wait it out. He's so classic. His dad slaps him in the face and all he can think about is drinking some old claret." She paused and looked at Blake and Maria. "Sorry, you guys, family crisis time."

Blake flinched and got up from the table and pulled a small phone from his breast pocket. "Hello," he said.

Maria looked at Jack and Sunflower with a puzzled look on her face. "Did you guys hear anything?" she asked.

"It's the old vibrating phone trick," Sunflower said, exchanging a wink with Maria.

"Petal, knock it off," Jack said, not approving of her innuendo.

"What?" she laughed. "Hey, do you think he'll let me borrow it? It gets so lonely in the vineyard."

Maria cracked up and took another swig of beer as Jack placed his face in his hands and shook his head. "How can we possibly be related?" he said.

Blake walked a few yards off the porch and continued his conversation. Pino and Vino were escorting him around the lawn as he walked. He turned to watch everyone at the table as he spoke, uncomfortable with his situation. "Yeah, Spalding, I'm here right now. There's three p-people watching me talk. I'll call you later, okay?"

"Did you get him to sign the lease?" asked Spalding. "Listen, Blake. These guys want to know what the deal is before they make a move to get this land. If they can renew the lease, great. If not, they sue for control. They have her signature on about a thousand documents; one of them is bound to be a forty year lease pretty soon, understood? I'm not paying you seventy-five dollars an hour to mess this up!"

Blake smiled at everyone as he listened to Spalding. The

familiar, prosaic speech was almost unbearable. He could feel his blood pressure rising as Spalding began to repeat himself for the third time without any hint of slowing down. The dogs were there to offer Blake their support and encouragement, sensing that he was just a few seconds away from launching the phone deep into the vineyard. Blake smiled, knowing exactly what they were thinking   fetch. He would have thrown it but he knew they would bring it right back, completely unaware they had become the faithful agents of Spalding West.

"Yeah, I'm on t-top of it," Blake said quietly. "I haven't had any time alone with him yet. He invited m-me to lunch, though. I'll try and get his signature before the end of the week. I've got to g-go. I'll call you later." He hung up as Spalding began his fourth round of threats.

Blake walked back to the table and apologized for the interruption. He opened another beer and, despite his reluctance, knocked it back in a hurry. The others watched him relax, as his face slowly returned to normal.

"What kind of beer is this anyway?" snapped Blake.

"That's my brother Skye's specialty. It's called Black Muddy Porter. It's kind of thick, isn't it?"

"Did he forget to ferment it?" Blake was obviously pissed-off about his conversation with Spalding.

"I guess they want my signature pretty bad, huh?" Jack said.

"Oh, there's a lot of stuff g-going down at the Seattle office," he said slowly. "I'm stuck in the middle of a couple of things." He looked at Sunflower and thought about Spalding; what a jerk, he said to himself.

"What signature?" Sunflower asked. "What do you do, Blake?"

"I'm a lawyer," he said, his face bunching up again.

"I'll tell you about it later, Petal. It's about Cherise," Jack said.

Maria suddenly felt out of place and got up to play with the dogs. Jack knew what she was up to and jumped down to join the game of fetch. He wrestled Pino to the ground as Vino jumped on his back. Maria pushed the dog off Jack and threw the tennis ball

[79]

at the winery. Vino bolted after it, grateful for the affectionate toss.

Sunflower smiled at Blake, wondering what he was up to. He couldn't hold her stare and he faked a laugh at the dogs. It was a pitiful attempt at distracting her and she knew it. His stomach knotted up as she asked the inevitable question.

"So, what kind of lawyer?"

"Probate," he said, trying not to drool on himself.

"Did Cherise leave everything to Jack?" she asked. She intentionally used her voice to massage his ears and calm his nerves.

"I don't know. I'm not handling the will."

"Hey, Petal, leave it alone. I'll tell you everything. You know that," Jack said, throwing the saliva-soaked ball at Maria as she screamed.

Sunflower frowned at Blake and his heart skipped a beat. He wanted to tell her about the grapes and recite the love stanzas of Romeo and Juliet without a stutter. He imagined her running naked through the vineyards in Yakima, her beautiful blonde hair flowing in the wind as her long stride carried her through the vines into his waiting arms. . . .

"Blake . . . hey, Blake . . . Blake!" yelled Jack, laughing at the lawyer as he dreamed about his sister.

A startled Blake looked up at Jack, trying to hide his embarrassment. His face was flush from his little Sunflower daydream and the beer he had just shot-gunned.

"Hey, Blake," Jack said. "Maria's gotta go and I've got to finish up some labwork. Do you want to get together tomorrow sometime? We can talk about this stuff after I talk to my dad."

"Sure, n-no problem. Noon, okay?"

"Yeah, I'll see ya here. Petal, you be good. Go get those guys back to work and meet me in the lab."

Jack and Maria cleared the table and went inside. Sunflower smiled at Blake as he tried to say goodbye, his words flowing like stones through a gall bladder.

"I'll be here tomorrow, too. We can have some more laughs. Do you like sushi?" she said, smiling as she walked to the vineyard.

He nodded and watched her walk away, speaking beautifully to her as she disappeared over the hill. He casually delivered an elegant soliloquy describing his kind heart and affectionate nature. Blake was shocked as the words were pulled from his mouth and rode into the vineyard on a invisible ribbon carried by Sunflower. His speech was flawless in every detail. He spoke fluently about her eyes, hair, and smile as Jack quietly listened through the screen door behind him.

Jack watched silently as Blake continued to speak. He was amazed at the beauty and clarity of Blake's dialogue. He was captivated by the emotion in his voice as the unfamiliar stanzas flowed like wine at a Roman banquet. Then he felt betrayed, wondering if Blake's stutter was just a tool he used to gain the advantage in negotiations. It had obviously worked on Sunflower. Jack hadn't seen her that giddy in months. In fact, just a few minutes ago he was ready to sign the lease on the property in Yakima. Damned attorneys, he thought. Those crafty bastards will do whatever it takes to close the deal.

Maria called from the kitchen and Blake abruptly stopped his oration, stumbling on the final verse in a clever finale. Jack ducked behind the door frame and waited a moment before answering, his confusion increasing as he pondered Blake's stutter. He walked to the kitchen and gave Maria a hand, wondering if he should confront Blake about his deception.

After a while, they heard Blake's car pull away and they walked outside. The sun was in full control of the day and Maria assured Jack that a rainout wasn't likely.

"Meet me at the park?" she said, walking down the driveway.

"Sure. I can't wait. Can I bring a glove?" he said, sounding like a kid.

"I always do. Come early and take some batting practice with me and Dad. You'll love it."

"Seriously?"

"Yep, I've got connections. See you at four," she said, bouncing as she walked away.

"Hey, where's your car?"

"Down the street. At the restaurant."

"Don't eat the croutons," he shouted. "Old Cornelius shovels those things into his pockets with both hands, and they're filthy." He watched her go as he walked to the winery to finish the titrations. Pino and Vino were on his heels the whole way, begging for attention.

He quickly scanned a bar code and watched the screen for the display. He was sampling five different types of barrels; all were from the same cooper, all were filled with the same wine, and each style of barrel imparted something unique, creating a different color, taste, texture and aroma in the wine. The various nuances are detectable not only with one's senses but by chemical analysis as well. The numerous acids, phenols, and aldehydes react with the wood to either enhance or destroy the vineyard's terroir.

The style of the barrel, like the style of the wine, is determined by many variables. The forest, climate, age, grain, assembly, toasting, and finishing of the wood all play a role in the barrel's overall quality. Again, like wine, the preference of one style over another is completely subjective. Thus, the commitment to an expensive barrel program should only be made after extensive research with your own vineyards and style of wine.

His dad experimented with several different coopers and forests before finding the right ones for his various vineyards. He decided on a mixture of new barrels with medium and heavy toast from the Limousin forest of France. He found, after a time, that these barrels infused just the right qualities to achieve the correct balance of fruit and acid. He used the lighter-toast barrels with loose-grain for the grapes high in acid, and the heavier-toast ones for the grapes low in acid. Usually, after about a year in oak, his pinot noirs were well-structured and ready to blend. Thankfully, they reach full maturity after only a few years in the bottle, a considerably short period of time compared to most other red wines. Anthony often joked that the rapid maturation was a small gift from the wine gods for trying to make pinot noir in Oregon in the first place.

Jack used the thief to draw another sample of wine and took it to the lab. He was checking the sulfite levels to compare the oxidative properties of the various barrels. He had found that over the same period of time, wine aged in a tight-grain barrel retained more fruit and free-sulfur than wine aged in a loose-grain barrel.

He was in the lab watching the iodine drip slowly into the wine, waiting for a color change to indicate the end point of the titration. After reading the amount of iodine used, he multiplied it by a normality constant to determine the amount of sulfur in the wine. The overall stability of wine is directly related to the proper levels of free-sulfur, pH, and alcohol. He entered the data into the laptop and retrieved another sample as Sunflower burst through the door.

"Jack's gonna get some yin," she sang cheerfully.

"What?"

"You know what I'm talking about," she said.

"Yin? What's that?" Jack said, being coy.

"Don't give me that, Shabby. I know what you meant last night when you said you needed some yin. You thought you were being sly, didn't you? We both know that yin is female, and Maria is definitely female."

Jack smiled at his little sister and gestured for her to grab a beaker and start drawing samples for the chromo. "I'm impressed that you picked that one up, Petal. I thought it was over your head."

[83]

"Oh, that'll be the day. So I'm dying to know, what's up with Cherise? Did that guy tell you anything?"

"Yes," he said.

Sunflower was looking at him as she dabbed little glass sticks into various wine samples and blotted them on a piece of paper. Her blots of wine crossed the bottom of the page in a straight line, about an inch apart from each other. She wrote the corresponding barrel number under each wine stain as she waited for Jack to continue. "What? What did he tell you?"

"That Cherise left me a lot of orchards up in Yakima."

"Really. How many?" she said, obviously excited but aware of her aunt's pain at the same time.

"Many. About twelve hundred acres, all in production."

"Wow. The Bhagwan liked his apples, huh?"

"I don't know, I guess. They've been leased for the last ten years by a co-op up there. They offered me a lot of money to renew the lease."

"Does Dad know?" she asked.

"No, not yet. I was going to call him after we finished this. I've been putting these chromos off for too long. I've already noticed a little fruit loss in some of Block Six. I may have missed it," he said, referring to the best time to add sulfites. The challenge for a winemaker is to let the wine develop and change, and then catch it and preserve it at just the right time with the smallest possible addition of sulfites.

"Jack, these smell great. Don't worry about a thing," she said, connecting the sides of the chromatography paper with a stapler and making it into a large tube. After she finished, she placed it into a gallon jar that had half an inch of liquid solvent in the bottom. The specially-treated paper immediately began to absorb the liquid. In several hours, the wine stains would be carried to the top of the page. Certain acids would be visible on the paper after it dried, their presence or absence indicating the status of the malo-lactic fermentation.

"Where did you meet Maria, anyway?"

"She was a waitress at the dinner I did the other night. Don't say a word."

"You dog," she said, returning his smile. "Like father, like son. She's cute, too."

"Definitely."

"Do you think she's going to do anything about the frog mutations?"

"I don't know," said Jack. "What can she do?"

"Shit, Jack, you know what I mean. Is she going to blame it on the vineyards?"

"Are they responsible?" he snapped.

"No, they're not responsible. You know I don't use anything except a little sulfur to control mildew. It's probably all that sheep piss. Why did Cherise plant apples?" she asked, changing the subject.

"I think she was trying to get back at Grandpa."

"Yeah, that makes sense. It's funny that she would leave everything to you, though."

"Why's that?" he asked.

"You know, the whole cabernet/syrah thing. It's kind of like she was admitting that the totem stuff is real. It just kind of surprises me, that's all. If she was really that upset about everything, why would she give Henry the pleasure of blending the two of you in his mind again."

"Blending the two of us in his mind? What the hell does that mean? Sometimes you're a little too weird for me, Petal. And I studied psychology."

"Can you believe Henry's going to be here in a few days?" Sunflower asked.

"I've been thinking about that a lot," he said, refilling the iodine to test another sample. "It's either going to be a real drag, or one hell of a party. He sent up five cases of wine, right?"

"Yeah, five cases. Have you talked to Skye lately?"

"No. He's a flake. Halle had the chicken pox last week, though. So, I guess that's some sort of excuse. Does he know about

[85]

Cherise?"

"Mom went up there today."

Sunflower was swirling a glass of wine, holding it up to the light. Her face was scrunched up as she contemplated the color. The information she gained from smelling the wine was being processed as she admired it.

"Did the pH go up much?" she asked.

"Yeah, from 3.27 to 3.58. It's done."

"How many p.p.m. do you want?" Sunflower asked.

"I'm gonna wait for those chromos before we do anything. I'm probably going to add thirty, though. What do you think?" inquired Jack.

"How long before you bottle it?"

"Fifteen months, at least."

"Are you gonna rack it again?"

"No," he said, without hesitation.

"I think thirty is a good call, Jack. Dad would puke, but after that fiasco in '93, I don't think we should mess around anymore."

"Tell me about it," he said, nodding at Sunflower to look at the maze of dirt still on the floor in the corner where eight pallets of wine had just been removed. "What a relief to have those out of here."

"How many did they buy?"

"Twelve hundred," he smiled. "They're fine for another year, Petal. Don't look at me like that. They weren't that bad, anyway."

"I didn't say anything. You sound like you're trying to convince yourself. In fact, you almost sound guilty of something, Jack."

"Yeah, guilty of committing to fifteen dinners. They have me going all over the place."

"You're such a goof. You know you love those things. I've seen you, remember?"

"The first two courses are like root canal," he said, whining like a little kid.

"Start drinking earlier," she laughed.

[86]

"You're a big help. Mom would love that advice. She could tell I was hungover from the last one."

"Alcohol was oozing from your pores, Jack. You stunk."

"B-B-Blake and I got hammered by some car dealer and a maitre d' that wanted to know what my sign was."

"That's not funny, Jack. He can't help it if he stutters. You're being mean."

"I wonder."

"What?" she asked, curiously.

"Never mind. Go ahead and top those barrels off, please. I need a shower before I take batting practice for the first time in five years. I don't want to look too bad."

"Where are you going?" asked Sunflower.

"Maria's dad coaches the high school baseball team. I'm going to their preseason opener tonight."

"Her dad coaches baseball?" she asked, shaking her head. "Looks like I'm going to have to make some room on the family cluster a little sooner than I thought."

19

The acrid smell of garlic and anchovies greeted Henry as he woke. He was confused, thinking he had overslept and missed breakfast and lunch completely. Then he remembered Antonio had said that that smell was always in the air. He could see that the sun was already up and that morning was well under way. It seemed a little early for anchovies, but he thought "what the heck" anyway, licking the thick film on his teeth. He could taste the forty year-old Port and Cuban cigars fermenting in his mouth as a knock sounded at the door.

"Come in," he said.

"Good morning, Henry," Rose said, as she filled a large bowl on the dresser with hot water. She looked lovely, despite the early hour. Her hair was shining and her smile was anxious and warm. "Come on, get up. We've got to get an early start if we're going to be back before dark." She left the room before he could answer, leaving the door open to let the smell of eggs mingle with the garlic.

He washed his face and got dressed, thinking about the day ahead. He still hadn't had a chance to communicate with Bennett. He was sure nonetheless that a rendezvous with some rare Cognac would be approved, even encouraged. The gamble on bottles shipped in individual wood boxes was a pretty good one. Some of the eau-de-vies he had sampled were worth far more than grand cru wine in the first place. And now they were even more desirable because of their high alcohol content. Many of the wines were feared to already have been spoiled because of improper storage and transport in the hot railroad cars. This was exactly the reason why Bennett now employed men like Henry in the field.

Vessini was already seated at the table when Henry entered the dining room. A large cup of broth was in front of him, steam rising from the bowl in the morning light. Antonio smiled at the young soldier, proud for a moment that he was still a part of the war in some way. Perhaps, he thought to himself, information about the location of his boys could be obtained through the help of Henry's employers. And, on a far lesser note but equally appealing to Antonio, maybe he could deny Hitler the satisfaction of another toast with Goebbels using wine stolen from his friends; the wine almost being as important to him as his sons.

"Good morning, Henry. You look well," he said, lying.

"Thank you, Antonio. So do you," he said, rolling his eyes and smiling at Vessini. "And thank you for the blanket last night. I would have frozen without it."

"I didn't give you a blanket."

Henry looked puzzled for a moment and then Rose entered the room. He realized suddenly that his dream about kissing Rose wasn't a dream. He blushed as soon as she looked at him. That crazy girl snuck up on the roof and kissed me when I was asleep? His heart was racing as she served him a plate with several ramekins on it. The little cocottes were filled with baked eggs, ham, and Fontina cheese. He was surprised how quickly the sight of them made his appetite return.

"Did you sleep well?" Antonio asked, frowning at his daughter as she served him a plate of eggs. He knew she had been on the roof with Henry and, on the outside, did not approve. On the inside, however, he was very happy that she liked the young grape grower from California.

"Yes, Papa," said Rose, disappearing into the kitchen.

Antonio had a suspicious look on his face as he turned his attention to Henry.

"And how did you sleep, Henry?"

"Good. Good. Fine. Boy, these sure smell good, don't they?" he said, not looking at a smiling Vessini.

"So, here's your map. You should be there in a couple of hours," Antonio said, no longer teasing Henry. "This is the man to ask for," he said, pointing to a name on the map. "You can use my name. He will be very anxious to sell his cache; his time is running out. How are you going to pay? Never mind. That's none of my business."

Henry ate his breakfast with Antonio. Corrina and Rose were nowhere to be found. His stomach knotted up as he thought about Rose and the long day ahead. He could only eat two eggs as they talked about farming and the past. Antonio was very curious about America and the opportunities that still awaited him and his family. He was only in his fifties, still young enough to start a vineyard and enjoy many harvests. Henry laughed, saying that he would never have to worry about grapes for as long as he lived.

"I must have my own vines, Henry. What else would I do?"

"Make millions of gallons of wine, Antonio. That's what," Henry said.

"Millions?" said Antonio, in awe.

"Millions. Merle is designing a factory for the grapes right now. When the war is over, there will be steel for everyone, lots of cheap steel. He sent me plans for huge, airtight tanks and automatic fermenters. He is very smart, and a wonderful winemaker. There are valves over two feet wide, Antonio enormous pumps and filters, too. Even the bottles will fill themselves," he said, gesturing with his hands.

Antonio mulled the numbers over in his mind. Henry could see that he was intimidated by the scale of their operation. To Vessini, the grapes were sacred. You were a part of them and they were a part of you. When you drank the wine from your vineyard, you were rewarded for your labor. If you had good land and water and worked very hard, you could sell some grapes and trade your wine for what food you couldn't grow yourself.

[90]

And that didn't leave very much for Antonio and Corrina to trade for. They needed little more than good food, wine, and family to be happy.

"Don't worry, Antonio," Henry said, sensing his apprehension. "The machines can never taste the wine. You will be in charge of making the wine. You will be there to supervise every step in the process, constantly refining and adjusting until the grapes taste like the land, not the machine."

Vessini smiled at Henry's good nature. He was very intuitive for a young man, Antonio thought, remembering how he had calmed the fears of both women during dinner   a very useful quality in any form of negotiation. I bet he gets the highest prices for his grapes, Vessini said to himself, feeling much better.

"Do you have enough fuel?" Antonio asked.

"Yes, many gallons. And more cigars, too."

"Do you grow the Spanna, Henry?" Vessini asked, enjoying his company immensely.

"I'm not familiar with it," he shrugged.

"I'm sorry, Henry. That's what we call the nebbiolo in this village."

"Not very much, no. There is some, but we don't own any that I'm aware of."

"What do you grow the most of?" Vessini asked.

"Cabernet, zinfandel, merlot, petite sirah, chardonnay and riesling."

"What's your preference?"

"Cabernet. Definitely," Henry said.

"And the Burgundies?" Antonio inquired.

"A little, but just the whites, though. The reds are far too fussy."

Corrina and Rose entered the room and were seated at the table. Corrina looked sternly at Henry. An unspoken warning was being issued and everyone knew it, especially Rose. The air was heavy and Antonio provided relief by commenting on how beautiful his wife was this morning. She was unfazed by her husband's remarks and continued to stare at the American who was shrinking in his chair. After a few moments, her face warmed and a small smile formed at the corners of her mouth. Henry sighed in relief as she offered him some peaches.

"Thank you, Mrs. Vessini. They look wonderful," he said, adding several slices to his plate.

Antonio left the room and returned with a satchel and picnic basket. His smile conveyed jealousy as he talked to the youngsters.

"I have packed a meal worthy of the king himself," he said proudly.

Rose and Corrina exchanged smiles without saying a word. They had been preparing a romantic meal all morning. The jeep was already loaded with enough food to last a week.

"Thank you, Papa. You didn't have to do that. You are very sweet." She smiled at him and gave him the little girl look that always made him so happy. She got up from the table and gave him a hug and a kiss and told him not to worry. "You take good care of Mama today and check the vineyards. We were lazy yesterday."

"Yes, yes," he said, hurrying them out of the room before he got emotional. He was talking gruffly, an obvious sign to Rose that he was sad.

They all followed them outside and watched as the two climbed into the jeep. Corrina gave another silent warning to Henry and waved goodbye as Antonio put his arm around her. Rose tried to look sad as her head swam in all the excitement and her father watched, knowing her feelings exactly. He smiled as they drove away, happy for his daughter. She had been devastated by the abduction of her brothers. Now she would smile and laugh as a young girl should, he thought, holding his wife's hand as it shook from her crying.

Rose took a deep breath and almost screamed as the jeep changed gears and sped out of the small village. Her breath was short as she climbed across the middle of the jeep and kissed Henry on the cheek.

"Did you like kissing me last night?" she said, nuzzling her nose into his neck.

He almost lost control of the vehicle as she bit his ear. His pulse had doubled since her kiss and he leaned away from her in an attempt to stay on the road.

"Be careful, Rose. I can't think if you're doing that," he said, trying to act mad.

"Okay," she said, climbing back to her side of the jeep.

"Wait a minute. It's not that bad," Henry said, hoping she would come back and start again, which she eagerly did.

"I can't believe you came up on the roof and kissed me," he said, leaning into her kisses.

"I was just going to give you a blanket, but . . . you looked so cute, I just had to kiss you." She moved her nose in small circles on his cheek.

It was another beautiful day and a handful of farmers were out, caring for their crops. Henry couldn't believe his current situation. He looked around and laughed as Rose's hair touched the side of his face. It smelled wonderful. He marveled at the diversity of terrain as they drove. The lazy river road carved through the valley and even turned back on itself at times, creating the illusion of driving in circles; this was fine with Henry and Rose. Neither one was anxious to arrive anywhere. The hills were growing taller and yet the vineyards still managed to cling to the sides of the mountains like enormous stairways. Despite the odds, the Italians' passion for the grape somehow managed to transform the steep Alps into fertile farmland.

After a couple of hours, they decided to stop for lunch. The station house hopefully containing the eau-de-vie was just a few miles ahead. Henry could hardly continue anyway; he was exhausted from driving with a constant erection. On the way, as she sought protection from the wind, Rose had curled around his body like a cluster of dark purple grapes on the vine. He was dizzy when they stopped and she knew it; his face was the color of a glass of young Beaujolais.

She (accidentally) brushed against him as she crawled from their seat. The inadvertent contact caused a sudden loss of strength in Henry's extremities. He tried to conceal his excitement as he stood behind the jeep blushing as his old Johnny stood at attention for all to see. He waited calmly for Rose to look away, fidgeting with something in the back of the jeep. She smiled coyly, and reluctantly turned and walked down the small hill, laughing along the way. She placed a blanket next to the river and waited, watching to her amusement as Henry walked awkwardly towards her carrying Antonio's satchel in front of him. She was anxious to lay next to him and feel his body again. He could smell nothing but food and was delirious from the excessive loss of blood from his brain as the blue, blue, blue sky glistened overhead.

🍇 🍇 🍇

20

The smell of freshly-cut grass was overwhelming Jack's senses. As soon as he walked on the field it became official; winter was over. For eighteen years he had been celebrating the end of winter the same way. Whether it was spring training with Henry in Arizona or playing catch with his dad at the winery, it didn't matter. The first toss of a baseball was the official start of the new vintage. The crush was now just a baseball season away spring training and pruning, crush and the World Series, the cycle goes on. "Yin and yang and a baseball game," as his sister would say.

He saw Maria in the batting cage. Her chin was firmly set on her left shoulder. Her hands were back, waiting, as she watched the ball approach the plate. She stepped forward with her left foot and pivoted with her hips as her hands exploded through the strike zone. The bat cracked as she ripped a line drive up the middle into the pitching screen. Her dad ducked and laughed, teasing his switch-hitting daughter as she jumped to the left side of the plate. He flopped his mitt over in a lazy gesture, signaling a curve ball as he began his wind-up. She had taken the advantage by switching sides; the ball's rotation was easier to read from the left side of the plate. The lazy curve ball dropped into her wheelhouse and again she ripped it up the middle.

Jack debated a trip to the jewelry store as he watched her bat being swung like a pro. Her swing was fluid and powerful from both sides of the plate. Style points were being scored like crazy as he observed her shagging the balls and waving to the team. She was obviously a favorite of all the guys, no doubt about that. She saw Jack and waved him to the cage.

"You ready? Or do you need to stretch or something?"

"Naw, I'm loose. I washed out some barrels and stacked some cases of wine," he said, trying to sound like a dork.

"All righty, then. Dad! This is Jack Miller. Jack, that's my dad, John Taylor."

"Hi, Jack," her dad said. "Get in here and let her throw you a few. I've got to get started on the line-ups. It was nice meeting you. Nice hitting sweetheart, see you later."

"Nice to meet you, too," he said, admiring her dad's goatee. He had the perfect look for a baseball coach. He wore short cropped hair with a Fu-manchu trimmed into a goat. He also had a well-defined beer belly   not a big stomach or butt, just a tight beer belly. It looked like it held about a six-pack comfortably without forcing him to pee. He wore his baseball pants long, just above the shoe   an absolute must for any ball player with a clue. The red stirrups were barely visible, vanishing into polished black cleats; his right one was protected by a pitching toe. The shiny, red coach's jacket was new and only the bottom two buttons were undone, adding a touch of definition to his beer belly. His baseball cap sat low on his head, hiding his eyebrows, the brim curving slightly.

Jack stood at the plate and took a few cuts at the air. He turned his wrist over quickly, snapping the end of the bat around in the middle of the strike zone. Maria was holding the ball, standing behind the pitching screen.

"How long did you play?" she asked, admiring his warm up swings.

"Through college."

"Where?"

"Stanford. Let's go."

"Stanford? No kidding? You must be pretty good."

"I was a bench warmer," he said, waiting for a pitch. He was no longer swinging the bat. "You gonna throw that melon, or what?"

He was shocked when she pushed her glove hand forward at him, indicating a fastball. Her wind-up was tight and efficient. A high leg kick and good torso rotation made the ball hard to follow through her delivery. The release was smooth, her arm motion fluid. There was absolutely nothing gender specific about it. The ball came down the middle in a hurry, a little faster than the usual B.P. tempo. He was ready, though. He sat back on it and delivered a compact swing, driving his back hand through the ball.

The ball shot back at Maria twice as fast as she had pitched it to him. Her smile was huge. She reached in the bucket and served up another. He repeated the swing with the same result as before. She grabbed another ball and flopped her mitt over using the lazy code, causing Jack to smile. The ball's rotation was flawless. Nothing about her wind-up changed as she fed him the hammer. Again, he sat back and waited, chin firm. The ball jumped off his bat and snagged in the upper left corner of the net.

"Nice deuce," he said, referring to the curve ball.

"Thanks. Ready for some heat?" she said, growing tired of getting rocked by the cocky scientist.

"Sure, I like a little mustard with my meat."

"Cute," said Maria, raising her hands above her head.

He could see her face strain as she delivered the pitch. The ball was by him before he finished his swing. His grin was hard to hide as he motioned for another ace.

"I could hear that one," he said. "Nice smoke."

Her face contorted again as she released the ball directly at Jack's face. He sat firm for a second and then backed off the plate as the ball just missed his head.

"Chin music, Maria?" he said, impressed by her competitive edge.

"What?" she laughed. "I'm sorry. You're crowding the plate. Back off."

The next pitch was a screamer in the exact same place. At the last instant, he rocked back on his heels and the ball broke away from him, dropping over the middle of the plate.

"That's bull shit in the cage and you know it," he laughed, shaking his head. A curve ball should never be thrown without notification during batting practice. It's a well-known rule throughout the baseball world.

"Oh, come on. That thing was telegraphed the whole way. You bailed like it was a hand grenade," she said, leaving the cage. "Lets go. The game is starting."

Jack's adrenalin was screaming as they climbed the bleachers and watched the teams take their infield practice. It was a relief to be away from the winery. He still had a lot of unpruned vines to deal with, and several hundred cases of wine to bottle before too long. The last couple of days had been full of surprises, too. Henry coming to visit, Cherise's suicide, and the land in Yakima were choking out the sounds of baseball in Jack's mind. He tried to block it all out and just enjoy the game.

"Hey, Jack, I'm sorry about your aunt," Maria said, with impeccably bad timing.

"Thanks. It's still kind of like it didn't happen. You know what I mean?"

"Yeah, it's going to take a little while for it to sink in. Were you guys close?"

"Not for a long time. I was there a lot when we were kids, though. She dated a lot of the Napa wine guys when I was younger. It was great. I was like the mascot for a lot of those places total access and free food and a lot of kisses from their big sisters and stuff. It was pretty cool for a kid. You know about the grape thing, right? Well, she was syrah and I was cabernet, and she always joked that they were a perfect match. So, that really got me into studying the different varieties of grapes when I was young. It was all I read about. And any effort you put into something when you're a kid, you know, you get back something like a thousand percent return on your time, compared to when you're older. Does that make any sense?"

"That makes a lot of sense, Jack. You were lucky to find something that interested you at such a young age. And your aunt had a lot to do with that, huh?"

"She had everything to do with it. If it would have been just my mom and dad at the time, I would have probably rebelled against the whole wine thing, just like every other kid who goes against what their parents want at a certain age. Cherise provided a back door, sort of. I don't know. She really enjoyed walking through the vineyards with me and Petal and Skye,

[98]

explaining all the trellises and different types of vines and grapes. She would have been an awesome teacher. . . ."

They stood for the national anthem, cringing as it bellowed about thirty decibels too loud from the public address speaker located right behind their seats. They could hear the kids in the scoring booth above them, laughing as they moved the microphone back and forth from the tape source, creating a Jimi Hendrix-type feedback rendition of America's most treasured melody. Maria nudged Jack and pointed to her dad, who was blue-veining as he stood on the third base line. He was trying to catch a glimpse of the clowns running the cassette deck and still look respectful at the same time.

"Oh, my god. Does he look like that very often?" Jack asked quietly after the microphone solo was over.

"Only when he's really pissed off. I feel sorry for those guys in the booth. I hope they're not in any of his classes."

"What's he teach?"

"Calculus."

"Well, I don't think we have to worry about those boners taking calc."

"No, probably not," she laughed. "Hey, what's up with your sister's name? Is it Petal or Sunflower?"

"Sunflower. Petal is her nickname."

"I thought it was Peanut," Maria said.

"It is. I come from a baseball family, too. You know how it is you can never have enough nicknames. Heckling gets kind of boring during tape ball if you have to use the same name all the time. When Sunflower was a little kid, like five or six, she chewed really big wads of gum all the time. And she would always fall asleep with it in her mouth, not just once or twice like you and me, but all the time. And, of course, the gum always got stuck in her hair. So, anyway, when Mom would cut out the pieces of gum, Sunflower would point at the big clumps of hair on the floor and say, 'look, Mommy, petals.' "

"Aren't some of the sunflowers' petals green?" asked Maria.

[99]

"That's part of the joke, too. Her hair had turned kind of green from being on the swim team. From the chlorine, you know."

"Petals," Maria said. "That's really cute. Does she still chew gum?"

"All the time," he said, watching the pitcher warm up.

"You guys play tape ball too, huh?" Maria said.

"Definitely. That and beer are the only things that get us through crush and the World Series," he added, flinching as the batter struck the ball. "You know what?"

"What?" she asked, watching the shortstop throw the runner out.

"We almost didn't move to Oregon to make wine because the grape harvest here is about a month later than California's. Isn't that funny? In Oregon, it's right-smack-dab in the middle of the Series it sucks. We used to always go to the games **after** the crush in California. When I was a kid, it seemed like it was either the Dodgers or the A's every year, so it was no big deal to go see a Series. This sounds snobby, but Henry Mueller could get tickets to any sold-out game on the planet. He still can. Anyway, my dad almost went crazy for the first few years until we got cable at the winery. Now we have a big-screen TV and Surround Sound going full blast, so it's not so bad; actually, it's almost more fun than being there. We play our games in conjunction with the real ones. And the beers are cheaper, too."

"I think baseball is better on TV anyway, especially if the game is on natural grass," Maria said.

"Wow, me too. You know, if both leagues are on TV, I'll pick the game on natural grass to watch, even if it's the American League game. Man, instant replay and close-ups, how can you beat it?"

"By knowing the signals," she said, teasing him.

"You're kidding, aren't you?"

"I don't know, maybe. The coach needs to practice with someone."

"Come on, tell me, please. Who would I tell? Oh, I have to

know, please. I want back on the inside again."

Maria looked at him and smiled. She was breaking another rule in the baseball world and she was enjoying this one even more than the last. She thought that watching him bail on the curve ball was pretty fun too, though.

"Is your dad a coach in Salem?" she asked.

"Are you kidding? My dad's asleep in Salem," he said, laughing at his dad's lethargy.

"Okay," she said, pretending to look around for a spy. "He uses the number system. His pants are worth three points, his jersey is two, and any part of his skin is one point. The plays are numbered: A bunt is seven, a steal is eight, a hit-and-run is nine, a delayed steal is ten, a safety squeeze is four, a suicide is five. Get it?" she asked, acting nervous and still looking around.

"Yeah, I get it. Man, I'm glad none of my coaches were calculus teachers."

"It's not that bad," Maria laughed. "Come on, watch."

"What's the indicator?" Jack asked.

"He doesn't use one. It's a continual count, that way the players are watching all the time. He uses an eraser sign instead. It starts the count over at zero again."

"Very cool. It's the hat, isn't it?" he asked.

"Very good. How did you know?"

"You didn't give it a value."

"Did you take calculus?" Maria said, afraid of the answer.

"Not a chance."

They watched the game for a while, not talking. Jack was absorbed by the signal system. He was enjoying the challenge and instant gratification when a runner would bolt for the next base after he picked up the steal signal from her dad. His smile was hard to miss and Maria laughed when she saw his fingers tracking the count as her dad moved his hands around his uniform, presumably swatting at invisible bugs.

"Coach gets upset when you count on your fingers," she said,

[101]

teasing the rookie. "It helps the other team out."

"Hey, I'm brand new to this system. Give me a break."

"Did you really donate all that money to Little League?"

"What?"

"The dinner the other night, you know?"

"Oh, that," he said, enjoying the perfectly executed hit-and-run. "It was their money. I just showed up and talked to them. If they want to pay five hundred bucks for dinner that's their business."

"So your dad's a baseball fan too, huh?" she asked.

"Oh, god. It's a religion to him. The parallels he draws during crush between wine and baseball are nauseating. But when you've been sorting grapes and running the crusher for twelve hours straight and the games are on, it's kind of hard to not get philosophical. All the beer and carbon dioxide helps too, though."

"What kind of parallels?"

"Goofy stuff. Your dad would probably like them. Like, how baseball is a mental game like winemaking, you know, all the strategy and planning by the coach and then the execution by the players. The history of baseball and the aging of wine, and how the seasons are exactly the same length and how the National league and American league are like red and white wine. How using sweet reserve is like using a D.H. and on and on."

"The American League is white wine, isn't it?" she laughed.

"Oh, yeah. And how the defense has possession of the ball in baseball just like Mother Nature controlling our business. And how there's no clock in baseball, like wine   that's his favorite one. And how pinot noir smells exactly like a baseball mitt. Oh, and the stats - that's the big one, the stats."

"I thought that the computer display for the barrel looked a lot like a box score, but I didn't say anything at the time," she said.

"Yeah, that was no accident. That was the only thing that got me interested in keeping track of all that stuff. It was my job to input all that crap, but he turned it into a baseball thing and, low

[102]

and behold. . . ."

"He sounds funny," she said, wanting to add that she would like to meet him.

"He's a good guy," Jack said. "Do you have any brothers or sisters?"

"My older brother Eric lives in Seattle."

"What's he do?"

"He's a Mooreman," she said.

"Like a missionary for the church?" he asked. He was a little surprised and he instantly thought about her drinking at the winery.

"No. He's a computer memory specialist. You remember Moore's Law? It's the one about computer memory doubling its capacity every two years."

"Yeah, I've heard of it," he said. "What's that have to do with the church?"

"No M-o-o-r-e-m-a-n," she said, spelling it out for him. "Not Mormon. It has nothing to do with Utah. It's a joke my dad made up about Eric because computer geeks are more devoted than missionaries. Get it? Cyber-junkies, Net-heads, you know? My brother's a full-blown techno-dweeb. He hasn't been home in, like, three years. He just sends e-mail. Well, anyway, if you study computer memory then, according to my dad, you're a Mooreman. He thinks it's funny. Eric doesn't."

"I think it's funny," Jack said, thinking about a hot dog. He watched her dad run through another series of signals. He could see the runner, slowly moving his fingers as the coach continued to swat the spiders on his uniform. "How can you taste wine if you're a Mormon? Ooh, I lost that one. Did he go to his ear or his hat? What was that? Ten or three?"

"Nine," she said, shaking her head.

🍇🍇🍇

21

Rose snapped the blanket at the air as they cleaned up their picnic. They were now in a hurry. The afternoon sun had somehow managed to cross the sky without gaining their suspicion. She was fussing with her dress, obviously flustered about something. Henry watched her and tried to act in a hurry also, hoping she would stop and jump on him again like she had the last three times they tried to leave. He was calm and relaxed. The pressures of war were not as severe as they had been before lunch. He had proposed marriage somewhere between the trout and the stuffed peppers. She'd eagerly accepted his proposition, savoring the bratwurst. Her frantic movements as she cleaned up were making Henry feel bad. He grabbed the basket and started for the jeep.

"I'm sorry, Rose," he said, walking up the hill. "I can't see the sun through my eyelids. I didn't know how late it was."

"You better hurry up and get us there or we will be very late," she said. Her scolding tone was light-hearted and flirtatious. He could see she was debating whether or not to jump on him again. Henry turned to grab her and she ran quickly to the jeep, jumped inside and laughed, then commanded him to drive as if she were a queen.

"My father will be angry with you. Let's go," she pleaded.

"Your wish is my command, my lady," he said, bowing gracefully as he climbed into the carriage. "Are you sure you know where the lake is?"

"Yes. It's just over there. You can see it." She pointed off to the right to a place where the valley separated. Several sets of railroad tracks were winding their way through the thin mountain pass. He drove quickly along the curving road, grinning as Rose tried to press the wrinkles out of her dress.

Henry could feel the lump growing in his stomach as he watched a train slowly climb its way north off in the distance. He wanted nothing to do with the remaining Gestapo agents, most of whom were now merely black marketeers, looking to trade their stolen items for new identities or gifts for the Führer. If at all possible, he only wanted to deal with the Italian man who Vessini trusted, avoiding direct contact with anybody associated with the Wehrmacht. He looked at Rose, who was also watching the train. He knew she was thinking about her brothers; her young face was unsuited to hiding emotions.

"Here is the place we want. Don't look so nervous, silly," she said, smiling at Henry. "You are a very bad spy."

He thought about what she said, realizing for the first time exactly what he now was   a spy. He smiled as the lump in his stomach broke apart into chunks of electricity and surged through his veins. He had nothing to fear. He was a representative of Be There Bennett, had connections to Antonio Vessini and was agent on a quest for some of the most sought-after items of the war, in certain circles. And besides, Antonio was right. Time was running out for the current landlords of these caches. They would be more than anxious to deal with a legitimate buyer connected to unlimited resources.

The station area consisted of several large warehouses and water towers. They lined the railroad tracks for nearly a half-kilometer. The signs on the buildings were in Italian and German. The place was deserted. Despite the assurances of Vessini and Bennett that the Germans had evacuated this portion of Italy, Rose and Henry shared a feeling of discomfort as they exchanged glances. Rose read the map and pointed to a building in the center of the complex. Henry took a deep breath and pulled the jeep up to the front of the office, parking the vehicle slowly and looking for any signs of activity inside. They sat quietly for a second, gaining composure and watching the door. The sun was setting as he set the brake and jumped from the jeep.

"Go get a sample and hurry back," Rose said, trying to be calm. "These guys are more afraid of us than we are of them."

Henry could see the stress in her eyes. "Then why are you biting your lip?" he asked, walking to the front door with the map in his hand. He pulled his hat down lower on his head in a nervous reflex, causing him to wince as it rubbed his bruise. "Wait here, okay? I'll be right back."

Rose looked around, wanting to be brave. Her stomach was in a knot, and felt like it was just behind her front teeth. She watched as Henry entered the office. She was in love with a stranger she'd only known for two days. In fact, she had hit him with a bottle of wine just yesterday, nearly killing him. The wrinkles in her dress made her smile, though, as he disappeared from view and she thought about their picnic. He was hardly a stranger now, she thought.

He walked into the office, leaving the front door cracked open behind him. The last few minutes of sunlight followed him through the narrow opening, adding a touch of light to the dingy room. He glanced at the train schedules on the wall, calling out as he walked to the ticket window.

"Hello." He spoke in Italian. "Is anybody here?"

A man walked out from behind a small glass cubicle in the rear of the room. He was small and round and obviously frightened by the appearance of Henry this late in the day. He looked exactly like the type of man who could make the trains run on time. His pants were held firmly in place by a thin set of suspenders. A thin, black tie matched his hair and moustache. He looked at Henry nervously, watching him carefully. Henry was well aware of the confusion his Germanic heritage could create. He used the man's name quickly, trying to alleviate the fears of a potential ally.

"Are you Brunaldi?" he inquired, stopping a few feet short of the window.

"Who wants to know?" the man replied, looking closely at Henry and checking for a weapon.

"My name isn't important. Who I work for is. I represent a group of buyers interested in beverages. Can you help me?"

The man placed his left thumbnail in the corner of his mouth. Henry could hear a faint clicking sound as the man bit softly on the worn nub. Rose was right, he thought. These guys are more scared of us than we are of them.

"Are you Gestapo?" the little fat man asked as sweat collected on his upper lip.

"Are you Brunaldi?" Henry asked again.

"Yes. I'm Vincent Brunaldi, Deputy Clerk of the Rails. Give me a name."

"Antonio Vessini," said Henry.

"Good, good," he said absently. "What kind of beverages are you looking for?"

"Only the best. I'm only a scout   a taster. On my authority, however, millions of dollars can change hands . . . quickly. My employers have a great deal of respect for my judgment. Antonio informed me of a large reserve of brandy in this area. He said you knew its whereabouts. I would like a sample, please. I am in a hurry to make contact with another scout."

The man was impressed by Henry's apparent credentials. He was eager to deal with an honest businessman (like himself). The last few months had offered him little hope of a cash reward for all his efforts. The future was becoming increasingly bleak, as well. Henry was obviously the right man to deal with knowledgeable, clean, and well-financed. After only a moment's hesitation, he took a chance on the young American.

"Cognac or Armagnac? I have both. Calvados, also. The wines I have are flawless, too. Remember, I control the rails. Nothing I possess sat in the heat without my knowledge. All the spoiled wines went directly to IL Duce and the Führer. I personally saw to that."

The little man spoke with pride as he explained to Henry how he diverted the shipments of grand cru wines to nearby salt caves for better storage. "The French had stopped labeling many of their wines in an effort to hide them from the Vichy loyalists, who were eager to sell them at low prices. Many of the bottles packaged in Bordeaux boxes were actually Burgundy-shaped, so they were easy to spot. The producers didn't know they had supporters on this side of the border. We only had to open one or two bottles per shipment in order to decide whether or not to send them on to Hitler. They have enjoyed some very bad wine in the Third Reich lately," he said, smiling at Henry.

"How many cases of wine do you have?" Henry asked, forgetting the brandy.

"Which region?" Brunaldi asked, smelling the money in Henry's coffers.

"Bordeaux. Top three growths."

"Only ten thousand. I couldn't keep so many of those. Even the dumbest of Nazis can pick those wines out. Many of the bottles went directly down their throats in the field."

"Incredible," said Henry, shaking his head. "How did you do this?"

"It was easy," beamed Brunaldi. "The Gestapo goons were only concerned with the gold on its way to the Vatican. Every one of them would drool at those boxes, and let me do anything I wanted with the shipments of wine. I simply told them I had to get the wine in a cave for storage or the Führer would be very displeased with them. They would sign anything I put in front of them as they watched the gold being transferred from one train to another. They didn't know that some of those French winemakers were alchemists, too."

Henry smiled at Vincent's clever observation about turning grape juice into liquid gold. "How far away?" Henry asked.

"What?" asked Brunaldi.

"How far away is the wine?"

"How far away is your money?"

"I must have samples, Vincent. We've been burned before."

He looked at Henry for a moment and then sighed heavily through his closed lips. The escaping air forced a thin strand of oily hair to move across his forehead. "Wait here," he said, obviously upset about getting some exercise.

Brunaldi turned and walked out a back door. Henry walked to the front door to check on Rose. She was sleeping in the jeep with a smile on her face. Darkness was taking over the day. The drive home would be slow but they would be back tonight, he thought, as he watched her sleep. He was anxious to take her home and introduce her to the rest of his family. He was sure his mother would love her, and his father would be grateful for someone who understood winemaking as well as the vineyards. If they were going to process their own grapes then Merle would need some help with the new winery.

He thought about the wine he had tasted and felt yesterday. It was certainly a quality effort, a fine piece of winemaking. He was trying to convince himself that his bride-to-be hadn't crushed a bottle of wine against his skull. It was the perfect start to a relationship and they both knew it the instant he awoke from his brief coma. Her beautiful grey eyes were now a part of him. He didn't like being away from her, even for a short period of time. He was rubbing his hat against the bruise on his head while he watched her sleep, waiting for Brunaldi to return with the samples.

Henry removed a cigar from his jacket and started to light it as Brunaldi entered the room with a wooden box. He carried it with two hands and set it on the table with an audible thud. He was visibly exhausted.

"Hey, don't smoke that," he said. "You'll destroy your palate."

"You're joking, right?" said Henry. "I'm adjusting my palate. If I didn't have a cigar, I couldn't taste a thing. I've been smoking these things since I was fifteen."

"I'm not surprised. You connoisseurs are a strange bunch.

Some of the blenders I've seen have a cigarette burning all the time. It amazes me that they can taste through that garbage," he said, smiling as he lit a candle.

He opened the wooden box with the teeth of a crow bar, removed bunches of packing straw, and lifted a bottle for Henry to see. He carefully placed it on the table as Henry moved in for a closer look. When he had emptied the box, an impressive array of wine and brandy stood on display. Henry admired the selections. A great deal of care had been taken to assemble such a collection.

"You obviously know your stuff, Mr. Brunaldi."

"Why, thank you. I try to please," Vincent said. "I gather I've stimulated your interests?"

"As well as my appetite," said Henry. "I haven't the time to try them now. May I trade you for the sampler? I'll enjoy them with Antonio and my employer tomorrow."

"What have you got to trade?" he said, very interested in Henry's offer.

"Do you like cigars? Cash? What then?"

"My girlfriend likes your chocolate that doesn't melt. Do you have any of that?"

"I'll be right back. You will be a very happy man when you give her some of the bars I have in my jeep."

Henry walked outside and tried not to wake Rose as he searched through his supplies. He found gum and bandages, but no chocolate. He searched another bag and found the lunch that Antonio had packed for them. He was shocked to find the humidor in the bottom of the satchel. After a few more minutes of looking, he found the famous chocolate bars from Pennsylvania. The newest daily ration of four ounces was very popular with all branches of the military. Containing six hundred calories and able to tolerate incredible heat, the bars were a favorite in the tropics and they could be traded for almost anything. He placed his hand on the humidor, sensing something strange about its appearance in the bottom of his bag. He shook off the strange feeling and returned to the office. Rose never flinched as he walked away.

"Are these what you wanted?" he said, holding a bag of bars up in the air for Vincent to see.

"Oh, I'm going to be a hero tonight."

"Why, thank you, Vincent. I try to please. I don't see anything wrong with these samples you have here. How many cases of this do you have?" he asked, carefully lifting a bottle of wine from the table.

"How many can you buy?"

"All of them. They only produced six hundred last year."

"I have a five-year vertical, fifty cases deep. And three hundred cases of the most recent release."

"I'm very impressed, Vincent. You've done your homework. You'll be paid well for your trouble. Are you looking to retire? Or are you willing to give us a fair market price for what is rightfully ours in the first place?"

"I'm on your side," Brunaldi said, exposing his palms in a display of pontification. "I never wanted IL Duce to enjoy those things. We aren't a fighting people we are lovers. Mussolini conquers Ethiopia with nerve gas, and all of a sudden he thinks we can beat the world? They should call him IL Dunce. Most of us didn't want this war. Is it too much to ask to be compensated for my efforts? I risked my life for those wines, you know."

"I know, Vincent, relax. We are prepared to offer a generous price. Are they loaded on trains and ready for transport?"

"They can be, very quickly. That's my job."

"Excellent. Let's pack these up. I have to go. I'll be back tomorrow."

"If it's not too much to ask, could you bring a deposit with you?"

"Of course. Name it," said Henry, knowing exactly what he wanted.

"Is five boxes of chocolate too much?"

🍇🍇🍇

22

Anthony was sitting on Jack's porch when he returned from the baseball game. Pino and Vino were behaving nicely, sitting quietly on each side of Jack's dad. His black T-shirt and grey hair were invisible from a hundred yards away, but the faint glow of his cigar and the reflection from his glasses confirmed his identity. Jack smiled to himself as he pulled in the driveway. He was glad to see his dad. He wanted to tell him about Maria more than he wanted to talk about Cherise. The fiasco with the land in Yakima was going to be nothing but trouble as far as he was concerned.

"Hola, Amigo," Anthony called to Jack.

"Hey, I'm glad you're here. I just came from a baseball game."

"Liar!" screeched Anthony.

"No kidding. Really. I met the coach's daughter the other day. She's a switch hitter."

"What? Like a lesbian, or in baseball?" Anthony asked, as a smile crept through his beard.

"Oh, that's some good stuff, Bear. You need some help. No, she's an awesome hitter. I took B.P. with her before the game. You should see her throw the ball. Unreal curve and poop on the fastball, too."

"Have you been getting enough sleep, lately? You look a little out of it."

"I'm serious. She's been playing ball all her life. She actually brushed me back after I lit her up for a few line drives."

"Chin music, eh?"

"Definitely. Guess what?"

"What?"

"She told me her dad's signals. The game was a blast to watch. He's an aggressive coach. They were running all the time. Bunts, hit-and-runs, delayed steals. I forgot what high school ball was like."

"It's spring ball, Jack. You've got to score a lot of runs or you'll lose. The batters are ahead of the pitchers right now."

"Yeah, I guess," said Jack, while petting his dogs. "So, Petal told you about Cherise, huh?"

"No. My attorney called me this morning. Some strange stuff, Jack. You want to go inside? I'm cold."

"Let's go to the winery first. I've got some chromos I want to check on."

They walked across the lawn, looking at the sky as the dogs ran ahead.

"So how many parts of sulfur are you gonna add?" Anthony asked, trying to pick a fight.

"I don't know yet. Some barrels need more than others; that's for sure. Sunflower thinks thirty parts would be okay, though. What about you?"

"You know what I think," Anthony said, conveying his dislike for the use of sulfites.

Jack opened the large jars that Sunflower had placed the chromatography paper into earlier. He carefully removed the samples and placed them on paper plates in the lab to dry overnight. He'd know the status of the malo-lactic fermentation in the morning.

"Why don't you just inoculate the malo during primary? Heck, if you'll use sulfites, you might as well use freeze-dried yeast from Sweden to convert your acids."

"My wines don't sell out two years before they're made, Bear. Some people worry about shelf life, okay? I tried that sulfite-free crap once. Remember?"

"What are you complaining about? You sold it, didn't you?" Anthony was giving Jack a hard time about selling his wine to

[113]

the hotel chain.

"Their buyer's a sharp dude. He knew that wine was fading fast. That's how he got me to agree to so many dinners this summer. They've probably already sold it by the glass anyway. You and Petal talk about what you're going to say to me behind my back, don't you?"

"You sound a little guilty about something, Jack."

"Oh, you guys are a classic team. I'm not guilty of anything." Jack paused, scratching Pino in her magic place. The dog was limp and nearly comatose from joy. "What did your lawyer tell you about Cherise?"

"That you're even richer today than you were yesterday."

"That's not funny, Dad. Syrah was up to something when she left me that land. Should I just renew the lease and be done with it, or what?"

"Do you believe it's really just an orchard?"

"What do you mean?"

"How could Cherise not plant a vineyard, Jack?"

"I don't know. Transition?"

Anthony had grabbed a thief and looked for a barrel to sample. "Which ones weren't topped off today?"

"Over there. Row two   in the white oak," he said, pointing to the barrels behind those he and Maria had tested earlier. "So, Henry sent you some wine, huh?"

"Yeah, that was really sweet of old Dad, wasn't it? About an hour after that, we got a bunch of big Styrofoam packs from Char's restaurant. According to her note, she gets here Thursday to start cooking for the weekend. Two days of prep   can you believe it? It's gonna be like crush . . . well, kind of."

"Mom and Char have a great time when they're together, though. That's cool. I'm glad she's gonna come up and help. Is she gonna bring any of her staff?"

"I don't think so, no. Rose might come a day early, though. I might stay here on Friday, if it's okay with you. That's a little too much estrogen in one place for me to handle alone. Sunflower, your Mom, Char, and Grandma can pull this meal off without my help. Henry will be there Saturday morning to open the wine. I'd appreciate it if you came up early on Saturday to help with the winery."

"Is Uncle Richard coming?"

"Yeah. Him and Henry are flying up together."

"Two peas in a pod," Jack said, offering his glass to Anthony and asking for a sample from the thief.

"Yep, the dynamic duo rides again - off to Oregon to spread the gospel about California jug wine. Hey, maybe Richard has found a way to use screw tops in premium wines again," Anthony said sarcastically.

"Oh, he was so close last time," Jack said.

Anthony poured a few ounces into Jack's glass and replaced the bung. They both placed their noses deep into their wine glasses, swirling and looking at the wine as they made mental notes about its various components.

"This is from my vineyard, isn't it?" his dad asked.

"Block ten. Do you want the scanner?"

"Fire it up, I say, hmm . . . 3.42, 7.8, 12.5. So, where did you meet this coach's daughter?"

Jack smiled as he rolled the tasting cart next to his dad. He placed the pH meter directly into his glass, stirring it like a celery stalk and thinking about Maria. Anthony frowned at the lack of formal laboratory procedure. The wand should always be rinsed with distilled water before touching wine. Any residual buffer solution on the wand will mix with the wine and throw off the reading. A tone sounded and Jack read the display.

"Ha! 3.51," he exclaimed, hoping his dad would forget about Maria.

"Rinse that off, you clown. Where did you meet her?"

"That wine dinner the other night," he said sheepishly, rinsing the wand with a small spray bottle.

"What's she do?" Anthony said, holding back his laughter.

"Knock it off, Bear. She works in the catering department on

[115]

weekends. She's getting her Masters in biology this year. I think I may be in trouble on this one."

"She gonna come play some real ball at the winery?"

"I hope so."

The new sample was being measured and they both waited as the meter adjusted itself to the various conditions.

"Beeeeep," Anthony said, mimicking the tone at just the right time.

"3.47," Jack said. "Not too bad, old man. You've still got it."

"Close enough. Where's the scanner?"

"Right here," Jack said, swiping across the barrel's bar code.

The screen flashed instantly and the contents of barrel #60 were revealed:

1995 pinot noir(104)-Salem,south block#10 C29, south slope@15 degrees

Planted '77 Date sampled-1-6-97   Samples F1   Menu F2

Barrel#60, racked, 10-4-95, 1-17-96, 7-17-96-5 ppm.per

Spray-21 day S.O.2–Petal's journal.	Degree days-1953
Crush temp.-68, 9-23-95	Must temp-68
T.A.-7.7	pH-3.22
Amino-2410.0 @ 28	K-678
Volatile-.04	R.S.-.11
Alcohol-13.3	Fining-none
S.O.2-22 free, 57 total	Brix-24.1
Clusters-22, 10.6#	Wind-Average
Irrigation-35 gal. per	Protien-Stable
Rain-3.3 inches, July-crush.	Sun-@ 1100 hrs.
Yield-3.5 tons per acre	Gallons-1050
Cooperage-Bluegrass	Toast-heavy
Vigor-Too much, four feet +	Trellis-Vertical
Canes-3	Botrytis-No

Petal's notes-okay, seeds 90% brown, small, clean clusters, no mildew.

Fermentation-F7/password. Racked to barrel's #55-75 on 10-4-95.

Tasting notes-Something different here. Color very good. Nice nose and tannin. Barrel wrong? All oak and caramel, where's the fruit? call dad:-(

[116]

Anthony laughed as he read the notes. "You never called me about the oak?"

"I knew you'd give me crap about those barrels," Jack said.

"Why? There's nothing wrong with those barrels if you're making cabernet. I just don't think we harvested very much cab in '95."

"Smartass. You really think Cherise planted some vineyards up there?"

"I'd check it out before you sign anything, Jack. How much did they offer you?"

"Half a million a year," he said, tasting his wine.

"Sign," Anthony said, spewing wine through his nose as he choked from obvious shock. "Who cares what she planted. Really? Half a million? Can I have a loan? It's a good thing I didn't cut Lupé's crew a check yet for pruning your vineyards."

"Our vineyards," Jack said uneasily.

"I know, just kidding. I had no idea her estate was that big. She must have pumped everything she had into that thing. When does the current lease expire?"

"I don't know. They sent an attorney down here to get my signature, though. Time must be pretty close to running out. Maybe they'll just buy it."

"Can't hurt to ask. Go up there and take a look at it. I've got a dinner up that way next week in the Gorge. I was gonna stay a few days and do some skiing. We can go out there and check it out. It's only a couple of hours from Portland."

"Where in the Gorge?"

"Hood River. Some old hotel on the bluff. It has a waterfall and one hell of a view. They're throwing in free ski passes, too. When's the last time you went skiing?"

"Since before I started this winery."

"Wanna go?"

"Sounds good. You gonna help me bottle this stuff?"

"Sure. Password still the same?"

[117]

"Yeah, go ahead. What are you looking for?" Jack asked, watching his dad enter the password for the fermentation notes.

"Did we crush this up there, or not? I'm a little curious about the source of all that pepper. I can't remember if some of these got too hot - can you?"

Anthony hit the F7 key and answered the request for a password. He typed in WILD CARD and the display rapidly changed:

1995 Block #10 9-23-95 Felix and Lupé Crew Chiefs @ 68 degrees

Triage-Sunflower and staff sorted to crusher on top of the truck
(never again) Too many dropped clusters. Bins go to Eugene from now on.
Great looking fruit-@10% rejection to blush.
Crusher rollers set to 1/3 inch, fair amount of juice. 20% whole cluster,
20% stems, mass earwigs and yellow jackets this year -Yum:-)
10-4x4x5 bins (plastic) filled 2/3 full. Need a bigger flatbed truck.
10 ml enzyme, 10 p.p.m. S.O.2. in bins w/nutrient.
Drive to Eugene - two trips.
Innoc-1pm 9-24 w/Red. All bins separate doses @ 2# Kgal
winery temp. up to 85 degrees, can't get much more.
Manual punch every five hours (Petal and the Muslims with their
daily prayer - the crossthreads continue, wash the chapeau, turn to
Mecca and pay homage, do the dance:-) Just kidding Petal.

BIN #5, indoors slot#5, west wall.   T.A.–8.7

11pm	9-23-95	Brix-24.1	pH-3.22	temp-68
1pm	9-24-95	23.8	3.24	72, smells good
11pm	9-24-95	22.5	3.22	75, very active
1pm	9-25-95	19.2	3.28	81, added ML.
11pm	9-25-95	15.5	3.27	83, smells great
1pm	9-26-95	14.5	3.31	85, nutrient
11 pm	9-26-95	12.5	3.30	85, 50 #
1pm	9-27-95	10.5	3.11	85, good color
11pm	9-27-95	8.5	3.23	85, smells good
1pm	9-28-95	5.5	3.26	85, added 100#
11pm	9-28-95	4.0	3.29	83, veg Petal?

1pm	9-29-95	2.5	3.31	81, hydrometer
11pm	9-29-95	1.0	3.34	77, foam
1pm	9-30-95	-.5	3.38	75, added 50#
11pm	9-30-95	-1.5	3.37	73, press time
7am	10-1-95	-1.5	3.38	71, stinger

10-1-95 T.A.=8.3: Great fermentation. Free run wine to tank #10005, 1st two press cycles to tank #5005@2Bar., others to tank #10006. Settled and racked on 10-4-95. Barrels #55-75, free run (600gal.) to heavy toast limo.#55-65, press juice to mix of U.S.(M)++ and French(M)++. Very smooth ferm. M-L complete-no problems to speak of. More compressors? Need better valves on press pan. Must pump? D.E. filter? Temp. control stainless fermenters on wish list soon. Dad's got it made:-)

Anthony shook his head as he read the remarks from Jack's log. He studied the numbers carefully and smelled the wine; with his glass tilted almost horizontal, he brought it to his nostrils from the left and then the right, trying to stimulate as many regions of the brain as possible. He was hoping to arouse an area that would trigger the most recall. Jack watched his dad as various connections were made between the wine and his vineyard. Anthony scrolled the screen back and checked some numbers.

"I think you overdid the stems, Jack. The pepper is nice, but there was too much heat during fermentation. I can't believe you're not cold soaking this stuff. If you're gonna pitch that culture, you gotta soak it longer to get more extraction. It ferments too fast with that stuff. That's probably why it's still gritty. Too many whole clusters, too. Add some more sugar next time, you wimp."

"I think it's the oak," Jack said. "It's not letting anything out. Fifteen months and it's still tighter than hell. I'm going to splash-rack it and bottle next week."

"Go for it, you Australian madman."

"Yep. I'm gonna shoot it into the air right through a spaghetti strainer and beat it to hell."

"Good idea," said Anthony. "Squirt it right on the floor. Use a

[119]

squeegee, though. You don't want to waste any."

"What's wrong with that?   The floor's clean," Jack said, laughing as they cleaned up their mess.

"So what kind of system does her dad use?" Anthony asked.

"What?"

"The coach. What's his system?"

"Well," said Jack, "I could tell you, but then I'd have to kill you. You know how it is."

"Come on, Shabby. What's the secret. I want to go watch a game sometime, too."

"Numbered clothes with the hat as an eraser. It's pretty cool once you get the hang of it."

"Indicator or eraser?" asked Anthony.

"Eraser."

"Sounds too confusing to me; I'd have to use my fingers."

They walked out of the winery, watching the dogs perform the circular dance off the porch, leap in the moonlight, and bark madly. Anthony offered Jack a cigar and they sat on the porch in silence as Pino and Vino retired quietly to their master's feet, an occasional grunt escaping their snouts. The smoke was sweet and moist, lingering on the porch in the windless night.

"Where did these come from?" Jack asked, contemplating his cigar.

"Henry. Not all the boxes he sent up were full of wine. There was a smaller one that said 'open now' on it. I think it was a peace offering of some sort. Twenty-five Havanas in an antique humidor. Wait till you see it. The damn thing is beautiful. I've never seen anything like it. It has the initials W.C. on the lid. Strange bird - that old Hank. His note said to enjoy the cigars and don't open the wine. You should see the humidor, it's amazing."

"You think there's some old Bordeauxs, huh? Like, from when she was born, or what?"

"Probably. I don't know. I can't believe my sister was hurting that bad and I never knew it, Jack. You stay close to Sunflower, okay?"

"Yeah, Bear. That'll be easy. She's not as weird as Cherise."

"You like the coach's daughter, don't you?" Anthony asked.

"A lot. She's smart, athletic, and beautiful. You and Mom are really going to like her."

"What's her name?"

"Maria Taylor. Her family grew up around here. She's balanced, you know, really comfortable with herself and me. She doesn't even notice the money or care about any of that I could tell that right away, and so could Sunflower."

"That's great, Jack. I'm glad you met somebody. All work and no play. . . ."

"Makes Jack a dull boy," Jack said, picking up where his dad left off.

"Columbia Valley," Anthony said after a long pause. His cigar was buried two inches deep in his mouth.

"What about it?" asked Jack.

"Good numbers up there. I could make some blends with those grapes. Wouldn't it be nice to have sugar, acid, and pH? I have tasted the future, Jack. It's cab franc and merlot, unfortunately."

"Your pinots are better, Bear, and you know it."

"Not consistently."

"That's why they're better," Jack countered.

"I don't know. Sometimes I think Skye was the smart one."

"Me too," Jack laughed. "Who would have thought it ten years ago, though."

"Well, there it is. It worked because he loved to brew beer. Not because some marketing survey indicated a niche. You know how many barrels he's cranking out now?"

"Hundred thousand a year, I think."

"Amazing," Anthony said, softly exhaling the tropical smoke. "By the way, Sunflower told me about the grandkids names."

"We figured she would. Skye doesn't care. It's pretty funny,

[121]

isn't it?"

"I can't believe I didn't figure it out," Anthony said. "It's hilarious. Halle, Cassy, and Kent . . . my own grandchildren named after hops. Henry's gonna poop. You know that, don't you?"

🍃 🍃 🍃

23

Rose snored softly as Henry ran through the gears. He was driving quickly as they returned to Vessini's winery. He was delighted to be on the trail of wine instead of brandy. This was more of a personal preference for Henry than anything else. There was absolutely nothing wrong with the brandies of France but according to Merle's letters, the recent glut of good vintages in America had saturated its brandy market. The eau-de-vies Henry hoped to recover for Bennett would certainly have no impact on the situation back home; however, he felt better about risking his life for something a little more esoteric than moonshine.

Antonio's contact in the railroad industry had proven to be very valuable, and clever. Henry laughed to himself as he thought about Hitler and Mussolini enjoying spoiled wine and not knowing the difference. He could see them languishing over their recent defeats, smelling wine better suited for jeeps and salads. Let the fucking Fascists drink all the vinegar they want, he thought, speeding through the valley.

Henry wanted to try his radio again and see if he could contact another scout about a possible meeting between Bennett and Brunaldi. He felt very confident about the quality of Brunaldi's cache. The little man's body language conveyed intellect and honesty, despite the fact that he was a downright thief. Sometimes, the level of trust shared among criminals can be as strong and binding as any military academy's honor code. He reached for the shortwave radio and called for one of Bennett's men.

"Rootstock One to Elevage, come in Elevage. Do you copy?" Rose stirred in her seat and Henry waited for her to fall back asleep before he tried again. The steep hills of the valley had given Henry the false impression of sunset earlier. Twilight would illuminate the road for at least another hour as they drove. The headlamps were turned on but they did little to light the way.

"Rootstock One to Elevage, come in Elevage. Do you copy? Over."

"This is Bacchus, Rootstock One. It's good to hear you're alive! We were wondering what had happened to you. Over," Bennett said. His excitement over Henry's well-being was easy to detect, even over the radio.

"Sir? Is that you? Over," Henry asked, surprised by his commander's voice.

"It's me, Rootstock One. Over," said Bennett.

"What are you doing out this way? Are you close? Over."

"I have a telegram from the States for you. It's urgent. Over," Bennett said. There was now a touch of sadness in his voice.

Henry felt sick to his stomach as soon as heard the tone of Bennett's voice. In nearly four years of war he'd never seen anybody get good news from a telegram. He immediately thought about his parents, fearing the worst.

"What is it, sir? My dad? Over," he said, his voice cracking as he thought about his mother. Rose woke up and smiled at him, unaware of his anxiety.

"I don't know, son. Meet me at checkpoint 12 on your map. You still have it, don't you? You didn't go swimming with it, did

[123]

you? Over."

"No, sir. I mean. . . . Yes, sir. I still have it. I'm not that far from there. I can be there in about thirty minutes. Over."

"One of our jeeps will be waiting to guide you when you arrive. Over."

"Roger, sir. See you in thirty. Over."

"Who was that?" Rose asked, curiosity getting the best of her.

"My boss," Henry said. "We have to stop and see him. It's on the way, okay?"

"Papa is going to be very angry with you," she said, teasing him again. She could tell he was upset about something but decided not to pry. The war had made her painfully aware of the many mood swings people are capable of during a crisis. She waited for the stern look on his face to soften and then crawled across the jeep, snuggling her nose against his neck and kissing him softly.

His mind wandered back to Napa as they drove, and he felt nothing but guilt as he thought about his father's failing health. He should have been there to do the traveling, not off running around Europe chasing Italian farm girls. Merle had warned him about their dad's chest pains, encouraging him to hurry up and win the war so he could come home and take over.

Henry slowly rotated his neck, caressing the top of Rose's head with his cheek. It was a warm night and the stars became visible as the headlamps took over the job of lighting the road. A thousand thoughts continued to race through his mind. Telegrams, he thought; why didn't they ever send funny ones or the ones with singing naked girls? It was always something bad.

"Are you feeling all right? You seem troubled," Rose said.

"There's a telegram waiting for me from back home," he said. "They usually mean something bad happened."

"I know. We have them, too. I'm sorry, Henry. I didn't mean to pry."

"It's fine. I'm a little worried about my father. Merle had written to me about his chest pains. He wouldn't go see a doctor.

The idiot is too dumb to get help."

"Papa is the same. Don't worry, Henry. They are probably just telling you about a very big order for some grapes. It could be good news, you know. It doesn't have to be bad."

He pulled the jeep over to the side of the road and checked his map as Rose held the flashlight and pointed the way with her delicate finger. Trying to lighten the somber mood, Henry grabbed the light and stuck it in his mouth, growling like a bear as his cheeks glowed like a Japanese lantern. Rose screamed and laughed, punching his shoulders as he moved in for a bite. He could smell roasting meat in the warm night air, and it added a touch of flavor to his appetite for Rose. They kissed passionately for several minutes, working to a frenzy as they both sought relief from the pressures of war. Under normal circumstances they would have courted for several weeks, but Henry was serious about his earlier proposal for marriage and Rose knew it. They embraced tightly and became one, losing all sense of reality for a brief moment. As fast as it left, however, a tidal wave of stress and guilt came back and flooded their emotions. They rode to checkpoint 12 in awkward silence, Rose sitting upright on her side of the jeep.

Henry saw the jeep ahead and flashed his headlights twice. The brake lights on the jeep signaled back with three quick flashes and he followed as it turned to the right, disappearing into a labyrinth of supply boxes. This camp was several times larger than the one Henry had first met Bennett in. Enormous stacks of munitions lined the narrow road and Henry quickly lost his way after a few turns. He would definitely need help leaving, he thought, as he looked for boxes of wine while following the lead vehicle. Rose was in awe as she gazed at the fortress of supplies. Taking a silent inventory, she correctly assessed the future of the Third Reich.

"Oh, my god," she said slowly. "Hitler is doomed."

"Welcome to America, Rose," he said, smiling with pride as they approached Bennett's main camp. His heart swelled when he saw a large American flag stretched above the gate. He could see Bennett shouting into a radio. His face was purple and his arms were waving hysterically.

"I think we'll wait here for a moment before we approach the general," he said. He could hear the profanities gushing from Bennett's mouth. Apparently, something wasn't where it was supposed to be and Be There Bennett was furious. Bennett saw Henry and Rose and started walking towards them, his conversation ending with his famous moniker: "It better fucking be there or there will be hell to pay, understood? Good. Over!" he said, smiling at Rose as he approached the jeep. Henry laughed, understanding at last why he was named Be There. It wasn't to compliment his efficient management of resources after all. It was an abbreviation of the closing remarks he directed to his subordinates when something was going wrong.

The general forced a smile and Henry remembered the telegram. His stomach knotted up as he greeted the commander.

"Problem, General?" he asked politely.

"Those lousy Navy bastards haven't got the port established in Salerno. Sorry ma'am," he said to Rose. "Who do we have here, Mueller? This doesn't look like any of the field scouts I've ever worked with." The general's smile was flirtatious and flattering. Rose blushed as Bennett kissed her hand and bowed, introducing himself in royal fashion.

"I am General Nelson Thomas Bennett, commander of this city of crates. And who are you?"

"General, this is Rose Vessini. Daughter of Antonio Vessini, the winemaker who helped us," Henry said. "She is the future bride of Henry Mueller, California grape grower and the world's greatest reconnaissance man." He emphasized the future bride portion, politely warning Bennett to settle down. The general had obviously been deprived the company of beautiful women for some time, not at all uncommon in a time of war.

"Future bride? What the hell are you talking about?" Bennett wanted to know. "You've only been gone for two days."

"It was love at first sight, General," he said, touching the bandage on his head as Rose smiled at him.

"Are you serious? You proposed marriage to a girl you've known for two days? No offense, ma'am."

"None taken," said Rose. It is a pleasure to meet you, General. Henry has told me very much about you. He admires you very much." She smiled at Bennett and he melted. Her grey eyes were the most beautiful he'd ever seen. After sharing a look of congratulations and envy with Henry, the general retrieved the telegram from his pocket; his personality changed from the competitive brother to the sincere father as he handed him the envelope.

Henry sighed heavily as he opened the telegram. He read it slowly as Rose and the general remained quiet, not watching him directly but politely aware of his progress as he continued to read the communique.

"I have to go home," he said softly. His face was muddled and confused as he explained why. "My brother, Merle, has been killed in a car accident. Apparently, a thick fog caused a traffic jam on the way home from San Francisco. His car was rear-ended. My father needs me for the harvest. There is much work to be done."

They all sat quietly, waiting for something to happen. Rose placed her hand on his arm and apologized. She knew exactly what he was feeling and wanted to provide as much support for him as he had for her. If he hadn't entered her life, she would have been devastated by the loss of her brothers. The general was, unfortunately, too accustomed to this situation and offered his support and guidance with a well-rehearsed but beautifully-delivered speech about death. He reassured Henry that anything he ever needed was at his disposal. It would Be There at anytime.

"Merle was the smart one," he said, shaking his head and thinking about the monumental task ahead. "I'm just the salesman. What do I know about making a million gallons of wine? Oh, my mother has got to be just wiped out. Merle never missed a meal in his life. They loved each other, so much."

"Why don't you two get washed up in my tent and rest a bit. Dinner is in a few minutes. I'd love to have your company, if you don't mind. Henry, again, I'm very sorry about your brother. I'll see you folks shortly. Nice to have met you, Rose. I've heard wonderful things about your father, and his wines."

Henry showed Rose the way to the latrine and made sure it was okay for her to use. He wasn't surprised to find it in immaculate condition, complete with towels and all the conveniences. He helped himself to one of Bennett's cigars and sat outside, watching the stars slowly fill the sky.

His mind was halfway across the planet; he was tending to the vines and working under the huge canopies. Ambitious plans to conquer the East Coast market for grapes would have to wait at least two more years while he trained a new salesman. He hoped that Merle had discussed the expansion of the new winery in detail with his father. Maybe they could process those grapes and maybe not, he thought. Antonio and Rose were the answer and he knew it. And Bennett was the key. If Be There could get the paperwork through, immigration would be a piece of cake for an experienced winemaker like Vessini. Of course, there was the little problem of Antonio being an Italian citizen. But what good were friends like Bennett if you couldn't take advantage of their connections? Besides, Antonio was almost a member of the French Resistance and his contact in the railroad department had turned out to be a gold mine. Surely, Bennett would pull some strings for a man like that.

"I'm so sorry, Henry. Is there anything I can do?" Rose sat beside him and remained quiet. His breath was heavy as he contemplated the strange turn of events. He thought it was strange that it took a death in America to make the war seem real.

"No, Rose. I'll be fine, thank you. I'm really sorry about your brothers. I want you to know that. Your father loves you very much, too. You know that, don't you? No matter what happens, you know he loves you very much."

"Yes, of course. Why are you saying this? You're frightening me, Henry. Stop it."

"I'm Sorry. I've got a lot running through my head right now. I want your family to come to America right away. The general can get the necessary documents. Your father has helped us tremendously, and he shouldn't stay in Italy any longer. It isn't safe. We can all work the vineyards in Napa. We need a winemaker, too. You and your father can be together and your mother can have a garden bigger than she ever imagined."

He could see that he was scaring her and decided to stop before he made things worse, forcing himself to relax and enjoy the view. He put his arm around her without saying a word. He kissed her softly and held her stare for quite some time, making her feel safe again.

Bennett's personal aide approached the tent and informed them that the general was waiting. His heavily-starched uniform was shockingly clean and wrinkle-free, amazing considering the heat and humidity. They walked to the mess tent hand in hand as dozens of soldiers loaded supplies into trucks with a sense of urgency. The strange glow of flood lamps turned night into day.

As they entered the tent, Henry couldn't help but notice the unmistakable aroma of military-issue canvas. It was something he would have never expected in a tent belonging to Bennett. The general's previous dwelling in France had been impeccable. In fact, Henry was looking forward to having dinner there again sometime. But this one smelled as if it had just been unpacked after two years of storage in the hull of a fishing boat. The walls had stains and the windows were dirty. Even the chairs were somewhat shoddy. The stench of mildew was reminiscent of a waterlogged sleeping bag, which had been made even worse by the hot afternoon temperatures. Henry looked at Rose and saw that she possessed the nose of a winemaker, too. He shrugged and smiled on behalf of the United States, unsure of what to say.

"Good God," Bennett said, walking into the room. "It smells like something died in here." With his busy schedule, he apparently forgot that Henry had just been informed about the death of his brother. He looked at the two of them and tried to recover from his insensitive remarks. "I'm sorry about the smell. This thing didn't get unpacked for several weeks. We've had some delays lately. The Germans keep sinking all of the damn boats in the harbors, slowing us down everywhere. Then they mess up the water supply every time they leave someplace. Bastards. How did your country end up on the wrong side of this thing, Rose?" He paused for a moment, pouring a glass of Champagne for his guests. "Never mind, Rose. Anschluss that's how. When Hitler claimed Austria, it was all over for your country. Mussolini had no choice but to join the fun; he's had a hard-on for Austria ever since World War I. Sorry about my language. I haven't been in the presence of a beautiful woman for quite some time."

The general sat down and gestured to an aide to serve the first course. He was quiet and reserved, obviously thinking about many things at once. The Allied Forces northern advances through Italy had been slower than anyone anticipated. The rugged terrain and German sabotage tactics had been very effective in allowing Hitler time to fortify the Third Reich's soft underbelly in the Alps. Therefore, millions of tons of supplies and troops were waiting for dispersal, and Bennett was pissed.

"This may not be the most appropriate time to discuss this, Henry. But I sure could use some good news right about now." The general looked at him and basically spoke without words. Henry knew what he was after and began his report.

"Yes sir, General, very good news. Antonio was very pleased

[130]

with your gift," he said, remembering that the humidor was now in his jeep. "He gave me the name of a man who worked for the rails. You won't believe what this guy has been up to for the last four years." Henry smiled at Bennett, using the moment for a dramatic effect.

"What?" the general said, smiling apprehensively.

"He's been diverting the grand crus to salt caves. The little bastard has everything ready to go. Cognac, Armagnac, Bordeaux, Beaune, D.R.C., and even some Calvados if you're low on gas for the jeeps." Henry looked at Rose proudly and continued. "He was just waiting for the right group to come along. The poor guy was ready to burst when I showed up. I think he's a little nervous that the Gestapo may have been sampling some of the stuff he's been sending to Germany lately. He said that Hitler and Mussolini have been drinking nothing but crap for the last few years. Can you believe it?"

"Do you have any samples?" the general asked, a touch of skepticism in his voice. He didn't get to where he was by being gullible.

"Yes, they're in the jeep. I'm sorry. I forgot them after I read the telegram." He tried to stay on track and not think about Merle. "The bottles were in perfect order. No sign of heat stress, bleeding, or ullage. He wants to meet you tomorrow. You'll never guess what he wanted for a deposit."

"What?" said Bennett.

"Chocolate bars. Isn't that a good one? An Italian wanting food from an American GI. He said his girlfriend was going. . . ." He stopped talking and looked at Rose, and quickly changed his train of thought. Rose shook her head, smiling at both the general and Henry. She was well aware of the effects of chocolate on a woman.

"How many cases did he say he had? Did he mention any numbers?" Bennett asked, bailing Henry out of his current predicament.

"Thousands. All well-maintained and cataloged, ready for

transport."

"Do you believe him?"

"Yes. It's hard to explain, but there was definitely something very trustworthy about him."

"Name?"

"Vincent Brunaldi. Ring any bells?"

"No. But I'll do some checking around after dinner."

The three of them ate slowly without talking for awhile. The pungent smell of garlic was rising from their plates, fighting and winning a first class battle against the mildew odor.

"How are things going with the war, General?"

"Slow. A mess is brewing with the Russians over invasion schedules and the Japanese are formidable. The Germans are still plundering Italy just a few miles from here. We thought we had the north all wrapped up but they're tenacious bastards. We bomb, and they rebuild the very next day. Make sure you stick to your routes on the map. It's more dangerous around here than we thought."

Henry looked at Rose to offer reassurance, letting her know with a comforting smile that everything was still fine in her village. Bennett realized his remarks were alarming her and changed the subject.

"I think this campaign will be over in a few more months, as long as Russia behaves herself." The general paused and poured more Champagne for everyone. His appetite was returning under the watchful grey eyes of Vessini's daughter.

"So do you work in the vineyards, Rose?" the general asked.

"Some. My brothers do most of the field work, however. They are very tall. I can't reach up to the canopy in most places. I work in the winery with my father. I've been making the wine for many years."

"She stirs the grapes with her legs. Her father says that's why her skin is so beautiful."

"Is that what they mean by 'nice legs'?" Bennett asked.

"No. That's from all the bugs in the grapes," Rose said,

laughing at the look on Bennett's face.

"So, Hitler has been drinking vinegar for a while, eh?" Bennett said, raising his glass to Henry.

"Yes, sir."

"Outstanding," said the General. He spoke absently, preoccupied with something else again. "Diverting the grand crus, how clever. And you think they're still in good shape?"

"I do. He struck me as an efficient man. At least he knew which wines to show me, that's for sure."

"We had an idea that someone would be on top of it on this end. Thousands of cases in one place . . . I'll be damned." Bennett chewed his food slowly, considering the news about a cache bigger than he imagined possible. He was going to build a nice house on a golf course in Virginia for sure now, and drink grand crus for lunch with the president and relax for another twenty years in the breadbasket of Southern hospitality. "You be sure and thank your father, Rose. He's been very helpful. His cut of this action will be substantial, too. Antonio had mentioned emigration to one of my scouts in a preliminary meeting. I'm certain it will be no problem now."

"We can't leave until my brothers are back home, but that will be very soon. Right Henry? This war will be over soon and my brothers will be set free." She was smiling from the Champagne, confident about the well-being of her family now that she saw the resources at the general's disposal.

The general looked at Henry, inquiring about her brothers without speaking as the entree was served. Henry tilted his eyebrows at Bennett, declining to comment further on the whereabouts of her siblings. He enjoyed seeing Rose smile and wanted her to stay happy. The general nodded discretely, understanding Henry's decision to avoid such a horrible topic; denial was a safe harbor at times, encouraged and reinforced by even the strongest of men during a crisis. Bennett knew that if the Germans had taken her brothers recently, the chances of their returning to Italy were slim   especially if they were

[133]

members of the military.

The thinly-sliced medallions of veal were prepared in a rich cream sauce. Enormous mushrooms overflowing with cheese and bread crumbs sat beside the tender meat. Bennett grinned at Henry as he reached below the table and retrieved a bottle of wine.

"Let's just see what our little Brunaldi has been up to for the last few years," Bennett said, placing the famous blend of cabernet sauvignon and merlot on the table. This one was from the small commune of Pauillac, about forty-five kilometers north of Bordeaux. Owned by one of the wealthiest families in the world, the Chateau's wines are best described as elegant, well-bred, and regal.

"You searched my jeep?" Henry asked, surprised by Bennett's initiative.

"I saw the box when you pulled up. You don't mind, do you?"

"Not at all. I'm anxious to see if he's as smart as he looked. How long ago did you open it?"

"Thirty minutes or so. I think it's ready. I'm surprised you couldn't smell it." Bennett looked at the stains on the tent's ceiling and sniffed the air. "Well, never mind. It would be hard to smell anything in this place."

He poured the wine and raised his glass to his guests. They all did the same, smelling their glasses and looking at each other as the aromas were processed.

"Very nice, despite the bumpy jeep ride," Henry said. "Great color. Do you like the nose, Rose."

"It's beautiful. Heavenly, really. I've never had this wine before."

"It has a little more merlot than most of the other Pauillacs. I thought it would be better with the veal. It's a little softer. Very fragrant and balanced." Bennett took a bite of veal and drank from his glass, blending the two in his mouth in a moment of extreme pleasure.

Henry enjoyed watching Rose devour her veal as she conversed rapidly with Bennett about the fate of the Third Reich. They chewed loudly and laughed with their mouths full of food. The transition from Champagne to red wine had been very smooth, as usual.

The general talked openly about the strange situation brewing with the Russians and how our involvement with the Japanese was more costly than anyone imagined. He said the war in the South Pacific was being won by our submarine forces, but the Japanese were using a weapon more terrifying than anything he had ever heard of before. Young boys and girls, trained to fly in only a few days, were plunging their heavily-loaded aircraft into the middle of our ships, killing themselves instantly with a devastating toll to our forces both physically and mentally; an enemy with such macabre conviction was ghastly to fight. He continued to describe the horror as Rose listened carefully, watching the general speak and still chewing her food with reckless abandon.

Henry rubbed his face with his hands, touching the bruise on his head to keep himself awake. His eyelids suddenly weighed about five pounds apiece, and each blink scratched his eyes like sandpaper as he tried to pay attention. He was dreading the drive back to Vessini's, imagining the wrath of Corrina when they showed up this late.

"Well, Mueller, it looks like you're about ready to hit the hay," Bennett said. He was terribly unimpressed by Henry's ability to fake having a good time.

"I'm sorry, you guys. I think I'm allergic to something around here. Either that or the dust from driving all day has set my eyes on fire."

"You kids go ahead and get out of here. There's coffee waiting in the jeep; I figured a farm boy from Napa might have trouble staying up late. Rose, there's some goodies in there for your mother and father, too. I'll have a scout contact you tomorrow, Henry. Let's wrap this deal up fast. If the rest of his wine is as

[135]

good as this, we don't want to wait too long. It's getting a little too hot to sit on something like this, okay?"

"Great, sir. We'll see you tomorrow then." Henry pulled the chair out for Rose, who was still gulping wine like there was no tomorrow. Her smile was contagious and they all had a good laugh as they walked out of the tent. She danced like a ballerina under the bright spotlights on her way to the jeep, twirling and waving goodbye to the general as he consulted with Henry in private.

"You lucky bastard, Mueller. None of my men said anything about a daughter in any of their reports about the Vessinis. Maybe they wanted to keep it a secret. She's the most beautiful girl I've ever seen. You're smart to marry her. You know that, don't you?"

"Yes, sir. I do. I wanted to talk to you about that. Can you get the paperwork necessary for something like this? I don't want to leave her here. I've got to go back, very soon. I know that's a lot to ask but Antonio doesn't think it's safe. He thinks that some people know he's been collaborating with us." Henry had a concerned look on his face that changed to a smile when he saw Rose blowing him kisses from the jeep.

Bennett was caught in the moment; watching a young girl in love was the best thing he'd seen in months. "Don't worry about a thing, Henry. Everything you need will be there. Just make sure I always get some of your finest wines back home, all right? See you tomorrow. I'll make the arrangements for her family. And Henry . . . I'm sorry about your brother."

They shook hands firmly and Henry ran to Rose's side of the jeep, smothering her with kisses as she tried to push him away. She was shouting goodbye to the general as she giggled like a child. Henry climbed over her to get to the driver's side and started the engine. They both looked at Bennett and waved as the jeep pulled away from the tent. Bennett was shaking his head and laughing, jealousy oozing from his pores. He stood and watched for a while as Henry crisscrossed the camp's exit route, turning every which way as Rose laughed and slapped him with each pass of the general's tent. Finally, Henry stopped and asked a soldier for directions out of the maze of supplies. Rose was laughing hysterically as he listened patiently to the explanation. The general pulled alongside in his shiny new jeep and honked his horn. "Follow me, you hay seed. You're like a little bear cub, Mueller," Bennett said, winking at Rose as tears streamed down her face.

When they reached the exit, Bennett flashed his brake lights and waved goodbye. He was still shaking his head. Henry gave his lights a flash and turned onto the gravel road as Rose stood and waved, the wind blowing her hair and dress into a frenzy. For some strange reason, she was now impervious to the cold weather. Henry drove faster than before and it didn't take long for the protective shield of alcohol to wear off and she finally sat down. She snuggled her face in the nape of his neck, shivering as she whispered teasing remarks in his ear.

"Do you think the general can get my family to America sometime?"

"He can do anything, Rose," he shouted over the wind. "He's famous for pulling off the impossible. He's a hero in America. I'm still nervous when I talk to him. He eats lunch with the president all the time."

"He seems like an extraordinary man. Is he married?"

"He's a widower. His wife died from pneumonia a few years ago."

"He was very happy with Papa's connection, wasn't he?"

"Very. Your father should get more than enough money to get everyone to America. Do you want to be a winemaker or come with me on the road to sell our grapes?"

"I want to be with you, always," she said, kissing him on the cheek. "I'm sorry about Merle. How old was he?"

"Almost thirty. He stayed home because our dad was sick awhile back. I volunteered before they could do anything."

"My brothers were very brave. They volunteered, too. They

didn't know Papa was helping your wine people. I don't think they would mind, though. They loved the wine more than IL Duce."

They drove through the night, talking some and kissing more. Rose wrapped herself around his arms and legs again, making him dizzy for the twentieth time that day. The caffeine was barely doing its job as he fought a losing battle against lust and exhaustion. He battled the urge to sleep by thinking about Napa, kamikazes, Brunaldi and, most of all, sex. The cool night air was the only thing keeping him alert.

Rose was once again snoring softly as the jeep wound its way through the mountains. He was relieved when he recognized all of the landmarks on the outskirts of her village and exhaled a large breath of stress, thankful there had been no contact with the German army. The last thing he wanted was a car chase in the middle of the night. He was pretty sure that the enormous box of cigars from Bennett could get him out of any trouble with the Gestapo traders that were left, but he had no desire to find out. Most of all, he was eager to get Rose home before Corrina turned him into soup; his anxiety over returning her so late was creeping back into his bones.

As he turned the last corner before reaching town, he saw a crowd of people holding torches. A pit formed in the bottom of his stomach when he saw their focal point. Several women were screaming, being consoled by their husbands. The light from the torches illuminated the night as shadows bounced high in the air against the branches of a huge oak tree. He could see the bodies hanging limply from the massive tree, their clothing tattered and torn and their lives extinguished.

He stopped the jeep slowly as Rose uncoiled from his arm. She was surprised to be home so soon and smiled at Henry without looking up, thanking him for a wonderful day. She saw the look in his eyes and turned to face the crowd of people approaching the jeep. Their faces were solemn. She recognized several neighbors and saw the tears streaming down their cheeks. Henry placed his arm across her chest when he saw the body of Antonio twisting in the wind. Corrina was hanging just a few feet away from her husband. They had their hands tied behind their backs. Their twisted heads were dangling awkwardly to the side. Their necks were broken. Several other bodies were hanging from the branches around them. Rose began to scream violently when she saw her mother's dress blowing gently in the warm night breeze.

Each of the bodies had a single letter painted on its chest in gruesome, red paint or blood. Henry struggled to hold her against the seat of the jeep as he read the letters. It was difficult to see in the strobing torchlight. The bodies were spinning slowly. He finally saw the words IL DUCE floating in the branches as Rose burst from the jeep and ran screaming towards her parents.

24

Jack drifted in and out of sleep as he listened to the weather report on the radio. It was, strangely enough, going to be another nice day in Eugene. Two in a row how bizarre, he thought. Maybe we'll get this place pruned after all. He watched carefully as Maria slowly took off her blouse and smiled seductively. She climbed from the creek, water dripping from her naked breasts in slow motion as they rocked back and forth. Each droplet struck the ground in perfect unison with Sunflower's pounding on his front door. He cursed his sister's lack of timing as his body chemistry sped beyond the lucid dream state and reality took hold of his senses.

"What?" he shouted, dreading the answer.

"Come on, Shabby. Let's go. Rise and shine," she yelled to her brother.

"I'll be right out. Give me a few minutes," Jack said, grumbling as the image of Maria faded from his mind.

The cuttings from the vineyard had to be gathered and burned. Usually, they just mulched them up where they lay and let them decompose naturally, but the soil was saturated with something and Sunflower wanted them removed this year. It was a pain-in-the-ass job as far as Jack was concerned, but Petal was the boss.

He showered quickly and finished his fantasy about Maria, wondering whether or not to call her today even though he had told her he would when they were at the game last night. He didn't want to rush things and could tell that she was pretty comfortable with the idea of them hooking up. Actually, he was more afraid of losing her in all the excitement with Cherise and Henry than he was of committing to someone, especially someone like Maria. He decided to call her tomorrow and ask for a few days to wrap up all of the Yakima/Cherise crap.

Pino and Vino were amusing themselves with a friendly wrestling match on the front lawn as he walked out to face the day. Their continuous gnarling and chewing usually resulted in a few scrapes and bruises, with the loser yapping for mercy or running away in disgrace. Today appeared to be Vino's day in the winner's circle. A quick nip to Pino's ear caused considerable damage for such a playful jab. Pino screamed foul and ran to Jack for protection as Vino basked in the glory of canine supremacy.

"Pino, you gotta stick and move, girl. Keep your head up. You can't let that vicious beast do that to you." Jack rubbed his dog's bleeding ear and checked for any serious damage as Vino sat proudly, watching his sister cry like a puppy. "Bad boy, Vino," he scolded, trying to hide his smile so Pino wouldn't get angry. "You know better than to bite your sister when it's cold outside. Bad dog!" Vino simply turned and began walking to where he last saw Sunflower, knowing exactly where to find love and easy hugs when he needed them.

Jack was thinking about the lease when his sister appeared from within the winery. She was carrying the chromo from yesterday's malo sample. Her baggy overalls were undone at the shoulder straps, flopping loosely around her side. A fanny pack, woven from hemp and containing related paraphernalia, was the only thing holding up her bibs. Her bright green shirt gave the false impression of a hidden power source; its ethereal color suggested to Jack that a use for radioactive waste had finally been found. A pair of black rubber boots completed the ensemble and provided the necessary ground if a bolt of lightning was to suddenly attach itself to her neon top.

"Oh man, Petal. It's way too early for a shirt like that. You're gonna suck all the sun away from the vines and we're not gonna get any buds."

[141]

"You don't like it? It's great. I think it's some new blend of fibers from the space shuttle. It's completely organic," she proclaimed proudly.

"Zero gravity textiles? What next?" he mused, shaking his head. The glare from her shirt was giving him a headache, causing him to rub his eyes and continue teasing her about the wardrobe selection.

"Stop it, Jack. It's not that bad. It brings out the green in my eyes, don't ya think?"

"Are you kidding? It's turned them purple. Is this thing dry?" He shielded his face and reached for the chromo paper, holding it up to the sun to examine the lactic acid's overnight progress across the sheet. As expected, the baseline dots of wine at the bottom of the page had traveled the length of the paper, leaving no trace of malic acid in the middle. They could now be sure that the wine had completed its secondary fermentation and was safe to bottle.

"Yeah, it's dry. Looks good, huh? When do you want to bottle it?" she asked, following her brother into the vineyard.

"I'm not really sure how many barrels are going into this blend. I want to mix some of Dad's with some of that Yamhill stuff we bought. I can't believe the fruit they get up there. I swear, some of that stuff has got to be petite sirah. I like the aromas you got with the eastern slopes, but it needs a big dose of fruit and I think Yamhill Valley might be the right call."

"If you wanted such big fruit, why did you start making pinot anyway?"

"Hey, Petal, just because you and Dad think it has to be some perfume-driven experience with hints of earth, leather, and tobacco, blah, blah, blah that doesn't mean I can't make them big and jammy. I like those big pinots from up north; they're chewy," he said, wrapping his lips around his teeth and chomping his jaws like a toothless old geezer.

"You're gonna confuse everything we've been trying to accomplish," she said. "Those jelly pinots have a one-

[142]

dimensional nose and you know it. It's not about the mouth; it's about the overall experience. You could have got that big fruit and nose if you wouldn't have pitched that friggin yeast from a packet in such a hurry. You rush your fermentations like a madman. I give you yields that are perfect in every way, with total mineral balance and you still add that crappy culture. And then, on top of that, you ferment it in a square building. What the hell do you expect?"

Jack looked at his sister and smiled while flexing his eyebrows. "A square building? Are you high? What do you mean a square building? You've got to stop reading that philosophical stuff, Petal. You're starting to scare me."

"Think about it, Shabby," she said, moving her hands like her fingers were emitting cobwebs. "The grapes are round, like the Earth. We harvest them into round buckets and then load the buckets on to tractors with round tires. Then, we ferment them in round tanks, age them in round barrels, and put them in round bottles. What's wrong with this picture?"

"I do it in a square building?" he stammered, scrunching his face apprehensively.

"Yes! Think about it. It's bad karma. To continue the cycle of the seasons we need to paint the walls of the winery green, or purple, or maybe both. No, one of each; that would create a flow of energy across the winery through the barrels and into the wine. That's about all we can do because the building is square. The corners absorb all of the energy that is extracted from the air by the white walls. Get it?"

"White walls?" he asked. He began to wonder if premature wrinkling would result if he didn't relax his face soon.

"Jack, listen to me. It's all about energy, right? Pinot noir has more pheromones than any other grape, doesn't it?"

"If you say so."

"I think it does. It's the horny wine, remember? Definitely an aphrodisiac. Just ask Mom." She was speaking very fast, looking over her shoulder at Jack as she checked the shiny new canes for any signs of trouble. "Anyway, pheromones enter our system through our sense of smell. They stimulate our brains and cause the release of various endorphins, making us happy, excited and sexually aroused."

Jack had stopped following his sister and was now standing at least fifteen feet behind her. This was a distance that he felt was safe enough to prevent anything communicable from reaching him, should his sister be infected. He was smiling as she continued her diatribe, unaware he had stopped a few feet back. She turned to say something and paused, smiling at his attempt to quarantine her next to the creek where Maria had taken her bath.

"You clown, cut it out," she said, waving him down to the creek. "I'm just thinking out loud. I think there's something to this. What if we rounded the corners of your winery and painted the walls in time to crush these grapes?"

"Rounded the walls of the winery, huh?"

"You know, with something like pressboard on the inside, curving around, sort of?" she said, twirling in a semi-circle and then stopping to look at the land across the creek that sloped upwards and off to the west. "I wish that darn sheep farmer would sell you that land." She was pointing to the huge field that bordered his vineyard. Its porous soil had excellent drainage and was thought to be the primary supplier of water to the creek. Made with infrared cameras, the aerial maps of their land showed that the 500 acres across the creek were ideal for grapes, too. In fact, Sunflower had pleaded with Anthony and Jack to pay anything for that land; its slope, drainage, and soil were exactly what she was looking for. Unfortunately, the corporation currently leasing the land was very happy with its current occupants, many of whom could be heard "laughing" in the background.

"We tried, remember? They didn't want to sell."

"I know," said Sunflower. "But that might be your answer to getting the big fruit you're looking for. Mmmm, just think of it.

Big, jammy mouthfuls of pinot noir with no nose."

"You're such a dork," said Jack. "If we add some big fruit to your aroma-therapy wines we might have something that tastes good and gets you laid, GET IT?"

Sunflower's mind had drifted into the creek. She was looking into the water as the morning sun pierced the surface, exposing the murky bottom and all of its inhabitants.

"Look froggies," she said.

Jack was disappointed that she hadn't heard his comment about getting laid and he almost repeated it, deciding instead to join her at the creek and watch the frogs. It was a whole lot more fun than riding the damn tractor through the vines and scooping up the canes. There was going to be enough of that for everyone, and real soon.

"What was Maria doing with the frogs?" she asked.

"Inserting micro-chips of some sort," Jack said, looking for the amphibians. "Checking the water depth where they live and the temperature and water quality and all that kind of stuff basic research."

"Micro-chips, huh?"

"Tracking their movements, I think," said Jack. "We didn't really go into it. I was too busy watching the baseball game to talk about anything. She told me her dad's signals. It was a blast to watch the game."

"You like her a lot, don't you?"

"Yeah. I think so," he said softly.

"So, I guess that means you're not going to call her again, huh?" she said, not looking at her brother. She was trying to make a point and he knew it. Maria wasn't the first girl that Jack had introduced to Sunflower and seemed to be excited about. To Petal, however, she was the most promising in a long line of hopefuls.

"I know what you're getting at, Petal. I've got a lot of crap going on right now and I need a little time to sort it all out. No big deal, okay? I'm going to call her, I promise."

"You don't have to explain it to me, Jack. I just hate getting to know your . . . friends, for lack of a better word, and then losing their friendship when you crap on them. They always call me and want to know what's going on, and I don't know what the hell you're thinking. What am I supposed to tell them, anyway? That you're a jerk and you can't make a commitment? I do, you know. That's what I tell them." She paused and tried to relax, closing her eyes and looking up to the sun for warmth.

"Gosh, Petal. What brought that on? It's decaf from now on, okay? I said I was going to call her and I will. She's awesome. I can't stop thinking about her. It's not my fault that Cherise freaked out. Gimme a break."

"Sorry, Shabby. Bad timing, I guess. I just thought Maria was really cool and I could tell she liked you a lot, too. That's all."

Jack turned towards the winery, surprised at his sudden motivation to work in the vineyard. Sunflower's jab about being noncommittal had gotten through and he wasn't in the mood to talk about it anymore.

"I've got a lot of work to do before Blake gets here. Let me know if you're going to be here for lunch. I'm going to call Juanita soon. See you later."

"No! I've got sushi coming. Blake's going to eat lunch with us," she said. A smirk on her face confessed to her brother her fondness for the crooked-faced attorney.

"Is that so? Wasabe riesling, too? Don't make him blow anymore spit bubbles, Petal. That thing was brutal."

"You are so mean, Jack. He can't help it and you know it, so knock it off. I don't think it's very funny."

"Yes you do, Petal. It was hilarious. I almost died laughing. You could still see the corn chips in his spit. That thing was thicker than gum."

Sunflower frowned at her brother, concealing her amusement extremely well. She wanted to laugh but she knew he was just trying to get even for her comments about Maria. Jack always had a way of making jokes when he was pissed off, and sometimes

[146]

his jokes got out of hand.

"You're a moron, Shabby. Go get the tractor." The frown had overpowered her smile and her face looked serious enough for Jack to soften up a bit.

"So, you told Dad about the Hops, huh?" he said, continuing up the slope to the winery.

"Did you tell Skye? Is he mad? I thought it was time for Dad to know, with Henry coming and all. Shoot. It's no big deal, is it? Those kids needed an Oregon totem to protect them from Grandpa anyway. You know he's still going to give them a grape totem. Now they'll be safe, though. Because they'll identify with the characteristics of the hop before the grape. Skye was a genius to break that hex. At least they can rely on hops. A person could go crazy trying to figure out a damn grape."

Jack was about thirty feet up the hill when he turned to look at his sister. Her use of the word "crazy" was unintentional and he had to see her face to realize it. He didn't think she was making a joke about Cherise, but he had to check anyway. It wasn't her style and he saw her expression change when she realized what she had said.

"This varietal totem thing is getting a little old, Petal," Jack said. "And Skye only made things worse when he brought beer into the equation. Now everyone is going to think of beer as being like wine and that's insane, too. Henry and Richard are gonna fry us on this one and they're gonna be right. So, whatever you do, don't tell Grandpa that his great-grandchildren are protected from any type of hex because of a beer ingredient, okay? Just let it go. I've gotta get going before Blake gets here."

"Hey!" yelled Sunflower. "What are you going to do sign the lease or what?"

"Yeah," he said, scratching his head. "I can buy a lot of cabernet with $500,000 a year."

25

Cherise was twirling in front of the television as a room full of people tried to watch the evening news. The anchorman was stoic as he counted the American casualties suffered that week in Vietnam. He read the list slowly, reaching the viewers as they ate their TV dinners and debated U.S. involvement in southeast Asia.

"Good grief, Syrah. Give it a rest. How can a person spin for so long?" Henry said. He was dodging to the left and right, trying to see around his daughter as she twirled to the thumping noise. The distorted music was escaping from the padded cups of her headphones. It was like listening to the sea in conch for everyone else in the room. "Rose, make her stop, please. I'm trying to watch the news."

"Cherise, honey," Rose called loudly, trying to catch her daughter's attention. "Why don't you sit down, dear?"

"For crying out loud, Rose, she can't hear a thing. She's gonna go deaf," Henry said, throwing his hands up in the air.

"In the Garden of Eden, baby. Don't cha know that I crave you, baby. . . ." Cherise sang to the music as Henry unplugged the power cord. He was shaking his head, smiling at the rest of his family. The cord looked like a dead snake hanging from his hand.

"She doesn't even know the words," Char said, laughing with Anthony. The two of them were sitting on one couch with flimsy portable trays holding up their dinners in front of them. Henry and Rose had their own recliners and it took a great deal of effort for Henry to put away his dinner and get up to unplug the stereo. Despite his smile, he wasn't pleased.

"How can you guys watch this garbage," Cherise said, taking off her headphones. Her long black hair stuck to the foam of the headphones as she pulled them away from her head. "All they do is try to make it sound like we're winning when we're really getting our collective asses kicked all over the place."

"How do you know more than everyone else, Syrah?" Henry asked. "All those demonstrations you go to don't tell you a thing about what's really going on. Your brother is over there right now, dammit. And I don't want to be fighting with you when they say his name on the evening news, understood?" He was shouting by the time he finished, causing the smiles to vanish from the faces of Anthony and Char. Rose sat quietly, waiting for the commercials to end.

The families had to be notified, usually by telegram, before they could say the name of a soldier killed in action on TV. This provided little comfort for the parents of boys fighting in a war. When the list was read, they invariably heard the name of their son with each new roll call as their mind played tricks with their worst fears.

Henry and Rose had been fortunate enough to return from World War II and start a family. It was a simple twist of fate that they would start having their sons eighteen years before another war would rob America of one of its most precious resources. Rose was simply stunned when her oldest boy returned from the recruiter, smiling big and proud and explaining that he'd enlisted to fight in a war 10,000 miles away from home. As she had done after the deaths of her parents, she completely immersed herself in the vineyards and winemaking, creating a gap in their family for the first time. She had managed to have four children in four years and build one of the most successful product lines in the California wine industry. Henry had hired to all of their weaknesses, operating the business with cunning efficiency and developing markets for the premium table wines that Rose produced a few short years after their return to America.

"Syrah is a hippy, Dad," said Char, referring to Cherise. "She knows everything."

"Shut up, Char! Don't you have a fund raiser to organize for the president?" Cherise snapped. "Maybe he'll make you ambassador to Squareville or something."

"Quiet girls," Rose said, watching the TV closely. The combat footage was unedited and the anchor warned everyone at home that there may be scenes unsuitable for young viewers. Cherise reluctantly joined her brother and sister on the couch and watched the report with the rest of the family.

"According to President Bennett," the reporter said as he ducked behind a car, "the current level of troops will be increased by twenty-five percent by the new year. Total U.S. troops will be at its highest level so far, approaching three hundred thousand soldiers. This latest word from the White House has been met with a flurry of debate and demonstrations throughout America."

"Oh my God," Cherise said quietly. "How can he do that, Daddy?"

"He knows what he's doing, sweetheart. He'll take care of Richard, too. Don't anybody worry about that. Old Be There has things under control, right Nebby? Besides, Zinny is as tough as nails, isn't he?" he asked rhetorically. He sat there quietly, thinking about his oldest son.

Rose failed to answer her husband, letting the pep talk rapidly dissolve into silence. She walked to the kitchen as an explosion rocked the hillside near their home.

"I thought they were through for the day," Henry said, looking at the window. "They like to scare me to death. Sorry guys. I give your mom fifteen thousand acres of prime land and what does she want to do with it? Nothing. Instead, she wants to terrace every damn hill in the valley, costing us millions. And for what? Less grapes, that's what! Unbelievable!"

All three of them sat quietly on the couch, unfazed by Henry's ranting. He'd been against the hillside vineyard program from the very beginning, but so far the results were amazing and even he was excited about the future. They knew better than to listen to him go on about her new projects. Since the day Richard left for Vietnam, Rose had done nothing but plant new vineyards, each one more innovative and expensive than the last. She was making Henry pay for his allegiance to President Bennett and they all knew it, especially Henry.

They all felt, in many ways, that it was their close association with the president that had prompted Richard to enlist. The macho, oldest son was eager to make them proud and prove his manhood. He worshipped the president and stood firm on any platform he chose. It was no secret to anyone that Richard was Bennett's favorite godchild. They were both college football stars and each one had a remarkable thirst for literature. Their only dispute had been over Richard's selection of Princeton over the Virginia Academy of Military Science, a decision that would better serve the family holdings when Richard took over the day-to-day operations of Mueller Vineyards. Despite Richard's role in the current escalation of the war, Rose trusted President Bennett when he told her that nothing would ever happen to her son. But, that didn't make his absence any easier on her or the rest of the family.

This was the first summer vacation in which all of the kids weren't home to work the vineyards. The usually-boisterous dinners featuring copious amounts of wine and yelling had been reduced to watching TV and trying not to say the wrong thing to the wrong person. Even Cherise knew when to back off the tannin and let things age, a quality that often impressed her younger brother Anthony and led to their close bond. Cherise was hanging out in Berkeley and came home to visit frequently, spending long hours with Anthony in the winery and convincing him to stay away from the military at all cost. He had to constantly remind her that his asthma prevented any military service, causing him to think that perhaps Cherise was volunteering for the strange experiments involving drugs at Berkeley. Char had purchased a restaurant in the Fisherman's Wharf district of San Francisco and hardly ever saw the light of day. Her voluntary role as family chef growing up would serve her well in the business world. She was creating a trend in cuisine that would combine food and art with wine and take California to a new level of culinary exploration.

It was now a rare occasion when everyone was together, and it tore Rose to shreds when the conversation festered to a level of cruelty that usually resulted in tears and long-term anger. She and Henry had done their best to create a stable environment for their children and now, as young adults, their voicings of differences in opinion was to be expected. It broke her heart, however, to have her children choosing sides and forming alliances against their father and one of his closest friends. She leaned against the kitchen table and listened to the explosions as they echoed through the valley, thinking for a moment that they sounded remarkably similar to the voices in her living room.

"Daddy, you can't seriously believe that President Bennett isn't being controlled by the military complex, can you? This war is great for the economy and everyone knows it. He doesn't give a hoot about the Communists or the South Vietnamese. He's just a puppet and I think it's sad, because I love him too."

Henry sighed deeply, resisting the urge to scream about the atrocities that he and President Bennett had witnessed at the hands of the Communists. He had seen the photos of the fields of corpses and knew first hand what kinds of horrors humans were capable of in a political free-fall. He looked at Cherise and bit his lip, walking to the window as he contemplated his strategy for attack.

"Cherise, I don't know how we can do this for the hundredth time," he said slowly. "You have your ideas, and God knows your mother and I encourage that, but I have mine too. We have to find a way to talk without being so mean. I'll do my best if you guys will, okay? President Bennett has done so much for us, you

[152]

know that. We wouldn't even be alive if it weren't for him. Please, understand that it tears me up to hear you talk about him that way." He gazed out the window in a moment of reflection and watched a bulldozer gouge a swath through the hill, leveling narrow plats as it plowed through the ruptured earth.

"Who wants ice cream?" Rose inquired as she entered the room. A large barrel with a crank was giving her fits as she struggled to carry it to the table. It was a welcome relief and everyone smiled as Henry lunged for the spoons, clanging them loudly as he threw them at each of his children. He grabbed the large serving spoon and swatted his wife on the butt. The resulting crack was surprisingly loud and obviously painful to a surprised Rose, who jumped in the air and turned after her husband with cat like speed. He saw the anger on her face and simply grabbed his ankles and moaned, mimicking a parochial school student in the headmaster's office. She played the role of disciplinarian with sinister familiarity, checking with her kids to see how severe the punishment should be. After receiving several dramatic nods of approval, she fired a flat bare hand into his buttocks with a shocking lack of mercy. The sound echoed through the living room, momentarily drowning out the explosions from the vineyard. Anthony and Cherise cracked up as their dad walked to his chair, still bent over and taking little baby steps with his hands clasped tightly around the tops of his ankles as he groaned softly.

Rose moved her hands up and down, clapping them lightly as if they were covered with flour. Her grin was triumphant. A silent apology was offered as she smiled at Henry and handed him a massive bowl of ice cream with several toppings, including hot fudge. Her look was pure love and they savored the moment as they watched Char, Cherise, and Anthony laugh like children with their faces covered with chocolate.

"Mission accomplished," Henry whispered, watching his grown children.

"You are such a wonderful father," Rose whispered. She

gently stroked the side of his face with the back of her hand, smearing chocolate across his cheek.

Anthony and Cherise stayed up late watching the Friday night thriller, eating popcorn, and talking about nothing. All things considered, it had been a very calm evening and they were both thankful for the lack of conflict. Anthony had learned to maintain eye contact with Cherise as much as possible during her bouts with their dad, playing referee in the clashes more than participating himself. What started as a simple dirty look to keep her calm had grown into an intricate system of eyebrow movements and heavy sighs that was complete with topic-avoidance grunts, toe jabs, and the ever-popular elbow to the ribs over political foes. She appreciated his concern, at times, and usually thanked him when the smoke had cleared, realizing his intentions were good although he seemed to be taking sides against her when it came to President Bennett.

Cherise had been drinking scotch for the last two hours without Anthony's knowledge, but her speech was becoming increasingly slurred as she talked to herself and laughed at the commercials with no hint of sobriety. Anthony was trying to follow the plot of the slasher movie, finding it easy to ignore his sister's drunken blather. His TV filters were in sterilization mode as he watched the poor and ridiculed artist kill a cat and cover it with clay. Of course, this first piece of work impressed the local Bohemians with his attention to detail and the artist was "discovered." Unfortunately, as his popularity grew, the artist had to improve with every piece, eventually using human subjects to express his sculpting talents. Anthony thought to himself that the artist would have made a good corporate winemaker; covering up bulk swill made from overcropped vineyards and labeling it Chablis or Burgundy was the source of many heated discussions between his mom and dad.

"Are you gonna go with me to the protest tomorrow, Anthony? There's going to be a lot of cute girls."

"Shut up," he laughed. "I can't. I've got to help Mom rack the reds. She wants to bottle next week while we're all still around. Besides, there's a dinner at Char's restaurant tomorrow night and we're all supposed to go."

"It's your summer vacation. They've got a hundred interns for that racking crap. You're coming to San Francisco and that's all there is to it. You need to meet a girl. It'll clear up your skin. We can go to the dinner after the rally."

He knew she was drunk and tried to ignore her as he watched the artist kill one of the more popular kids who'd discovered his secret   creating his final masterpiece out of a bitter enemy, much like the conglomerate wineries destroying the reputations of the little French vineyards in Burgundy, he thought.

"You should grow a beard," she said. "It would cover up your acne. You have such beautiful eyes, Anthony. A girl is going to look into them tomorrow and fall madly in love with you, I promise. Come with me, okay? Please."

"Only if you promise to stop fighting with Dad about Be There. I know you're nicer than that. Why do you have to give him such a hard time? Be There has never done anything but be nice to you and you know it, Syrah. Stop trying to be such a rebel, for once. You don't have to agree with what's going on, but that doesn't give you the right to make everybody else miserable. Mom's worried sick about Richard and all you do is make things worse, so knock it off." He didn't look at her the entire time he was talking. Her comments about his acne were true and his feelings were hurt. He hadn't gone to the city in a long time because his face looked like a pizza. He'd been hiding in the winery for a couple of weeks and he didn't like Cherise calling him on his insecurities.

"I'm sorry for teasing you about your pimples, Anthony. I just want you to come out and have some fun. I didn't mean to hurt your feelings."

[155]

He continued to watch TV and ignore her, looking straight ahead. He could tell she was waiting for a response, staring at him as the cathode rays pulsed off the walls and provided the only light in the room. "I said I'd go, so shut up about my face. This stuff doesn't only look bad, it hurts."

"I said I was sorry," she said. She leaned over the side of the couch and took another straight shot, carefully avoiding his field of vision; she let the alcohol sit in her mouth and burn as its soothing effect caused her to cringe and almost vomit. "Are you going to go to the draft board, or what?" she blurted loudly. The garbled words were stuck in her thick saliva causing her spit them at Anthony. They hit him like a wet towel.

"God, Cherise. How many times do I have to tell you that I got a medical release, okay? My asthma is enough to keep me alive. How's that for irony? If you'd stay off the drugs for more than a hour, you might remember the conversations that you THINK we enjoy so much."

"You're so mean," she said softly, the booze finally depressing her. She fell asleep while he watched the rest of the movie in silence, regretting what he'd said and thankful just this once that she probably wouldn't remember what they'd said to each other.

The following morning Anthony drove to San Francisco as Cherise nursed a hangover, groaning for him to stop and let her buy a bottle of vodka for her headache. She let out a caterwaul every time he changed lanes as she used the open window as a basket for her head. She let her hair hang out and cried to the strangers for sanctuary as they passed. Anthony was laughing, trying to concentrate on the road, and watching the tail lights ahead as he tuned into the radio for an update on the rally. The fog was thick as they approached the city causing Anthony to drive slow enough for Cherise to hold down the contents of her empty stomach.

"You gonna be all right, Syrah?" Anthony asked. "We're

[156]

almost there. Do you want to stop and get some OJ or something?"

"Or something, dammit. I need a drink, you brat," she said. Her voice was cracking from a mixture of laughter and pain. She hadn't opened her eyes for at least an hour, wanting to be completely immersed in the protective shroud of fog before attempting to blink. She was afraid that if she opened them, her head would explode from the flood of light and the ensuing sensory overload. She turned to Anthony with her eyes still closed and spoke very slowly. "I need some damn sunglasses too, Pinot." She rested her head on the back of the seat, obviously fatigued from the energy required to speak such a long sentence.

"Nice mouth, Durif. Clean it up a little."

"Don't call me that," she said. She was mumbling through a crumpled up T-shirt that she was using as a pillow and the words sounded more like gibberish than coherent speech. "I've got enough problems trying to keep up with petite sirah, shiraz, Hermitage, syrah, Durif, or Chateaunuef du poop and whatever else they can find from the Rhone. I'm tired of all these of nicknames. They freak me out."

"Blah, blah, blah, blah," Anthony said, mimicking her speech pattern. "What a waste of a perfectly good liver."

"I heard that."

"How far away should we park?" he asked. "I don't want to get stuck in some log jam later on. Remember, we're going to dinner at Char's tonight. It's important."

He decided on a spot about five blocks from the park. He could see the crowd of people, moving like a herd of cattle through the street. A sea of tie dye, bell bottoms, and banners caught his eye and caused him to question his presence at such a political brouhaha.

Cherise smelled the crowd's intensity and suddenly began to light up like a Christmas tree. The osmotic flow of energy provided instant nourishment to her damaged soul like a car getting filled with gas. She jumped from her seat and retrieved a blanket from the trunk, looking like she'd been to a beautician for a make over. Her eyes were gleaming and her face sparkled with joy as she listened to the noises coming from the park.

"Okay, Anthony, this is it. Stay close and don't drink anything, especially the water. Everyone is cool, but don't get pushy if someone gets in your face, got it? Stay calm." Her breathing was erratic and hurried as she spoke. She was almost on the verge of hyperventilation.

"Relax, Cherise. I've been around this type of thing before."

"When?"

He paused, searching his mind for an answer that wouldn't seem too stupid. "Lots of times," he said, looking at the park. "You don't know about everything I do."

"Whatever, Anthony. Just stay close and whatever you do."

"I know," he interrupted. "Don't drink the water."

"No. Whatever you do, don't get on TV. Dad will kill you and me, okay?"

"Yeah," he laughed.

They walked towards the surging crowd looking for a place to merge without being squashed. Even Anthony was getting excited as their tempo gained speed and they matched the crowd's rhythm, walking in unison up the street in a frenzy of hormones, anger, and shouting.

The assembly was already approaching about 5000 protesters, all chanting one stanza or another and hardly ever using the same one at the same time. Depending on where they were, they were either shouting something about not going somewhere or something about Bennett; either way, Anthony just watched, listened and absorbed, searching the herd for the mate promised by Cherise.

"Go get 'em, stud! They're out there and they're horny," she yelled.

"What?" he laughed, knowing that she'd just seen him check out a nearby girl. He was bursting at the seams. Women were everywhere.

[158]

VARIETAL TENDENCIES

He followed his sister through the crowd to the polo field, then helped her spread out the blanket and secure a spot with a view of the stage. A poet was standing behind the microphone, calling for the lives of the young men to be avenged for their parents in the form of angels floating through Congress, staining the pressed suits and starched shirts of the politicians with the blood of the draft lottery losers.

Anthony fought the urge to listen, avoiding guilt at all costs for the moment. Because he was a chronic asthma sufferer and a virgin, his protesting was driven by lust instead of fear and anger, making him lighthearted, romantic, and successful. Cherise was right about the women, he thought, as he began to sweat. He rubbed his hands together and looked around, watching Cherise select her path to the stage as the sun finally pierced through the fog and exposed a blue sky. His glands were producing pheromones at a clinical rate, quickly arousing the interests of a beautiful young woman seated next to him.

"I'm going to go walk around for awhile. If we get separated, meet me at the car at 6:30 and no later. It's barely eleven now, so we have lots of time." She saw the eye contact between Anthony and the girl and took her cue, smiling at him as she walked away. "Don't drink or eat anything, understand? I'm serious."

"Go save the world, Syrah. I'll see you later."

He waved a dismissive hand at his sister, turning his attention to the blonde seated to his right. Her hair was filled with scarlet flowers and sunshine, and her face was painted with hearts. A long, white cotton skirt with hundreds of pleats caressed her legs and barely touched her sandals. Little silver cat bells hung off her foot straps, ringing softly as she flopped her feet left and then right. He could tell she was ringing them intentionally slow, listening to the crowd's rhythm and matching its pace as it filled the huge lawn. She was naked under her velvet vest and her breasts were almost visible from the side when she reached for her spray bottle. The sight of her dark nipples made Anthony blush, but not turn away.

[159]

"Are you kind?" she asked. Her look was warm and inquisitive, highlighted by a row of pearls behind soft lips that she slowly spread as she watched him ponder her question.

"I'm sorry. What?" he murmured. He was startled by the depth of her voice. Its low, raspy tone was effeminate and beautiful but he was surprised by how powerful it was, too. He had to watch carefully as she spoke, making sure it was really her voice.

"Are you kind?" she repeated.

"I dunno, I guess so. Why?"

"Because you look kind." She gazed right through him, watching the people move about the field and never letting the warm smile fade from her face.

Anthony watched her chest swell as she breathed deeply through her nose and then exhaled softly through her mouth. She repeated the cycle for several minutes as her face flushed with color and waves of energy rippled through her body like bugs crawling under her skin. At times, she looked like a pole in front of a barber's shop, the colors climbing and circling around her face. He realized how strange it was that he could actually see these things happening to her. He was sweating profusely. His heart began beating faster with her every breath. His lungs swelled with hers in an erotic syncopation that was almost perverse. He was afraid she was going to stop and ask him to leave her alone. He didn't want her to catch him in his debut exploration of voyeurism.

She turned to him slowly, filling her mouth with air with her lips slightly parted. She exhaled loudly, smiling as the final rush escaped her body. "Wow!" she said, almost laughing. "I'm glad that's over."

Her eyes were now on fire. They were full of water and blinking slowly. They appeared to be sending a lot more information to her brain than they were just a few moments before. He was still incredibly turned on from her strange breathing exercises. His mouth was dryer than it had ever been before as he tried to speak; sweat ran down his forehead.

"W-what . . . happened?" he asked.

"I think I just got on the bus," she said. Her voice was now more seductive than powerful.

"Oh," Anthony managed, not having a clue what she meant.

"You look really uncomfortable. Do you want some water?" She offered him her bottle in a casual, un-threatening way.

"No thanks," he said quickly. "I'm fine, really."

"Here, let me just spray you with this one." She reached into her bag and pulled out another spray bottle, exposing her breast again. She squeezed the plastic handle several times, launching a rainbow of water through the air at Anthony. After a few blasts she turned the bottle on herself, holding it above her mouth as she tilted her head back. She gently squeezed the handle, spraying herself with the water and then pointing it at Anthony again.

He watched the liquid arc through the air and become a gossamer mist of relief suspended in the blue sky; its soothing chill caressed his skin as it landed softly on his upturned face. He saw the rainbow again as it glowed like a peacock's reflection in a pond. The brilliant colors created something out of nothing as more of the water danced on his body. The brief hydrogen bond between them lasted only a few seconds, but it exhausted Anthony beyond belief. He was completely satiated, no longer feeling hot or uncomfortable. He simply sat, smiled, and hummed softly as he watched a band set up its equipment. The girl chimed her bells, sandals flopping left then right like a metronome.

"You should lick your lips," she said, yawning powerfully. Her mouth flexed open incredibly wide as she continued to breathe with some difficulty.

He was enjoying the sensation of the droplets on his face, well aware of the exact location of every liquid kiss from the beautiful stranger. Each one of them had warmed in the sun, touching the stubble on his face as he breathed. He could feel them joining forces when he blinked his eyes; two drops becoming one then sliding away and tickling his skin as they rolled into his ears and hair.

"Why should I lick my lips?"

"Because you look thirsty," she said. She sounded very casual as she drew deeply on a cigarette, holding the smoke in her lungs longer than normal.

He thought about what she said and let his upper lip slide beneath his lower one, drawing the moisture from the short abrasive hairs. The small amount of water was sweet and warm and only made him thirstier. He wanted to ask for a drink but thought about what Cherise had said and decided not to, choosing instead to savor the water still resting on his face.

The band began to play and the crowd responded with a round of cheers and thunderous clapping as they surged towards the stage. Anthony stood and tried to see the stage but the crowd had filled in, leaving him and his blanket with a well-obstructed view. He turned to the water girl to ask who was playing, but she was gone. He panicked for a moment but then saw her purse and spray bottles and relaxed; he sat back down on the blanket to enjoy the music. The band was hacking their way through a Chuck Berry cover, laughing out loud as their P.A. cracked and distorted for no apparent reason. They apologized for being out of tune and took a few moments to adjust, begging the crowd's indulgence as they played another song in the key of A.

Anthony wrestled with his dry mouth while he laid back and watched the clouds change shapes. His hands were folded behind his head, making the worst type of knuckle pillow. The crowd had stirred up so much dust that he felt like he was eating a peanut butter sandwich. He massaged his lips with his tongue, searching for the last few drops of water on his skin. He closed his dehydrated eyes slowly, sliding the folds of skin over a gritty layer of dirt and checking one last time for the girl of his dreams. She was nowhere to be found.

"Hey! What's that cloud look like to you?"

Anthony let the animated voice pass through his head without a thought, writing it off as a ringing in his ears. It sounded like someone had taken a big breath of helium just before speaking, using all of their wind to manage just a few high-pitched words and then rushing through them like they were speaking to someone who was closing a door in their face.

"Hey! Hee hee hee. What's that cloud look like to you?"

Again the voice came, this time using inflection similar to a trumpet ripping through a smoke-filled jazz club.

Anthony did a quick head shake, trying to rattle the hearing impairment out of his head before turning to face the cartoon-like voice. He could tell before looking that he wasn't going to like what he saw.

"Hey, sleepy, get that suberin out of your ears."

He turned to where the girl had been just thirty minutes before and took a deep breath as he opened his eyes. His stomach turned violently when he saw a fuzzy, yellow bear smiling at him.

"Suberin?" Anthony asked, rubbing the dirt into his eyes and helping nothing.

"Yeah! Suberin, you clown. Don't you remember what suberin is?"

"Cork wax?" he asked slowly, amazed by everything.

"Wow. You're right on top of it. Look at that cloud. What do you see?"

Anthony was checking to see if anybody was watching him talk to an imaginary bear. His skin was hotter than hell all of a sudden, and he was breathing in waves of hot air like that girl had been doing earlier. The bear appeared to be glowing slightly. His bright yellow fur looked like it was charged with static electricity as it stood on end like an Angora sweater. A velvet, turquoise collar with jagged edges, similar to a clown's, was floating around his fuzzy neck. He patted Anthony softly on the shoulder while pointing at the sky.

"The cloud, Anthony," said the bear.

[163]

Anthony looked up at the sky and instantly recognized the pine-cone-shaped cluster of grapes. They were bursting with sugar, way too plump and almost overripe. He felt exactly the way they looked.

"Grapes," he said, yawning deeply to relieve the stress in his neck.

"What kind, Anthony?"

"Pinot noir, but they're not balanced; something's wrong." He was watching the cloud as it floated by, tasting the innocuous wine that it would eventually yield.

"Why?" the bear asked. His voice had dropped several octaves, falling to a level detectable only by Anthony and the Richter scale.

"Too hot, I think. There's no character left. The acid is all gone."

"Very good. That's your varietal totem, isn't it?"

"My what?" Anthony laughed, thinking about an Indian story he had read as a child.

"Your varietal totem, Anthony. Pinot noir. You share all the same qualities as pinot noir when you're in the right environment. You've tasted La Romanée-Conti. You know how amazing pinot can be." The bear was sitting casually on the girl's blanket. His arms were folded over his knees, waving the occasional paw at the cloud as he spoke.

"It's not a varietal totem – it's just a nickname," Anthony said. "You don't know what you're talking about. What am I talking about? You're just a bear!"

"I'm a California bear," the bear said, taking another hit off the invisible balloon while pointing to the state flag flying above the stage. "Richard is going to be fine, don't worry."

"How do you know about Richard?"

"Duh," the bear said, flopping his paws outward. "I know everything you know and then some. Richard's totem will see him through any trouble. Zinfandel is tough and very adaptable, but it can be light and fruity when treated right. That's the quality that will see him through Vietnam."

"Richard is light and fruity?"

"Kind of," said the bear. "Bennett has him on a special assignment. He's in charge of all the menus and entertaining guests but he'll never admit it to you guys, so don't say anything."

"Why did Dad make him zinfandel and me pinot? I'm tough, too."

"No you're not. You're a wimp. Really! You need to get out of here and find your place. You're turning into a momma's boy."

The cloud transformed itself in the light winds and became a tighter cluster of grapes. It was now almost cylindrical, balanced in color and temperature with just the right amount of energy. Neither Anthony or the bear saw the transformation.

Anthony gazed upwards at the cloud, sensing a new vision as if their dialogue had indicated a motive. He could feel the harmony of sugar and acid in the new grapes as the wispy stratus formed the beautiful cluster overhead.

"Richard's doing fine, huh?" Anthony asked.

"Yeah. It's Cherise you have to worry about, but you know that, don't you?"

"What can I do? She's wild like her nickname," said Anthony.

"Totem," said the bear. "Syrah, Durif, Hermitage, Rhone, Syracuse, Sicily, petite sirah, shiraz I feel sorry for her. At least you know who you're supposed to be."

"Shut up! They're just grapes."

"They're not just grapes, my little Pinot," said the bear. "They're a reflection of your every fiber. You can pursue pinot noir and do it right, if you want to."

"Why me? What do you mean?" Anthony asked. He was flustered and having trouble breathing again. He inhaled sharply through flaring nostrils, swiveling his head to release the tension that had built up in his neck again.

[165]

"You hate being called Pinot because you know it's an insult, right?"

"Yes."

"Well, Rose has shown you how to handle pinot noir properly. Smaller yields from the hillsides, and proper exposure with wild yeasts and some whole clusters with a small percentage of stems, right?"

"Yeah, but they have the money and Dad won't even try to make pinot."

"You're the son of a famous winemaking couple, Anthony. You also have a lot of money. What's the one thing that you really lack?"

"To make pinot noir?"

"Yes, to make pinot, you dunce. Is that suberin still in there?" The bear was very animated in his anger with Anthony, flailing his fluffy arms around like a grizzly on the attack.

"I think I need a cooler climate. It's too hot out where we are."

"Exactly, Anthony. Do you get it now?"

"What?"

"That you're the one who's supposed to leave. Go find yourself. You have the resources and knowledge to make pinot noir a powerful totem. Rose has been showing you all along. You don't really think she went through all that trouble just to make a better zinfandel, do you?

"What do you mean?"

"She's been making pinot noir all along, dummy. She wasn't wasting Henry's money to make a superior cabernet or merlot, even though she did. She was spending all that money to process those grapes to show you how to make a great Burgundy. Every step along the way has to be more precise and expensive to get the varietal character out of that finicky grape. Soil, slope, sun, elevation, water, yield, quality, yeast, treatment, and barrel, Anthony   they all matter."

"Where should I go? Sonoma? The Pinnacles?"

"North," said the bear. "Remember, the furthur north you go,

[166]

the better."

"Mendocino?"

"Furthur. You must always go furthur, Anthony."

The way the bear said "further" sounded funny to Anthony, but he wasn't sure why. He could tell the bear was emphasizing something but he didn't know what. He thought about it for a moment as the music crashed through the crowd, pouring sound into his lap like a tidal wave. The band had been climbing to a higher level without Anthony noticing. They were now rupturing the air with the force of a thunderstorm, rolling their music through the mass of people with a violent clapping of drums and echoing guitars. Anthony stood up to see if an orchestra had joined them on stage, doubting seriously that the same guys who had trouble tuning up earlier could be generating such power. He had trouble focusing on the stage. The switchboard operator in his brain had accidentally plugged his audio receiver into his visual output causing every note to pulse like a silent movie. The music ripped through his soul as he thought about what the bear had said about moving north.

"Plant some eastern slope grapes, Anthony," the bear instructed. "Who cares if you only get one ton per acre. If you pay homage to the east, you'll be rewarded with the aromatics that you enjoy so much. Varietal character disappears with big juicy yields."

"But estimated profit disappears at one ton an acre," Anthony groaned. "I can't pay the bills at that level of production."

"Yes you can, Pinot, because you're famous. You don't even have to work at it. You're a member of the lucky sperm club."

"I'm not afraid of hard work and you know it! Good winemaking is ninety percent mop and only ten percent microscope."

"I know, Anthony. You're a very good janitor," the bear said. His voice climbed to its original animated pitch and he laughed uncontrollably, swatting his thigh with a big fluffy paw.

"Very funny," said Anthony. "How much should I plant to the

[167]

east?"

"About a third, maybe more."

"I'll never pay the bills," mumbled Anthony.

"So," said the bear, watching the drummers do their thing. The other musicians had left the stage, leaving a pair of drummers to perform what sounded like an African funeral march blended with a Harley Davidson and a steam locomotive. "Van Gogh."

"Van Gogh killed himself!" screamed Anthony. "Why would I want to pursue a stupid grape that will drive me crazy and even make things worse for myself by reducing yields just for aroma."

"Because you can and you know it. People will buy your wines because of your connections at first. If they suck they won't keep buying them, though. So you have to do it right the first time. Go north, change your last name to Miller, and plant on hillsides with some eastern exposure, and always ferment in an open-top fermenter."

"I can't change my name," said Anthony.

"You have to, Anthony. It will make you stronger in the long run. Look east, Miller. Go north and taste the soil from the eastern slope."

"And you think that will give me the right stuff, huh?"

"Terroir, Anthony . . . terroir," the bear said. He was speaking like a prophet. His voice had become rich and full of depth, lingering in the furrows of Anthony's brain.

"Terroir?"

"Not 'terror'. Tear-whar," the bear said slowly. "Go north and make a red wine with soul."

"What kind of barrels should I use?" Anthony asked.

"How should I know?" the bear shrugged. "Experiment. The vineyards will determine that. The most important thing to remember is to always keep the barrels happy."

"Happy?" Anthony said, yawning as he scraped the layer of white mucous that had formed around his lips from dehydration.

"Wine is alive, Anthony. It picks up your vibes and negative

[168]

energy. If you and your future wife have arguments in the winery, the wine will suffer I promise. But it will also synthesize any good vibes you have, like the ones that love and romance generate. Trust me. Never yell at someone near your wine. Always fill the winery with good thoughts and fun, especially during crush. Crush is like developing film, Anthony. You're taking a snapshot of Mother Nature when you crush grapes and make wine. Nothing else can do it with more accuracy than a well-made bottle of wine from a carefully-tended vineyard. If light gets in the darkroom during the process, the photo is ruined. It's the same thing with wine. Henry and Rose produce millions of photos every year. But they're just copies and Rose knows it. That's why she started the Sonoma project in the first place. She wanted to paint some portraits. You can create originals, too."

Anthony was thinking about the bear's words, consuming everything he said like a puppy nursing milk. He had been thinking about pursuing his own project after college, but pinot noir had never been an option; common sense had always been his strong point as a child.

"Okay, yeah. I get it now," Anthony said. "The bottle can be a canvas, filled with depth and texture and flavor and tear-whar, or it can be a paint-by-numbers book, mass produced and synthetic."

"Don't be so dramatic, Anthony. That's my job," the bear said. "Just remember what you saw in the cloud. Balance, Anthony acidity is the key. Pick with lower sugars and a better titratable acidity. Go somewhere where you can add sugar. The yeasts don't know where the sugar comes from; they convert it anyway."

"That's sacrilege. I can't add sugar to the grapes," Anthony said.

"I'm just a blasphemous bear, Anthony. What do I know? Rose must have been getting up at midnight all the time to check on all of those pies she was baking, huh?"

"She was adding sugar?"

[169]

"Not all the time - just to the gold medal stuff."

The bear laughed again as the drummers left the stage. A lone guitarist was plucking his strings with his back to the crowd, slowly using the feedback to communicate with the purple aliens orbiting Anthony's blanket. The faint whine of his guitar was being drowned out by the protesters in the adjacent park who shouted about Bennett and his use of their brothers to fight the Communists.

"You're embarrassed that your family is responsible for Bennett's election, aren't you?" the bear asked. He could see that Anthony was straining to hear what they were yelling about his godfather in the park.

"Be There is a good man. He doesn't deserve all of the negative crap they're throwing at him," Anthony said, still listening to the protesters. He could see Cherise leading a small group of people around a burning barrel as they chanted and threw draft cards into the thick grey smoke.

"Syrah's just a little confused, Anthony. Her heart's in the right place, though. She wants to fit in at school, but it's hard because your dad is Bennett's best friend. She has to be a rebel. She can't help it."

Anthony watched as the bear leapt to his feet and began circling his blanket; his fur pulsing from green to blue and then orange to yellow as he danced and twirled to the music. Anthony shook his head as the image of the dancing bear became vaporous against the blue sky, looking like a mirage at the end of a paved road on a hot summer day. The music trickled into Anthony's head like a spider, slowly circling his earlobe and then attacking the eardrum like a fly caught in an acoustic web of bass guitar, filling Anthony's head with sound. His breathing became erratic and hurried as he tried to process all the information being gathered by his senses. **[FULL SENSORY OVERLOAD]** Anthony was now just waves of energy, sweaty palms, and a dry mouth. "Help," he whispered.

[170]

"Relax, Anthony," the bear said softly. "You're in a good place with kind people all around. Don't freak out, okay? It's cool. Breathe slower, then close your eyes and relax. Enjoy the eyelid theatre for awhile. I think it's going to be a very good show."

🍇 🍇 🍇

26

Skye was sitting in the shade on a bench near the winery when Jack walked up from the creek. He was still a little mad at Sunflower for calling him a jerk and was walking with his head down as he climbed the slope. She had no right to give him a hard time about not calling Maria in the middle of all this stuff with Cherise, he thought. It's not like I do this all the time, is it? He was surprised to look up and see Skye reading a book and sitting casually with a leg on each side of the bench.

"There you go again, trying to act like you can read," Jack said.

"Shabby!" said Skye. "What's up? Besides your weight."

"Good one. What are you doing here? You're gettin' a little tired of smelling like wort all the time, aren't you?"

"Tired of smelling like money is more like it," Skye said, teasing his nearly-bankrupt brother. The microbrewing empire that Skye and his wife had started was doing all of its sales under its own roofs, avoiding middlemen and distributors whenever possible   a lucrative practice learned from their dad that Jack thought was entirely too much trouble.

"Yeah, that's true," Jack said reluctantly. "You heard about Cherise, huh?"

"Bummer, man," Skye said, shaking his head. "That's really something. Old Syrah finally bailed. I know how close you guys were. I'm sorry. Dad says you own some apples now. You wanna make some hard cider?"

"Nah," Jack said, surprised by Skye's question. "I'm gonna renew the lease to some old-timers up there. I can probably get you a good price, though. Where's the Hops?" he said, referring to Skye's children.

"In town with their mom. Where's Petal?"

"Looking for frogs."

"Again?" Skye laughed. "Is she on another trip about pesticides?"

"Oh, I met a biologist that's doing some research on the frog mutations around here and I think she shook up Sunflower pretty bad."

"I was only kidding. Really? Mutations, huh?" Skye's face looked like he had taken a bite of an apple that was full of maggots.

"If eight legs can be considered abnormal for a frog, then yeah, mutations. Maria says it happens every once in awhile they're adjustments to environmental changes or something. But who knows?"

"Galapagos, eh? Who's Maria?"

"The biologist."

"Is she cute?" Skye asked.

"Oh, man. She's gorgeous."

"I knew it," said Skye. "I could tell the way you said her name that she was hot."

"Bull crud. Petal told you about her, didn't she?"

"Yeah," Skye laughed, closing his book. "Let's get a beer. Or is it too early for the little winemaker to have a drinky pooh?"

"Shut up," said Jack. "I've got some of your brews in the

winery. Let's go."

"I'm packin'," Skye said, reaching into a canvas cooler under the bench. He pulled out a couple of long necks and handed one to Jack. Skye twisted the cap off of his beer in the fold of skin inside his elbow by inserting the bottle, squeezing his bicep, and then twisting the bottle. It was a simple drinking game started by their Uncle Richard.

"You're still doing that?" asked Jack. "Grow up. I'm not playing."

Skye slowly unfolded his arm, trying to keep the bottle cap attached to his skin as long as possible. The little dimple marks in his arm were pink and red, similar to a seam in a pair of ugly designer jeans. The cap was dangling by only two creases before it finally fell, landing upside down on the grass below.

"Shit," Jack said, taking a huge swig of beer. If the bottle cap had landed right side up, Skye would've had to take a drink.

"You better get used to it, little man. I'm the master."

"Quite an accomplishment, Franky. Mom would be proud." Jack finished his beer in two long chugs. He was pretty sure that the vine cuttings weren't going to get harvested now that the beer-drinking demon from Portland was here for the day.

"You drank that pretty fast; I'm impressed. Something wrong?" asked Skye.

Jack was surprised at how fast he drained his beer too, wondering if he was ready for another bender so soon after the last one. "Oh, Petal was giving me crap about not calling Maria the biologist I was telling you about. She said I was a jerk. I'm not a jerk. I'm just a little stressed over this whole thing with Cherise."

"Whatever, Shabby," Skye said. Despite winning the drinking game, Skye drained his beer too.

"Are you gonna give me a hard time, too?" said Jack.

"Let's just say you don't have the best track record lately when it comes to relationships."

"I know," Jack said. "This winery has been a financial

nightmare. Maybe that's why I haven't had any luck lately. If you and Monica hadn't helped out, I would have been buried by now. If I sign this lease on Cherise's land, though, I can pay you guys back."

"Hey, Jack, we don't care about the money. Monica loves being invested in the winery. She thinks she's gonna get you to plant some gewürztraminer."

Jack shook his head while opening another beer. "No way. Does she still think she's spicy enough to be gewürtz? She's stuck with chenin blanc as a totem and that's all there is to it. Henry made the call. She shouldn't have kissed his butt all the time. He thought she was so sweet. She blew it. Besides, I'll never make a white wine as long as I live. Dad can mess around with the refrigeration and clarification and filtering and cold stabilizing. I'm never going there, no way. I don't care how popular pinot gris gets."

"What about a wasabe riesling, Grasshopper?" Skye said, using a thick Japanese accent.

"Don't laugh. It's on the way," said Jack.

"What, really?" Skye asked, overcome with fear.

"Oh, yes. Be afraid . . . be very afraid. Axis powers reunite in a culinary collision. She's got sushi coming and she's wearing her wasabe shirt."

"Whoa! I can see it from here," Skye said, watching Sunflower climb the slope to the winery. "That's ghastly, Jack. Where did she find that thing?"

"Guess."

"Catalog?"

"Nope. The Internet, baby. Organic textiles from the space shuttle, hand woven by vegetarians in Veneta, Oregon."

They both watched Sunflower as she walked up the long row of cane-pruned vines. The severed bones were crunching under her rubber boots as she checked the remaining limbs on the trellis. She would stop and look up at the sky and then turn her attention back to the vines, looking for the shiniest canes to make sure the pruning had been done correctly. The shoots that got the most sun the prior year would be shiny and healthy, eager to produce fruit this year, and thankful to be clinging to the trellis for another season. The darker canes with crusty bark were now covering the ground, continuing the cycle in another way. She looked up and saw Skye and Jack and smiled, waving to her brothers as her bibs dangled loosely around her stride.

"You know," said Skye, "our sister is probably the smartest person I know right up there with Dad but she scares me sometimes. Really." He was squinting now, trying to avoid direct eye contact with her shirt.

Jack was draining another beer, applying a protective shield to his stomach before the wasabe riesling made its appearance. Designed to cleanse the palate of any residual fish oils that the sushi might leave behind, Sunflower's unique blend of Oregon dry riesling and Japanese horseradish was a disaster in a glass. She'd been "perfecting" the mix for over three years. At first she added the powder directly to the must with horrifying, almost toxic results. Then she tried blending it with bentonite after the primary fermentation and proceeding with cold stabilization and filtering as usual; the yield was clean and floral but too weak surprisingly potable. This year's outcome was a cloudy-looking grog of mustard and ethanol, blended just before bottling to insure an aggressive start and finish on the palate.

"She looks happier than usual, if that's possible," Skye said. "Has she been getting the happy-stick lately?"

"Maybe. She's ga-ga for the attorney handling Syrah's lease. You should have seen the two of them when they met. It was hilarious. The poor guy almost puked on himself when he saw her. I wouldn't be surprised if they hooked up last night. It was pretty funny."

"Why?" asked Skye, laughing as he watched Sunflower wrestle with Pino and Vino in the vineyard.

"Don't say anything to Petal, okay? But he's got palsy like you had for awhile. You know, really bad muscle spasms and a thick lip   remember?"

"Hell, yes. It was my freshman year in high school. How could I forget. That God is a funny guy."

"Well, anyway, Petal comes running up to the house and Blake has a mouthful of carnitas, and he sees her for the first time and he tries to say 'Hi' but his stutter is so bad from shock that he practically has a seizure." Jack was laughing and having a hard time finishing his story.

"What, he has a stutter, too?"

"I'm not sure. I think so. It's a long story. Anyway, you know how Juanita's tortillas have all that yellow corn? Well, it was like a paste and he's trying to talk through it and he blows this beauty of a spit bubble right in front of us   and I mean thick, big, and chunky. I thought he was going to die. But Petal was totally into him for some strange reason. BANG! Fish on, she's hooked."

"Sounds like the old wounded bird syndrome to me," Skye said, still watching Sunflower.

"Exactly," said Jack. "How many half-dead critters do you think she brought home when we were kids?"

"Thousands."

"Skye baby! What's up?" Sunflower said, running towards her brother.

"Hey, Petal, long time no see. You look great," Skye said. He gave his sister a big hug, lifting her off the ground.

"Whew, you guys smell like a brewery. No offense, Franky," she said, rubbing the top of Skye's head.

"None taken," said Skye. "Nice shirt."

"Thanks, you like it?"

"Yeah, it's very subtle. Is it supposed to control mildew or something?"

"Very funny. Where's the Hops?"

"Getting new shoes with Mom. Run faster, jump higher. Gotta look good for Henry."

[176]

VARIETAL TENDENCIES

"Can you believe he's coming here? Dad's freakin'," she said, helping herself to a beer. They both watched as she rolled up her sleeve and inserted the beer into the socket of her elbow. "Me and you, Skye," she said, choosing her opponent. She twisted the bottle until it opened then slowly uncoiled her arm. They all watched as the cap fell, bounced twice, and landed right side up.

"I am such a stud," Sunflower said, watching as Skye reluctantly guzzled his bottle of Black Muddy Porter.

A slight breeze was blowing across from the west as the sun climbed towards noon just above the roof of the winery. Their protective shadow was creeping out from under their feet like a magic carpet slowly disappearing into the cellar behind them. The formerly-shaded drops of morning dew still clung to the grass as they fought a useless battle with the sun like a hungover vampire waking up miles away from her coffin. Sunflower, Jack, and Skye all laughed as the dogs provided their usual entertainment gnarling and biting, jumping and whining, and such.

The pruning crew was now visible as they climbed a knoll in the vineyard to the west. They were in groups of two covering six rows at a time, one cutting away the old while another secured the new. They looked like a very slow three-legged race from a distance. In fact, if you were a betting man like their Grandpa Henry, you'd probably wager on a team as you sat on your porch with your military buddies and watched them work while you drank martinis and smoked cigars, just to pass the time. Hourly labor was never as fun to bet on, though; the pace was far too slow. It was always the piecework during crush that got the teams moving fast and the wagers moving faster. Henry and the president would laugh and make plans for the upcoming elections as the buckets of grapes reached the bins and tipped the scales in favor of one wager or the other. Henry always had the advantage because he knew which team had the oldest members;

[177]

he watched discretely as the younger pickers dumped one out of their ten buckets into the older pickers' bin to pay their tithes for the pleasure of working in a Mueller vineyard. Impressed by Henry Mueller's apparent hospitality, President Bennett was always happy to have the youngest team of pickers   they were obviously stronger and faster; he was completely unaware that the plebe system wasn't limited to the Virginia Academy of Military Science.

"So, Skye," Sunflower said, "did Jack tell you about his waitress friend?"

"I thought you said she was a biologist." Skye said, looking at his sister.

"I did. She is. Huh, Jack?" Sunflower was beaming. She enjoyed watching Jack as he tried to get out of the impossible situation that lay ahead.

"So, who's the waitress, Shabby? Are you seeing two girls at the same time again?" Skye asked.

Jack smiled at Sunflower until his left cheek tightened his face into a smirk that said "you bitch." "I met her at the wine dinner I did the other night."

"Who?" asked Skye, winking at Sunflower.

"Maria."

"I thought Maria was the biologist," said Skye.

"She is, but she works part-time at the restaurant as a waitress. That's where I first met her."

"A chip off the old block, huh?" asked Skye. "Does Dad know?"

"Yes," said Jack. "I've heard plenty already. If I want any more crud out of you. . . ."

"You'll squeeze my head?" Skye said, laughing in unison with Sunflower.

Jack slapped his knee and acted like he was laughing too, although no sound was coming from his mouth. "You guys kill me. You really do. Did you all get together with Dad and plan this out, or what?"

"Easy, Shabby," said Sunflower. "You know it's funny, admit it."

"It's no big deal, so drop it. You guys need to get a life. So she's a waitress, so what? That doesn't mean I'm going to marry her," said Jack.

"I think Shabernet's a little tense from all that money he inherited. What do you think, Petal?"

"Yeah, he's trippin', Skye. You're trippin', Jack. Relax. Hey look! It's Cornelius."

The flock of pigeons worked their way up the driveway, cooing and squawking and rapidly flapping their wings to jump two feet at a time. Old Cornelius was throwing handfuls of croutons at them in as much of a defensive posture as one of generosity. The abnormally-large pockets in his new coat had expanded his capacity for charity beyond his throwing range, attracting ever larger flocks of hungry birds from greater distances. What had started as a random act of kindness was now a daily commitment to feed dozens of birds. Cornelius was tired and cursing the birds. He was shaking his long twisted finger at them as he laughed some-but yelled more. He was hoping the birds wouldn't leave but just relax. "Yei, yei, yei, yei," he yelled, waving at Skye.

"Wow, he's still around. How's he doing, Jack?" Skye asked, vacantly waving back to Cornelius.

"He cruises by every day. He seems to be doing a lot better. I think his new coat has got him in over his head, though."

"What do you mean?" asked Sunflower.

"Well, before he could only carry so many croutons, but now he's probably got half the damn salad bar in there. Look at the size of those pockets."

"That's the first time I've ever heard him say anything," said Skye.

"He looks a lot better. A few years ago he used to talk all the time," said Jack. "But he hasn't said anything in a long time."

They watched Cornelius battle the birds for awhile as he waved at the three of them. A blank stare crept into his eyes and the emotions slowly faded from his face. He suddenly looked dead. He wiped the butter from his fingertips and patted his empty pockets to show the birds he wasn't being selfish. A flicker of disappointment registered in his eyes as the birds flew away one by one to find a more generous host. He looked like a confused drunk who couldn't find his car in a large parking lot as the Alzheimer's tightened its grip on his senses; he mumbled something about "those ungrateful bastards" as he turned slowly towards the bar at the end of the street, still quietly cursing the birds.

"What time is Blake supposed to be here?" asked Sunflower.

"Around noon, I guess," said Jack.

"I'm gonna go get the sushi," she said, walking towards her jeep. She turned around and crouched down low with her hands in front of her, her fingers forming a dangerous set of claws. "I'm bringing the wasabe riesling, too," she snarled.

"Ah geez, Petal, I brought some nice crisp raspberry ale," said Skye. "How does that sound? Hmmm?"

"Mmmm, Snapple Ale. I can't believe we're related, you wimp. Man up, okay?" She laughed and waved goodbye, swiping her harmless claws at the two of them as Pino and Vino jumped after the dangling straps of her overalls.

"She's psycho, Jack. You and Dad need to make her take a vacation."

"She's doing just fine," said Jack. "So how's the brewery? World domination and forty percent growth, or what?"

"Well, it doesn't suck, but there's a lot of new players out there. And each one's getting hipper than the next. Friggin' barrel-fermented beer out of California is a classic example of 'mine's bigger than yours'. Leave it to the people who put caviar on a pizza to poop in the brew kettle. But we'll ride it out. We were one of the first so we'll always have a position, hopefully."

"You gonna get a distributor?"

"Monica seems to think that we can keep deliveries in-house

right through the next expansion, but who knows? Portland's a loyal town and we haven't disappointed anyone so far. Granted, 35 pubs is a lot to manage, but there's a lot of P.h.Ds who wanna brew beer. And as long as they'll work for ten bucks an hour, we'll do just fine. I'll refurbish every old building in the city for 300 percent profit and have my weekends off."

Jack finished another beer and gazed into the vineyard, watching Felix motivate his crew to keep up with Lupé's. He laughed to himself over the thought of betting on the younger crew with Skye.

"You heard that Petal told Dad about the Hops, didn't you?" said Jack.

"She did, huh?" said Skye. "That's what I mean about her scaring me. She went off for about an hour about the hex and totem thing, saying that the kids would relate to hops easier than grapes or some darn thing."

"I know, she did the same thing to me, too," said Jack. "She's into this Feng Shui thing lately. She wanted me to round the corners of the winery and paint one wall green and one wall purple. She thinks the square fermenters have to go, too."

"Feng Shui?" Skye repeated.

"You've heard of it, haven't you? Furniture placement and color schemes for optimum energy flow and conductivity? Never mind. I sound like Sunflower."

"What did Dad say about naming our kids after hops?"

"He thinks it's pretty funny," said Jack. "He said he was surprised he didn't figure it out. I think he's sorry he ever started the whole totem theory."

"It's more than a theory, Jack. You know that. I know it's strange and all, but you have to admit it. I did. Hence the names Halle, Cassy, and Kent. Don't repeat this to Petal, but Monica and I did think about that stuff when we named the kids."

"I know that," said Jack. "But I thought you did it as a joke. You weren't really worried about some varietal tendency determining your kids' future, were you Franky?" Jack was

[181]

teasing his brother, moving his hands in elliptical orbits while his fingers emitted invisible cobwebs.

"Knock it off, Jack. Look at you. All of a sudden you own a thousand or so acres of the world's best land for cabernet and merlot and you think it's a coincidence? Come on. There's some strange ju-ju going around, Shabby. Think about it."

"Serendipity, Skye. That's all."

"Cherise knew exactly what she was doing. Don't give me that serendipity crap. Luck had nothing to do with it. She wanted to haunt everyone with another episode of prophecy. Trust me. I bet there's a whole lot more than apples up there. Let's go up to Yakima and check it out. Five hundred thousand dollars is a lot of money, Jack. I wouldn't sign that lease if I were you. Dad thinks you should wait to sign, too."

"No, he doesn't. He almost gagged when I told him how much they offered me."

"Well, I wouldn't trust some attorney, Jack," said Skye, opening another beer.

"What am I gonna do with all that land, Skye? Work it? Hell no. A lease is perfect. I'm signing. I can retire and pay you guys back. I thought having my own little winery was going to be a snap. It's almost killed me! And now you want me to worry about running some huge vineyard with no money? Shit."

"You should at least find out who wants the land," said Skye.

"It's some cooperative. Big deal," Jack said lazily.

"What if it's **THE GUILD**?" asked Skye, his voice dropping very low. He was trying to make it sound as if he was speaking through a synthesizer when he said the guild, hoping to sound like the ruler of a dark and evil empire.

"So," said Jack.

"Oh, so now you don't mind if the whole Northwest is owned by one big conglomerate."

"That'll never happen, Skye. They wouldn't touch Oregon with a ten foot pole," Jack said, laughing at his brother. "The yields are way too low."

"Hey, I'm serious, Jack. Monica and I can help out with whatever money you need to farm that land. Don't let the mod squad diversify into everything. Next thing you know, they'll have ten more labels and every slot in the supermarket, just watch."

"Oh come on, Skye, they're not that bad. They use really cute cartoon characters in all their ads. Don't you like Rocky Riesling? And what about Joe Cabernet? He's a stud. He always made me want to drink wine when I was in high school. They've done a lot for the wine industry and we owe them a little something, don't we?"

"I forgot what a smart ass you were, Jack. It must be all that tannin from the cabernet, huh?"

"Very funny. We don't even know if it's **THE GUILD** or not. Besides, I don't want to mess with them if it is, that's for dang sure."

🍇 🍇 🍇

27

Anthony's nostrils were full of dust from the long day on the blanket. He'd managed to sleep through the worst of his dehydration; he opened his dry eyes through a crusty film of boogers, not quite sure what to expect when he finally regained his vision. He immediately looked for the water girl, hoping to see her asleep on her blanket. No luck.

Taking his time standing up, he looked through the crowd for Cherise, the blonde, or the dancing bear. They were nowhere to be found. The sun was almost even with the top of the stage, indicating a significant passage of time. He checked his watch. "Shit. 5:30. Dinner at Char's soon," he said, talking out loud to himself.

He plopped back down on the blanket and laughed as he thought about the fuzzy yellow bear. He wiped the thick layer of oil from his face with his hands, then wiped them on his pants leaving visible stains. His lips were sticking together.

"Oh my god. What happened to you? I thought I told you not to drink anything," Cherise said, looking at her little brother.

"I didn't, I promise. Man, I feel like I've been demagnetized. Something's wrong, you know, like every mineral has been stripped from my body."

"You could say that," she said, smiling at Anthony. "Do you feel alright? You don't look so hot, but you sound pretty normal."

"I'm really thirsty."

"I bet. What the hell happened?"

"Nothing. I just sat here and watched the band and listened to the music. It's cool, Cherise. I feel great!" he chimed. He gazed at the sky for a moment, forgetting who he was.

"I bet you do," she said, wondering if it would be alright to take him to Char's restaurant. "Make sure you wear your sunglasses tonight. It looks like you got a little too much sun. Your pupils are a mess." Cherise shook her head as she offered Anthony a hand up from the blanket. Her little brother was growing up, she thought as she smiled at the look on his face. "What happened to your little friend?"

"You saw him, too?"

"Who?" Cherise said.

"The bear," said Anthony.

"What bear?" she said, laughing at how drunk he sounded.

"Never mind."

"I meant the girl that was sitting next to you. What happened to the blonde? Isn't that her stuff?"

"Yeah, that's her spray bottle and purse. I don't know where she went, though. We talked for awhile and she sprayed me with some water and then she disappeared." Anthony's voice was higher than usual, almost lyrical. It sounded as though he was going to start singing at any minute.

"She sprayed you with her water bottle, huh?" Cherise said, biting her cheek. She was trying to keep herself from laughing out loud at her little brother. The last thing she wanted to do was scare him about tainted water bottles.

"Why?" he asked, swatting at a mosquito. He carefully watched his hand as the insect slowly traveled across his field of vision and landed softly on his arm.

"Nothing, Pinot," said Cherise. "Everything's cool. Come on, we need to get moving. I'm in the mood to drive, if you don't mind."

"Be my guest," he said. "I'm kind of tired." Anthony followed his sister through the dwindling crowd, looking everywhere for the girl with flowers in her hair. He checked the state flag flying above the stage and smiled. The golden bear was there, waving in the breeze, his big fluffy paws planted firmly in the fabric.

They drove to the wharf, found a place to park, and took a few moments to compose themselves before entering the restaurant. They had a few minutes to spare and Cherise used them to smoke. Anthony checked the radio for the next time the band would be playing a concert, wanting desperately to be there and knowing full-well that the blonde with bells on her shoes wouldn't miss it for the world. She was too kind.

"I'm glad you changed your pants, Syrah," said Anthony. "Those things were ugly."

"Hey, I made those. Be nice," she said, exhaling softly. She'd inserted large pieces of faded denim just below the knees of her new jeans, causing her pants to flare dramatically around her calves and ankles. "So, what did you think about at the show,

[185]

Pinot?"

"What do you mean?"

"Your mind tends to ramble at one of those things. I think it must be the music. I was just wondering if you came up with anything new."

Anthony wasn't sure if he should share any of the excerpts from his conversation with the bear. He still wasn't sure if he'd been dreaming or not. "Umm, well, I thought about growing pinot noir somewhere north of here. And I think I figured out what it will take to make a red wine with soul. And I figured out the varietal totem thing. And I know that Richard is going to be fine and that eastern exposure is important and that yields need to be reduced by at least fifty percent and that. . . ."

"Whoa, whoa, whoa, hold on there! What was that about Richard? And what? A varietal totem? Yields? Shit, Anthony, we're going to be late. Hold on to that thought . . . wait, never mind, that's impossible, even I know that. Try hard to remember everything you were just talking about or you're going to lose it. Trust me, okay? Let's go."

Char's restaurant had been open for only a few months but it was already extremely popular. Her commitment to presentation and fresh ingredients (and her lineage) made her a hit with food and wine enthusiasts throughout the Bay Area. It was no secret that her parents were Henry and Rose Mueller, and that she had catered both of President Bennett's inaugural dinners. Char was famous for her work ethic, and the fact that she could usually be found working the line or seating the guests didn't hurt her reputation either.

The old warehouse had been restored to a barely-presentable level. Not caring a bit for fancy lighting or plush interiors, Char relied on her plates to create the atmosphere. Using a variety of sauces and colors on every dish was a must at Chez Panacea - an example of "Color, taste and texture, the Legos of cooking"

[186]

according to Henry. "That and one hell of a view," agreed Char. One third of Chez Panacea was windows, all facing San Francisco Bay.

Cherise pushed a giggling Anthony through the front doors and immediately pointed him towards the restroom. "Scrub your face and make it hurt. I mean it. Rub so hard that your skin burns," she said, barely controlling her laughter.

"Why, Syrah? I feel good," he sang, stumbling away.

Cherise paused, looked for her parents, and sneaked behind the elevated hostess stand to dim the lights before Anthony returned from the restroom. Where normally stood a simple podium, Char had erected a cathedral. Even a teenager could control the dining room from such a powerful position. It's very hard for a psycho-celebrity to assume a position of power when they're looking straight up at the hostess, begging for a table. The coast was clear. Cherise felt like she was in high school, sneaking in late with her panties in her pocket. She dimmed the lights and headed for the dining room.

She passed through the foyer, smiling at the well-behaved guests who were waiting to be seated. Her heart was racing as her eyes met her mother's. Rose was seated at the far end of a very large table. The chair next to her was vacant. Oh no, where's Dad? she thought   not the bathroom, please, not the bathroom. Rose held up her hand and pulled Cherise across the room with a sculpted forefinger. A polite smile was stretched tightly across her lips, her grey eyes disappearing into the lazy fog behind her.

"Hi, Momma. You look so beautiful. Sorry we're a little late. Traffic was a bear from the protest. Where's Daddy?"

"In the kitchen with your sister, opening the wine. How's Anthony doing? Did he stay out of trouble?" Rose was speaking through her smile, not looking at Cherise as people joined them at the table.

[187]

"He met a girl and got a sunstroke, but other than that nothing much happened," Cherise said, making room for a waitress who was filling the water glasses. The waitress smiled at Cherise in the usual 'excuse me' way that servers do. Cherise nodded back, smiling at her in a friendly manner and taking a moment to think about where she knew her from. She looked strangely familiar to Cherise, almost like a friend she'd known for many years. Then she remembered the face painted with hearts, the scarlet flowers in her long blonde hair, and the cat bells on her sandals ringing softly in the park . . . on the blanket next to Anthony.

🍇 🍇 🍇

28

Sunflower waved her brothers over to the porch while opening a bottle of unlabeled . . . something. She poured the "wine" quickly, hoping to dispose of the clay-like sediment before the critics arrived. The liquid bubbled and burped, fighting itself in a fury of escaping gases as the colloidal suspension revealed its unstable nature. She involuntarily winced as the vapors reached her nose. A sinister smile spread across her lips as the boys approached somewhat timidly.

"I hope," said Skye, "that you've paid your life insurance premiums for the month, Jack. The Hops are still listed as your beneficiaries, aren't they?"

"Stop it, Skye. It only looks hazardous," Sunflower said, looking at the wasabe riesling.

"Hey, maybe this is another conspiracy between you two to get my money, huh? I never thought of that," said Jack, scratching his temple.

"What money, Jack?" asked Skye. "I thought you were broke."

"Oh, yeah. Hey, I'm rich again now, though. Remember? I'm not poor anymore. Thanks, Aunt Cherise," he said, looking up at the sky.

"You guys stop teasing and go wash your hands," said Sunflower. "I'm going to put the food out as soon as Blake arrives. Is Monica going to be back soon, Skye?"

"Nah, they're having lunch at the golden crotches. It's playtime at kiddy-land."

"When did you get as tannic as Jack?" she asked, shaking her head at Skye.

"Hey, haven't you heard? I'm the next big grape in New York City. Heck yeah, they're gonna name restaurants after me. Just you wait and see. The Cabernet Franc and Grill is coming soon." Skye saw that Sunflower wasn't amused and he changed his tone. "Sorry, Petal. These movie promotion, happy-feast collectible boxes with their limited-supply plastic toys are really getting to me. There was a time, before I had kids, that I thought there was no possible way any of my kids would want to eat that garbage and have those toys and see those movies, but we had to get cable TV and the rest, as they say, is history. 'Collect all five, while supplies last.' What a pain in the ass."

"Are you through?" Sunflower asked, looking at Skye like he was talking way too much. She was nervous about seeing Blake again and she wanted to have everything just perfect.

"Hey, Petal," said Jack, "if you're so nervous about seeing Blake, you should probably change that shirt. That thing's gonna give him a seizure. Do you know CPR, Skye?"

"Yeah, we just had a training session at one of the breweries. I can help if there's a problem." They both laughed and exchanged pointing fingers at each other, shooting blanks across Sunflower's path. She lifted two glasses of wasabe riesling at them like they were turds and used them to chase her brothers into the house.

"Wash up, boys! Now!" she yelled, laughing as they flexed their bodies like they were playing a game of tag to avoid contact with her.

Jack entered the house first with a powerful lunge, looking at the glasses of wine over his shoulder. "Oh man, did you see the sediment in the bottom of those things? We're gonna die!"

"I heard that," Sunflower said. She was using a spoon to extract the clumps of green mustard from the bottoms of the glasses, hoping to have them almost presentable before Blake arrived.

Skye was washing his hands in the kitchen sink, giggling as the coarse fibers of the plastic brush tickled the palm of his hand. "Are you really going to sign that lease without seeing the property?" he asked.

"It's a lot of money, Skye."

"I know it is, Jack. Have you asked that guy what's planted up there, or are you just going by what Cherise always told everyone?"

"We all know it's apples. She was so sick of everything to do with grapes that there's no way she would have planted a vineyard. Think about it, Skye. I'll ask Blake, though. He has to tell me the truth, doesn't he? He's a lawyer." They both laughed as Jack took a turn at the sink. He looked at the phone hanging on the wall and thought about calling Maria. It was the perfect time to call, he thought she'd be in class for sure; just leave a 'hit and run' message on the machine and everyone's happy.

"He might have some client confidentiality thing he's dealing with, Jack," said Skye. "But I'm pretty sure he'd have to tell you. Hell, you own it. Why hasn't one of our lawyers contacted us about this, anyway?"

"Dad said he was trying to find out who's holding all the papers, but you remember how frustrated he got the last time he

[190]

dealt with all those guys, don't you?"

"He was a madman," said Skye, faking a shiver to make his point. "I've never seen him like that   except when they canceled the World Series."

"That's understandable, though," Jack said, shrugging as he pondered the phone call.

"True," said Skye.

Blake Stewart was a nervous wreck. He was wrestling with some documents on the passengers seat of his car, waiting for his face to relax while he watched Sunflower set the table for lunch. She had seen him pull into the driveway and waved at him, causing muscle spasms throughout his body. He thought it was an optical illusion that she was glowing under the shade of the front porch; she appeared almost angelic, like a bright green aura was surrounding her body. He shuffled the papers into his briefcase and took a deep breath through his nose, begging the Lord for the strength to control the involuntary convulsions in his face, and thinking hard about what to say first in an effort to prevent himself from stuttering. He walked towards the house with his head down.

"Hi, Blake," Sunflower said, casually placing a platter of sticky rice on the table. She was careful to avoid eye contact with him as she worked diligently to set the table. "Can I get you anything to drink?"

Blake was watching the straps of her overalls flop around the chairs as she spun around the table. Now and again, the clasps would briefly snag on a chair, pull the sides of her bibs down an inch each time, and momentarily reveal the thin strings of her fluorescent green panties in the space between the double set of buttons on her hips. He almost fainted when he saw the milky white skin between her shirt and underwear.

"N-no thanks, I'm fine," his voice cracked. He smiled at how high his voice was when he said 'I'm fine.' A strange smell was burning in his nostrils.

"You've got to try this, and please pretend you like it, okay?" Sunflower said.

He was surprised to be feeling so normal. She had seen him looking at her panties and simply smiled. She actually likes me, he thought, as he reached out for a glass of death. He tasted the beverage without apprehension, then used the front lawn as a spittoon after trying to endure the assault on his palate for several grueling seconds.

"I'm supposed to like this?" he asked, coughing through his nose. His sinuses were flushing like a toilet as his head expanded from the increased oxygen flow. It felt like someone had jammed a jalapeno pepper in each nostril as the hot vapors reached critical mass in his nasal cavity. The tears began to flow as the finish registered on his palate like a sledgehammer. He was trying to regain his composure as Jack and Skye walked out of the house.

Jack took one look at Blake and laughed, shaking his head at Sunflower as she handed him a glass of wine. "No way, Petal. I'm gonna have to eat a lot of eel before my tongue has a coating thick enough to stand up to that stuff."

Skye quickly opened another beer and put it to his lips before Sunflower could suggest the dreadful alternative. He held out his hand to greet Blake. "Hey, how ya doing? I'm Skye."

Blake's breathing was still erratic. His eyes were on fire and his mouth tasted like a caustic mix of breath mints and paint thinner. He shook Skye's hand without saying a word, letting his deformed smile and pink complexion speak for themselves.

Skye nodded politely, acknowledging Blake's pain and trying hard not to laugh. He looked at the table that Sunflower had prepared, and commented on its use of the key culinary elements. "Very nice, Petal. Great colors. And the wasabe riesling should provide some nice textures, huh Blake?"

"I-i-i-it's alive," he said, exaggerating his stutter for Skye. He could tell there was something very likable about the brewer from Portland.

"So, Blake," said Skye, "how many acres of vineyards did my little brother inherit?"

"God, Skye, can't we even eat our lunch first?" Sunflower said, rolling up a fatty of sushi.

"Let's just cut to the chase, shall we?" said Skye. "We all want to know what's up there, and we're all too polite to ask. But, seeing as how we should have some respect for the dead and all I guess it's not the best time to talk about it - is it, Petal? I'm sorry. I'll take one with some of that crab."

"Roll it yourself, butthead," said Sunflower.

Jack was cramming handfuls of rice into his mouth and chasing it with soy sauce. "Have you ever noticed that there's always a ton of rice at the end of every sushi party? What's up with that? I'm taking it upon myself to see to it that there is no rice left."

"Perhaps you could wait until everyone's had a roll, Jack?" said Skye.

"Mmmm?" Jack said through a mouthful of rice.

Sunflower rolled several different types of heavily-oiled fish into the sheets of seaweed. She wanted to lube their palates with as much salve as possible, hoping the protective layer of oil would soften the blow of the wasabe riesling. She looked at Jack and Skye with a sad face, trying to make them feel guilty for not tasting her latest blend wine and spice.

"Come on, Blake. What gives?" said Skye. "Is it grapes or what?"

Blake had covered his tongue with a piece of cured salmon in an effort to relieve the pain. It was sitting in his mouth out of everyone's sight, making his speech even harder to control than usual. "I'm not s-sure. But I advise you to visit the property before you s-sign anything." He was stunned by what he had just said. He could now, he thought, consider himself officially unemployed; Spalding would fire him for sure. He looked at Sunflower to let her know that he didn't like being a lawyer right now.

She smiled seductively at Blake, thanking him with her eyes. She looked at Jack, who was oblivious to everything being said; his mouth was full of food, his head was tilted back, and the soy sauce was dripping slowly into his gaping craw. Skye was alert, nodding his head at Blake. He understood what Blake had just done and smiled at him. He raised a glass of Sunflower's truth serum to suggest a toast.

"So, here's to the Columbia Valley and Aunt Cherise," said Skye as he shook his head at Jack, who was choking on his food. "May we find the answers she was looking for." He slowly tasted the "wine." He let it rest on his tongue for a few moments, and tried hard to not breathe through it. The last thing a person should ever do is add oxygen to an unwanted flame. He had been careful to avoid the chunks of green clay laying on the bottom of his glass, choosing instead to live another day. "Not a bad effort, Petal. It approaches the mid-palate with a little force, though. I imagine it's about the same as a pitchfork plunging into the soft spot of a baby's head. And, the finish is somewhat abrasive. In fact, it feels like my mouth is full of fishhooks. No, wait broken glass, that's it."

Blake chuckled and nodded his head in agreement, wishing he could express himself like Skye. Sunflower was frowning at her brother, but in the back of her mind she was thinking about what Blake had just said. Jack was watching Skye to see if he should administer any kind of first aid.

"It works though, doesn't it?" she asked, hopefully.

"It works, Petal," said Skye. "My mouth is absolutely free of any residual fish oils whatsoever. Nice job." His eyes were bleeding and his heart rate had accelerated by 30 beats a minute. He wasn't sure if he could maintain his composure much longer. He turned his attention back to Blake, trying to get Jack to pay attention to what was going on.

"So, you advise Jack to check out the property before he signs the lease? Is that right, Blake? Did you hear that, Jack?"

"Hmmm?" he said, shoveling rice into his mouth. "What was

that?"

"Blake here," said Skye, "thinks you should go to Yakima and check out Cherise's orchard. Or is vineyard the right term, Blake?"

"I think I should call m-my employers," said Blake, his face scrunching up like an arthritic hand. "They're prepared to offer more money if necessary."

"You hear that, Jack? What the hell have I been telling you guys? She planted grapes! I'll be damned." Skye was smiling with pride as he accidentally took another drink of wasabe riesling. "Gah!"

"Blake, is that true?" asked Sunflower. "Did Cherise really plant a vineyard?"

🍇 🍇 🍇

29

Cherise could hardly believe her eyes as she watched the waitress fill the water glasses around the table. The girl appeared to be floating. Her lazy smile was unfocused and kind, and it lit up the room as she poured water in (and around) each glass without a care. Cherise couldn't help but smile, thinking about Anthony and wishing she had a camera. He was gonna shit when he saw their "waitress" for tonight's dinner.

Rose watched Anthony bump into the door as he entered the dining room. He turned a clumsy circle and then continued forward, looking at the pretty chandeliers. His face lit up when he saw his mother, and he called to her with glee. "Momma-mia, bellisima! Bella, bellisima!"

[195]

Every head in the room was pointed at Anthony and he relished the attention. Absorbing their stares, he smiled with pride as Cherise crumbled under her mother's gaze.

"Don't look at me like that, Mama," Cherise shrugged. "I didn't do it."

"I suppose he looks that way from his allergies. No, let me think, it's a sunstroke, right?" Rose asked, still smiling politely at her guests.

"He said he felt fine when I asked him what happened. He doesn't look that good, though, does he?" Cherise wondered softly.

Anthony grabbed a chair and plopped himself down. He took a huge drink of water, emptying his glass. A loud breath of cool air escaped his lungs as he scanned the room for a waiter, hoping for more water. He smiled at his mother and winked at Cherise, still looking for more water. His eyes were bloodshot and bleeding; his acne was on fire. He greeted the people seated next to him with subdued enthusiasm, losing his composure, and sensing the tension. He suddenly felt out of place.

About 20 people were now seated around the large table. It was nearly full. Rose and Henry's seats were at the head with their backs to the Bay. A dozen or so candles were burning throughout the room, glowing with almost the same intensity as the bulbs in the chandeliers overhead. The sun was evaporating on the horizon, sinking into the ocean like a forgotten rubber ball deflating slowly in the dead of winter. Anthony could feel the light from all three sources playing a minuet on his zits, highlighting the blemishes for all to see in a symphony of puss, scars, and scabs. He wanted to hide his oily face for a year, hoping today's sunburn might give him a fresh layer of skin in a day or two. He sat up straight in his chair when he realized the source of his discomfort wasn't the lighting or his acne it was Rose, glaring with soul-piercing force and commanding decorum with astonishing stealth as only a parent could. He nodded politely to his mother, surreptitiously asking for a second chance. She held his attention for another second of reprimand, then answered with a twitch of a smile that was faster than the flap of a hummingbird's wings. It said that he could stay if he behaved, and that she loved him very much, and that she was glad he was here and safe but that he'd better shut up with the bellisima crap. Anthony watched her carefully, understanding every word she didn't say; he translated her encrypted message easily after so many years of practice. After a moment, he was breathing easier and feeling better about his complexion, relieved to be back on her good side.

Cherise found a seat near the middle of the table and selected a view of the kitchen door, her parents, and Anthony. She was searching the room for the waitress, anxious for the drama to unfold and wondering how their little Pinot was going to react under the watchful glare of their mother. She was enjoying the little circles of fate that humans experience, thinking about her valence theory of attraction she'd explored, but not conquered, as a test subject at Berkeley. Her acidic thesis was molecular bonding of the heart (love or hate); two people colliding with no control or understanding of their situation, simple victims of chance, their realities determined by a sequence of explosions 50 billion years ago. Each encounter today is an echo of the big bang so long ago, rippling through time like wakes through a pond and uniting unsuspecting masses for a chance at the greatest (and most unstable) chemical bond of all love. If an opening in the outer shell exists, and the right person comes along BANG! valence filled. She'd tried to fill her shell with love several times and failed, eventually switching to drugs and alcohol as most people do. But the pace was grueling and the hangovers atrocious. She was currently considering God for her next addiction, but the 10-percent solution still seemed a little drastic compared to her free drug habit.

Henry entered the dining room in a flurry of swinging doors and

[197]

greetings, carrying a bottle of wine in each hand. He kissed the air towards Rose, and smiled to everyone as he began to pour around the table. "Lovely, lovely Hollywood style, baby," he said, schmoozing the well-dressed room of guests. "Lovely." They all laughed and responded with a polite round of applause, clapping as if Henry had sunk a 10 foot putt.

Char followed behind her dad with two bottles of her own, twisting them carefully as she poured. She smiled at Anthony and kissed his cheek. "Thanks for coming, Anthony. I'm glad you could make it. Mom says you can have a little red with dinner, once we know everyone here. You know, make sure it's cool and all. I don't want to lose my liquor license for serving a minor."

"No problem, Char," he said.   "The place looks great. Congratulations on the good crowd. Hey, if you get a chance, I could use some more water, like maybe a pitcher, if you don't mind."

Char looked into his eyes and shook her head, immediately turning to Cherise with a frown on her face. "How could you?" she whispered.

Cherise shrugged from across the table, holding Char's stare. "I didn't do it," she said helplessly. She scanned the room for the waitress, growing tired of taking the blame for Anthony's condition.

Char decided to claim Anthony's side of the table for the evening, hoping to prevent Henry from looking into his eyes. She'd never seen Anthony messed up, but the times they were a changing. She was afraid for a moment that she might have to get used to it, but her gut feeling told her otherwise. Anthony was a smart kid. He'd experiment with that garbage and grow out of it like she herself did, she hoped.

"Ladies and gentlemen," said Henry, "on behalf of my wife and family, especially my beautiful daughter Char, I would like to thank you all for joining us to celebrate the release of our '65 Sonomas. It is truly a momentous day in the long history of

[198]

Mueller Vineyards. We've waited two and half years for this moment." Henry bowed to Rose, gesturing for her to stand and take a bow. She reluctantly did so, managing to lift herself a few inches off her chair. Her embarrassment was easy to spot and everyone instantly knew why "Henry the Ham" was speaking. "Rose has created a truly remarkable ensemble of wines, and our daughter Char has composed an equally exceptional menu. You are all in for a treat. I hope you all brought a pen and paper to take notes, and buckets in which to puke." He winked at Char, turning the floor over to her for a description of the first course.

"Gee thanks, Dad," she said. "First up are seared strips of duckling breast with a blend of ginger and mandarin orange. The wine is a medium-dry gewürtztraminer. We at Chez Panacea are committed to finding the answers of life through the pursuit of aesthetic cuisine, creating balance and harmony with a myriad of colors, tastes, and textures. The Chinese word *tom* means using contrasting elements to achieve harmony, and we find the identity of the food or wine through the use of opposites. In addition to these concepts, we are always thinking of the wine when we cook, too. It is our ultimate goal to create a dish that thirsts for a wine and vice versa. And, oh yeah . . . get drunk."

"Here, here," Henry chimed.

The staff filed in slowly to serve the thinly-sliced pieces of duck. Cherise was watching for the flower child as the butterflies circled in her stomach. She was incredibly excited about seeing Anthony meet the girl of his dreams in a crowded restaurant, in front of his parents, high as a kite. She saw the waitress enter from the kitchen, holding a pair of tongs and a large basket of bread. She began serving rolls just a few people away from Anthony, moving to her right at a snail's pace on a collision course with her brother for sure. Cherise wanted to scream with joy.

As the waitress approached her brother's chair, Henry stood and asked for everyone's attention in a solemn, fatherly voice.

[199]

"If I may, everyone, it is a sad time for those of us with children fighting in Vietnam. While I'm not suggesting prayer, before we begin I'd appreciate it if we observed a moment of silence on their behalf."

Everyone (except Cherise) bowed their heads in silence and closed their eyes in a show of respect (including Anthony, who enjoyed the opportunity to take a little nap). In fact, he kept his eyes closed while the water girl dropped a roll in the middle of his duck. She was giggling softly as she floated around the table, unaware of whom she'd just served a roll to. Cherise just had to laugh as she quietly cursed the war, wanting to protest Richard's involvement in Vietnam even more than ever. The girl continued around the table, slowly dispersing rolls as if they were daisies. Anthony was stoned and completely oblivious to everything that had just happened as he worked to open his eyes; he focused on a candle in the middle of the table. Cherise watched the waitress disappear into the kitchen and then turned to smile at Anthony, watching the candlelight dance languidly in the deep pools of stupidity where his eyes should have been.

"Thank you, folks, very much," Henry said, clearing his throat. He lifted his glass and smiled, looking at Char with pride. "To my beautiful, little girl - Salud, Char. This looks like crap!"

"Here, here!" blurted Anthony. He was gazing at the psychedelic mural on his plate. The colorful blend of sauces was moving before his eyes, merging in a frightening display of abstract expressionism. He couldn't decide if it was a Jackson Pollack or a Picasso as the straight lines from the duck fused with the splatters and drips from the mandarin coulis. He took a deep breath as the cartoon continued to strobe in the candlelight, deciding that perhaps it was more of a Rorschach than modern art as he grabbed for a utensil. He used the prongs of his fork to move the mysterious roll aside and blot the ink, changing the test image from a butterfly to a bear. "Whoooa," he giggled softly.

"I see that the bottle here says 'unfiltered.' What exactly does that mean?" a man asked Henry.

"Good question," Henry said, swirling his wine glass. "There's a lot of debate about the merits of filtration. Rose and I based the entire Sonoma project on a few simple ideas, one of those being a philosophy of no filtering whatsoever. We rely strictly on time and gravity to clarify our wines. Whether that's good or bad, who knows? Some people think that an unfiltered wine contains more fruit character or a creamier texture, but the jury's still out on that one. It does, I think, contain a lot more pollen and dust, that's for sure. Because we bottle directly from the tank or barrel, we think it's necessary to label our bottles appropriately so that people who suffer from grass allergies or hayfever will know that there's a chance of a reaction. Take a look at my boy Anthony over there. That poor kid suffers from every allergy imaginable."

Cherise nearly spit her wine across the table as the attentive guests smiled at Anthony with empathy and concern. Their hearts were bleeding for the spaced-out son of the famous winemakers. It was obvious to everyone that he could barely breathe. His eyes were nearly swollen shut and his face was covered with what appeared to be hives or some sort of nasty rash. That poor kid, they all thought. Cherise watched him coil up like a snake ready to strike. Henry had made too many jokes about their little Pinot suffering from every allergy known to science. She waited for Anthony to snap, and watched his lower lip quiver in the candlelight as he shrank from their stares.

"Don't get my father wrong," Anthony said, feeling naked and looking like he wanted to spit. "You'll look like me if you **DON'T** drink our wines. I can't wait till I'm old enough to embalm myself with this stuff. Maybe then I'll be able to breathe." He winked at Rose, who was petrified. He could tell she was expecting a violent reaction from him, and it made him feel good to see her smile as they all laughed at what he had said. His personality softened as he glanced at Cherise and nodded like everything was cool. Tonight was Char's night and he knew it. He wasn't going to let Henry spoil it with a few "harmless" jabs about his genetic maladies.

"That's right," said Henry, sensing that he'd crossed the line with Anthony. "A bottle a day, that's all we ask. Have you ever noticed that it's the teetotalers who are always calling in sick and missing work? Drink up!"

Rose watched carefully as Anthony had a private conversation with the liquid bear on his plate. She could see that he was completely engrossed with the image in his sauce. She was hoping that the other guests would chalk it up to boredom instead of psychedelic enrichment. She'd dealt with Char and Cherise's mental vacations enough to know what was going on in Anthony's muddled brain. Perhaps these people have kids his age too, she thought, as she watched him giggle and snort.

"What are some of the other philosophies behind the Sonoma wines?" that same man asked Rose.

Henry looked to Rose with a polite "may I?" expression on his face, symbolically asking if he could answer on her behalf. Everyone in the family had seen this maneuver a thousand times and Henry always did it with grace and candor. There wasn't a chance in hell that Rose was going to get up and talk, but Henry always made it seem possible. Since the day she'd seen her parents hanging from the largest tree in her village, Rose always stuttered after a few minutes of speech in front of an audience. Henry smiled at the table and touched his wife's hand.

"Sonoma is based on tradition," he said. "It's that simple. Rose comes from the old school of winemaking, and we've tried to blend the most recent technology with the oldest methods, cutting no corners. The per-unit cost of these wines will always be substantial and so will the price. There's been a renaissance in wine consumption and appreciation lately and we have no fear that we'll find buyers for our efforts. California will soon emerge as the center of the wine universe, thanks to this beautiful woman you see right here. Her attention to the vine and soil, and to the wine's individual character, will seduce even the staunchest of jug-wine drinkers. If you want to drink cheap wine and still enjoy it, never buy a bottle of M.V.S. Mueller-Vessini-Sonoma is now a reality." He held up his glass and nodded to the table, still holding Rose's hand.

Anthony burped and laughed. Cherise wanted to puke. The entire table was suddenly in love with Henry and Rose. They all savored the flavors and drank with passion as the candles became torches in a cavern of lipstick and polyester.

"So, you're saying that the product line of Mueller Vineyards wines that I've been drinking for years is now garbage?"

Henry was shocked by the man's question. "Don't get me wrong. What we've done at M.V.S. is take varietal character to the next level. When you see our name on a label you can always count on the wine inside being wonderful, even our jug wines. Today, however, represents a new mark in quality. Our wines are distinguished by extremely low yields and spontaneous fermentations with a minimum of handling and processing. Every step is determined by Rose's palate and nose. That's it. No recipes or formulas, just skill   artful winemaking with one goal."

"Profit?" said a smiling Anthony, thinking about the bear.

"Exactly," added Henry. He raised his glass to his son as the table enjoyed a round of laughter.

"What do you mean by spontaneous fermentations?" the man asked.

"We can either let nature do her thing and let the wild yeasts have their way with our grapes, or we can add cultured yeasts from any number of laboratories and be pretty sure   I repeat, pretty sure   of the outcome. M.V.S. wines will always be very distinctive. Sometimes they'll be leathery and pungent, and sometimes they'll be fragrant and balanced. We can never be sure."

Cherise watched the flower child fill Anthony's water glass as he dabbed his fork in his sauce. She almost shouted at her brother as the girl's hip rubbed his shoulder, but she didn't want to interrupt the table's silence. She couldn't believe they weren't going to connect again with such similar orbits. Anthony looked up to say thanks as he took a drink from his glass, pausing for a moment to pour water in his lap while he processed the image before him. He looked at his plate to make sure he wasn't dreaming in his sauce. He'd seen her face several times in his Rorschach of mandarin orange coulis. The waitress smiled back casually, tilting her head like a puppy as she thought about where she knew him from. BANG! valence filled. They held each other's gaze for several seconds while Cherise watched with joy.

"Bear?" the waitress asked. She was pointing at Anthony like a little girl pointing at a butterfly bouncing through a field of wildflowers.

"Huh?" whispered Anthony. He was squinting his eyes at her, trying to make the illusion vanish. "Bear?"

The girl crouched down to avoid the stares coming from all angles, and put her mouth just a few inches away from Anthony's. "You kept calling me Bear at the park today. Why?"

"Is it really you?" he said quietly, glancing at Rose. "What are you doing here?" His heart was racing. Her breath was intensely erotic; he'd never experienced a more stimulating moment in his life. The puffs of warm air from her mouth massaged his face and lips like the spray from the water bottle had done earlier that day. Her low raspy voice was incredibly sexy, especially as a whisper. He could feel a warm wave of energy climbing across his face. He felt like he was going to explode.

"I work here, Bear," she said softly. Her eyes twinkled as she smiled and stood up to leave. "I'll see you in the foyer." She turned and walked out of the dining room, glancing over her shoulder at Anthony.

He turned to look at Cherise who was in tears from biting her cheek. A thin strand of drool fell from his mouth as he shook his head in disbelief. He was in shock on the verge of paranoia as he glanced around the table at the smiling guests. The faint smile on his face turned into a look of bewilderment as he silently asked Cherise for help. She nodded towards the door and told Anthony to follow his future wife. Her thoughts drifted to her dissertation about the valence theory of attraction as she tasted her wine.

"Do you use sulfites in your wine?" the man asked Henry quietly.

🍇 🍇 🍇

30

Jack choked on a mouthful of rice as he watched Blake gag on Sunflower's question. It was now apparent to everyone, especially Skye, that Cherise had done a little bit more than plant an orchard up north in Yakima. Jack began to daydream about owning a vineyard that produced Bordeaux varietals with balanced numbers; with sugar, pH, and titratable acidity all present no assembly required all the intoxicating elements of winemaking contained in one of nature's most beautiful packages. He visualized a gelatinous shell of glucose, amino acid, and money just waiting to be crushed into a tank and made into a French Omelette. He saw himself breaking the tiny eggs of sugar one at a time into a fermenter and crying about the high labor costs to his dad, as the hourly workers slowly cracked their eggs one by one and dropped them in the tanks, bin after bin piling up behind them on the crush pad.

"Have you been there, Blake?" asked Sunflower.

"No."

"So you don't know for sure what's planted up there?" she

asked.

"A lot of things," said Blake.

"Who's been leasing the land?" asked Skye.

"I'm n-not at liberty to say."

"Is it **THE GUILD**?" asked Skye, sounding evil again.

"We should take Henry and Rose up to Yakima and spread Cherise's ashes on her land," Jack said, recovering from his Bordeaux daydream.

"Mom and Dad want Cherise nearby, Jack," said Sunflower. "We want to spread them in block two, around the mural."

"What mural?" asked Skye.

"I painted a family cluster on the barn in Salem. You guys should check it out on your way home. Oh yeah, I need a new photo of the Hops. I didn't get them in there yet."

"Family cluster? What varietal are we?" asked Skye.

"Seedless," she said, smiling at Jack.

"That works for Jack," said Skye. "But what about the rest of us? I've definitely got seeds."

"You guys kill me. You really do. You're all so funny that it hurts." Jack was dangling his tongue at his siblings, rolling his head and eyes.

"Just kidding, Shabby," Sunflower said.

Jack was suddenly serious. His face was calm. He looked as if he was experiencing some sort of heightened awareness from the wasabe riesling. "It's her best piece of work so far, Skye. You really should check it out," he said. "I've been thinking about that thing a lot, Petal. It's pretty impressive."

Sunflower was surprised by Jack's sudden sincerity. She was expecting the usual outburst of tannin that these little volleys of insults so often produce. For years now, Jack had always been the target of their teasing because he could defend himself so well. It wasn't any fun to pick on someone who wouldn't or couldn't fight back. Jack, however, could play doubles without a partner, easily covering both sides of the verbal court. His reluctance to fight back caught Sunflower and Skye off guard. They exchanged glances and watched as he pondered his glass of wasabe riesling.

Jack took a sip and did everything he could to smile. He looked at Blake with a calm face and casually ate a large piece of eel. He was hoping this macho display would break down Blake even more. Any man capable of drinking this stuff and smiling was a force to be reckoned with. He could feel the wasabe crushing his ethmoid bones as he began to speak, thinking for a moment that perhaps the smell of ether did permeate the earth. "Come on, Blake. What's going on? How much more money are they prepared to offer? If it's grapes, and it's **THE GUILD**, then I'll be happy to sign the lease. You just have to be honest with me."

"What?" exclaimed Sunflower and Skye simultaneously.

"I told you I'm not in any position to fight with those guys over something they want," said Jack. "Right, Blake?"

Blake looked at the three of them and thought about what was happening. If he was honest with Jack, it sounded like he was going get the lease signed and perhaps another glimpse of Sunflower's panties. If he didn't tell them who wanted the land right now, this thing was going to drag on forever and he might not stay on Sunflower's good side. He managed his words carefully, thinking about the milky white skin just below her buttons. "You can't win with these guys, Jack. There's no way. They have her signature on about a thousand documents and one of them is bound to be a thirty-year lease pretty soon."

Jack watched Sunflower as she listened to Blake's eloquent speech. He hadn't missed a beat or stumbled on a syllable. His words were firm and direct, spoken with clarity and confidence.

"See what honesty will do for your speech?" she said, smiling at Blake and caressing him with her eyes.

"So who's been leasing the land, Blake?" asked Skye.

"You were r-right. It is **THE GUILD**," said Blake, thinking about career alternatives as he mimicked the way they said the name of the huge corporate empire.

"Is it all grapes?" asked Jack.

[207]

"I'm not sure. I don't think s-so."

"What else is there?" pushed Jack.

"I really haven't been there, Jack. I don't know for sure. That's why they sent m-me to get the signature."

"Why's that?" said Jack, unrelentingly.

"Plausible denial ability," said Skye, seeing the big picture.

"Exactly," said Blake, gulping more truth serum. The flood of fresh air from the wasabe inspired even more commentary. "I can go as high as six-fifty a year, Jack. You should t-take the money," he gasped, thinking about unemployment.

"Grandpa will shoot you if you sign, Jack," said Sunflower. "You know how he feels about them."

"Shoot, Petal," said Skye, "Grandpa's practically one of them."

"I know," she said. "What the hell was Cherise thinking when she signed that lease over to the Bhagwan?"

"She was no dummy, Petal," said Jack. "She's getting even for the nouveau totem he gave to the twins. You guys were exactly right. She had it planned out all along." Jack looked at Blake and nodded his head. "Tell your employers to have a cashier's check in my hands in two days if they want to continue to harvest my land."

"Well, Jack," said Skye, "this makes naming my kids after hops a lot easier to cope with. You've turned a potential train wreck into a flat tire with a mere autograph. Thanks. I'm actually looking forward to the wake now."

"You think Henry will really give a damn about **THE GUILD** raising her grapes?" asked Jack.

"Do screw-top wines suck?" volleyed Skye.

"What a quagmire. Maybe I should talk to Dad first, huh?"

"Take the money and buy some more land around here, Jack," said Sunflower. "Everything's going to be just fine. Grandpa's not a crabby old man yet."

"Yeah, he's still getting laid," said Skye. They don't get grumpy until the sex is all gone. Take the money and buy some oak that actually works with pinot noir."

"Excuse me," said Blake. "Is there a chance that any of you will be looking for an attorney in the near f-future?"

🍇🍇🍇

31

Anthony stumbled away from the table, walking towards the foyer as Rose answered the man's question about sulfites. She knew it would distract everyone's attention from Anthony if she was the one to speak. She absently explained the ancient Greeks as she watched her son bounce off the wall on his way out of the dining room.

Anthony glanced around quickly, expecting to continue outside. The waitress grabbed his shoulder as soon as he was clear of the door and turned him around, putting her mouth next to his once again. "What are you doing here, Bear?" She was obviously excited, almost on the verge of laughter.

"Char's my sister," he said, breathing her in deeply. His head was reeling in the narrow hallway. At first, the foyer had appeared to be a hazy shade of purple, but it was beginning to pulse with red now that his hormones were catching on fire.

"That's so groovy. I was hoping I'd see you again," she whispered. "I'm so sorry about the water bottle. It wasn't mine I promise. It was a friend's. I must have grabbed it by mistake. What a day, huh? I freaked out and walked around town for about six hours. I almost didn't show up for my shift, but your sister is about the coolest person on the planet. I couldn't think of a safer place on earth."

"What is your name?" he asked, savoring the warm energy as it surged through his veins.

"Lisa."

"I'm Anthony," he said. "It's a pleasure to finally meet you."

"You're not mad at me are you?" she asked. "It was an accident. I promise. I didn't know what was in that bottle."

"It's cool, Lisa. Cherise can keep a secret. No one has to know. Everything's going to be just fine," he said. "So . . . are **you** kind?"

"Oh yes, Anthony. I'm kind." She looked deep into his eyes and saw the love he was capable of as he thought about children and vines and good wines. "Look at those eyes," she said, smiling sweetly at Anthony. "Why did you keep calling me Bear at the park today?"

"I don't know," said Anthony. "I guess I freaked out, too. I had a very enlightening conversation with what I thought was a bear. I guess it was you, huh?"

"I don't know," she laughed. "What did it look like?"

"Fuzzy . . . yellow, um, glowing kind-of-static-electricity type of . . . thing." He was laughing like he'd had five shots of tequila. "Never mind."

"No," she said. "I didn't see him. I saw a lot of other things, but I didn't see him." They shared a smile and touched hands briefly.

"Hey, goofballs! Come join the party," said Char, leaning through the door. "Anthony, you don't want to miss the salmon and chardonnay, do you?" She was smiling at the two of them, completely unaware that her favorite waitress was about to become her sister-in-law.

"Hey Char," said Anthony, "what wine are you serving with the main course?"

"Guess."

"I'm afraid to," he said.

"Sonoma Zinfandel, baby," said Char, rolling her eyes. "Big and strong, just like Richard."

"Light and fruity is more like it," he said.

"What was that?" laughed Char.

"Nothing," he said. "I can hardly wait."

"Lisa," said Char, "if you get a chance, could you come give us a hand clearing the duck?"

"I'll be right there," Lisa said, smiling at his sister. "See what I mean? She's the coolest. You're a lucky guy."

"Oh yeah, lady luck's always knocking on my door."

"Hey, you found me, didn't you?" She winked at him and touched his hand as she walked away. "Let's go for a walk after dinner. I've got to go back to work now. Char's cool, but the chef can be a real idiot sometimes."

Anthony laughed, watching as her blonde hair disappeared around the corner. He thought about the Nazi working behind the line that everybody hated and cringed. Lisa ducked her head back through the door and smiled at the surprised look on his face. "Bear! What's terroir?" she asked.

"Not 'terror' tear-whar," he said, laughing out loud. He could see the bear casually flopping his paws outward.

"What is it?" she asked again. "Tear-whar. You kept saying it at the park today."

"Let's go to France and find out." He watched her think about what he said, surprised by her sudden concentration. She appeared surreal, like a dream come true. He imagined the cat bells ringing softly on her sandals, her feet flopping left and then right. The velvety aroma of scarlet flowers filled his nostrils. . . .

"When?" she asked.

"Uh, I've got the summer off. Anytime, I guess."

"Groovy," said Lisa. "See you inside."

32

Jack sat and stared at all the zeros on the cashier's check, his eyes getting lost somewhere between the fifth and sixth digit. If he gazed at them long enough, his eyes would cross and cause the numbers to overlap and stack on top of each other, forming a crude cluster of grapes. He looked at Blake and smiled, wondering if now was a good time to bring up his stutter. The dogs were at Blake's feet asking for a game of fetch. Pino had the ball in her mouth while Vino lunged a foot at a time as if the ball had already been thrown   how could anybody resist such a tempting offer? they thought.

"Hey, Blake?" Jack asked casually, looking at the igloos of dead canes spread throughout the vineyard.

"Yeah."

"What's up with your stutter, If you don't mind my asking?"

"I wish I knew," said Blake.

"Huh?" said Jack. "The other day I heard you go on and on without any trouble at all when you were talking about Sunflower. Then when people are around you can't even manage a sentence. It just seems kind of strange, that's all."

"Tell me about it," said Blake. "The palsy is going away but the stutter is a real bitch. And your sister only seems to make it worse."

"Don't worry, Blake," Jack laughed. "She makes a lot of guys nervous. For awhile there, I thought you were faking the stutter to make us feel sorry for you so we'd sign the lease."

"D-d-d-d-did it work?" he said, joining Jack at the table on the porch. He handed him several documents and a pen, reaching for a beer as his watch chimed noon with a digital beep.

"It started during my cram sessions for the bar exams. I almost snapped from the stress, I guess."

"Well," said Jack, "then there's a good chance you'll get over it sometime soon, huh?"

"I sure as hell hope so."

"My degree is in psychology, Blake. And I remember something about stuttering and sexual deprivation being related. Are you gettin' any?"

"Not enough."

"W-w-w-who is?" stammered Jack, winking at Blake. He looked at the first page of the pamphlet and smiled, apparently agreeing with something he read in the first paragraph. "They agree to sell me ten tons of all three varietals at cost if the sugars exceed twenty-three brix. Outstanding. I didn't think they'd go for that."

"Like I said before, Jack," said Blake, "they had a good relationship with Cherise, and they w-want it to continue with you. You're dealing with a tenant that has virtually unlimited resources."

Jack was leafing through the numerous pages one by one, stopping to look at the aerial schematics. He gazed at the photos, thinking about Cherise. She really did think of the three of them as her own children . . . planting huge amounts of unheard-of crops in a place that was known for apples and cherries. He studied the pictures carefully, surprised by what he was seeing. There, on a terrace overlooking the Yakima river, Cherise had created a massive tribute to her love for family and nature. The upper level of the mesa was dominated by tall pillars of cedar trellises suspending long rows of hops   the huge flowers that gave zest and flavor to Skye's lifelong passion. The majority of the acreage was devoted to cabernet sauvignon, cabernet franc, and merlot. All three varietals were basking in eastern exposure and drip irrigation. The seemingly endless rows of Bordeaux varietals fell down the slope, connecting the hops above to a massive field of sunflowers located at the river's edge. Jack could

[213]

hardly believe his eyes. There must have been at least 30 acres of the tall, yellow flowers caressing the wind, each stalk defying gravity and profit motive in the middle of a corporate endeavor.

"Sunflowers?" asked Jack.

"Check page six, Jack," said Blake. "I was shocked when I saw those, too. There's a provision regarding the sunflowers. There always has been."

Jack turned to the end of the contract, laughing out loud at what he saw. He was on the verge of tears, pursing his lips as he read the provision.

Blake turned to the dogs and retrieved the ball from Pino's mouth, allowing Jack a moment of privacy. He faked a few throws towards the winery, but Vino didn't bite. Blake smiled at the clever dog and finally let one fly into the vineyard, watching as the dog bolted around a pile of dead vines in pursuit of the ball.

"I'll never call her Crazy Cherise again, that's for sure," Jack said, clearing his throat.

Anthony was scratching his beard as he walked out of the house and joined Jack and Blake at the table. His bare feet sounded like someone slapping bread dough as he walked across the hardwood floor of the porch. He was wearing baggy boxer shorts and a gray shirt that was too tight for him. His frizzy hair and beard were still asleep. In fact, there was nothing awake about him at all. He leaned over the table, looking at the photos as he thought about a cup of coffee.

"My, Bear," said Jack, "don't you look charming this morning?"

Anthony was searching his mouth for moisture with his thick white tongue, considering a beer despite the early hour and his old age. "It's been a long time since I've had a night out with the boys, Jack," he said. "Take it easy on the old Bear, huh?"

"Did you call Mom back?" asked Jack.

"Did she call?"

Jack laughed at his fat dad. "I stood there and talked to you for five minutes with the phone in my hand, you sloth."

"You did?" mumbled Anthony.

"Man, you're cut off for the weekend," said Jack. "Here, check these out." He handed the photographs of Cherise's estate to his dad, watching as Anthony skillfully deciphered the terrain from the plane's point of view in spite of his headache. "Don't get dizzy from up there, Bear."

"Hops, grapes, and sunflowers. . . . God, she was a gem," Anthony said, pausing to think about the many secrets that had died with his sister's suicide. "She always did have a real spark of creativity, didn't she, Jack?"

"Yes, she did, Dad," said Jack. "You about ready to head up north and party with the California folk? Skye called from Portland awhile ago. He's on his way with Monica and the Hops."

"I've got to get g-going to Seattle, Jack," said Blake. "Say goodbye to Sunflower for me, will you? Bear, thanks for a good time last night. It was good to have m-met you. Don't let Jack fool ya; he's hurting too. He put out those beers just to impress you. He didn't drink any."

"Shut up, ya gimpy bastard," said Jack. He smiled at Blake and shook his hand. "Thanks for bringing that stuff down here in person, Blake. I'm sorry Petal wasn't here, though."

"Win some, lose some," Blake said, shrugging as he walked to his car.

Jack handed the cashier's check to his dad as he watched Blake walk away with the dogs at his side. He was pretty sure he'd see him again for some strange reason   Petal had a way of getting under anybody's skin after a few days, especially if it was someone she was attracted to. It was only a matter of time before you missed her so bad that it hurt. He figured Blake would be smart enough to create a scenario in the lease that required his immediate attention . . . and if Sunflower happened to be nearby, oh well.

"Jesus, look at all those zeros," said Anthony. "It looks like my pruning bill from your vineyard."

"Yeah, that should about cover it, ya think?" Jack said sarcastically. He looked at the photos again, thinking about the sunflowers, and shaking his head as he opened a beer. "Thanks a lot for your help with the contract, Dad. That was a lot to cover so fast."

"I think you did the right thing, Jack. They could have drawn this thing out for years. I'm surprised they agreed to terms so fast. But, I guess ten consecutive gold medals will make you want to keep your grape supply, huh, rich man?"

Jack grinned and looked at his watch. He could hear his mother's voice in the back of his head saying that they had better be there before 2:00. That left them exactly 20 minutes to shower, and get dressed, and then drive like hell to Salem.

"How's the waitress, Jack?" asked Anthony.

"Maria? I haven't talked to her for a few days. We've been playing phone tag, I guess. That's about it. We gotta get moving, Dad. Henry and Richard are gonna be there any minute. Mom wants us there when they arrive. I think she's afraid of dealing with them without us."

"Relax," said Anthony. "I'm gonna let Sunflower handle Henry. And Skye can put Richard in his place. You put a sugar coating on Grandma and this weekend will be over before you know it."

"So all the girls were having a good time when you left?" said Jack.

"Yeah, it took them about two hours to catch up. Actually, I think I got my first word in around the three hour mark. That's why I had to come down here   between Sunflower and those other three, the place was turning into an estrogen palace. They had Cherise's ashes on the coffee table the whole time. Toasting to life and crap like that . . . too bizarre, man."

Jack could see that his dad was having trouble with his allergies in addition to suffering from his first hangover in a couple of years. Anthony's eyes were watery and he was rubbing them continually, inserting the top two knuckles of each fist deep into his eye sockets in search of relief. Jack didn't think it was from the pollen. He knew Henry could still get inside his dad's head and cause a histamine reaction despite Anthony's accomplishments with pinot noir here in Oregon. "Come on, Bear. Grab a shower and get dressed. We gotta go," said Jack. He watched his dad walk away and wondered what it would have been like to have lived in fear of him for his whole life; thankfully, he'd never had a clue.

The drive to Salem was a quiet one. Anthony scratched and Jack thought about being a millionaire. Cherise rested quietly in the bottom of an urn on the coffee table. The dogs were grabbing mouthfuls of Oregon air from the back of the truck, biting bugs and turning circles with their tails wagging. Jack took a deep breath and turned the old truck into the winery's entrance, slowing down to look at the new mural on the side of the building. A small crowd of people was gathered nearby, staring at the image. Smoke from the burning piles of vine cuttings obscured their view as they strained to see who was standing by the barn.

"Nice touch, Petal," whispered Anthony. He leaned forward in the cab of the truck, trying to see better.

Jack agreed with his dad, delivering a brilliant oration about Petal's use of sepia tones with a reverberating "whoa" after searching his extensive vocabulary. The vehicle stopped and they got out slowly. After a slight pause, they exchanged glances and sighs before starting towards the barn. Sunflower had created a scene from a Viking funeral. She didn't want the vines harvested into piles to get them away from the soil; she wanted them harvested so that there would be dozens of pyres burning throughout the vineyard to symbolize her aunt's ascension to the next level. The sweet-smelling smoke was lingering all around as

[217]

they crossed the parking lot.

Jack waved at his grandma and smiled as she began walking towards them. "Geez," he said, looking at Rose. "Nebbiolo, how appropriate."

"That's funny, Jack," said Anthony. "I was just thinking the same thing. She hasn't aged in twenty years. I wonder if the bottle's been re-corked," he said, winking at Jack. He was speaking metaphorically about a facelift or two.

"Nah," said Jack. "Really? You think so?"

"No way," said Anthony. "Not in a million years."

"Hi, Jack," said Rose, giving him a big hug. She reached for Anthony's hand while still embracing her grandson. Tears as thick as glycerine were clinging to the smooth, dark skin of her cheekbones. She smiled at Anthony over Jack's shoulder. "Hi, sweetheart," she said, trying not to cry out loud.

"How are they doing?" Anthony asked, looking at the rest of the family but not seeing Henry.

"Fine, Tony," said Rose. "They look better than you." She winked at Anthony, intending no harm with her little jab about his numerous allergies.

Jack backed away from his grandma in a fluid motion while still holding her left hand. He lifted it slowly to suggest a spin as if they were dancing the two-step. Rose knew the move well and obliged, showing off her figure as she turned around slowly, laughing some but blushing more. "Stop it, Jack. You're embarrassing me," she said, softly slapping his arm.

"You look beautiful, Grandma. You really are improving with age," said Jack.

"Well, I'm older," said Rose. "I'm not any smarter, though. I'm still with that jackass Henry. I thought I would've traded him in by now, but . . ." she shrugged.

Jack gave his grandma a smirk, knowing full well that they'd never been apart for more than a day since the first time they'd met. "Yeah right, Grandma. I'm surprised you guys made it this far, too," he laughed. "So, where's he at?"

"He and Richard are in the winery. I hope you don't mind, Tony."

Anthony's face turned white as he thought about his dad in a winery full of pinot noir. "Ah, I'm sure they're fine. He won't yell at my barrels will he, Momma?"

They all laughed and walked over to the barn, raising their heads to look at the mural. Sunflower had spent the last two days painting the faces of Halle, Cassy, and Kent into their respective grapes. As a joke, she had left the little blotches of red on Halle's face from her bout with the chicken pox. Halle wasn't amused and she was currently chasing Sunflower through the grounds. She could be heard in the distance yelling "Stinker! Aunty Petal is a stinker!" The dogs were punctuating her shouts with intermittent barks, adding another layer of depth to the mayhem.

Jack got a hug from Char and kissed his mother while nodding to Skye and Monica. The other Hops had him surrounded and began jumping on him to express their affection for their Uncle Jack. Despite the reason for their gathering and all the smoke, the mood was incredibly light. Jack was relieved. He watched his dad talk to Lisa and head for the winery. He decided to follow, nodding discretely at Skye to come with him.

"You don't look any richer," said Skye, teasing his brother.

"We are."

"Just like that, huh? Those guys are amazing. Did you get the twenty-three brix clause?"

"Yep. Thirty tons, F.O.B. Eugene."

"Unreal. You kill me," said Skye.

Jack was focused on the winery, watching as their dad passed through the door. He was nervous and excited, hoping quietly that Henry hadn't become an old man in the last year. Seeing Cornelius walk by his house every day was a constant reminder of his own mortality, and of the inevitable demise he was going to witness in his legendary grandfather. If Rose was any type of barometer, though, Henry was going to be just fine.

[219]

"Are you ready for this?" Skye asked, sensing Jack's tension.

"I think so. How's he look?"

"Awesome," said Skye. "He's still tough as nails, but he moves a lot slower now. Richard looks really cute, too."

"Knock it off, Skye," said Jack.

"What?" laughed Skye.

"Don't start in on Richard yet. Let's get through the dinner before you make him cry again, alright?"

They entered the winery through the side door, carefully looking around for the trio. Jack felt a shiver as he glanced upwards at the primary fermenters. His hair stood on end when he saw his thin, strong grandfather throwing a ball made of shipping tape at them from above.

"Look at you two bastards!" Henry yelled. "I can't believe you haven't rusted in this goddamned rainforest. My god, Shabby, you look like a love-sick puppy." He laughed at the boys as they ducked their heads and took cover, watching them carefully for any signs of retaliation.

Anthony was crouched beside a row barrels, waiting for the carnage to end and laughing at Skye and Jack as they counted the tape balls laying on the winery floor.

"You're kidding me," said Jack, whispering to his dad. "Did he bring those with him?"

Anthony nodded, quietly searching the building for Richard. "Blushman is around here somewhere," he said, having a genuinely good time.

"I heard that!" said Richard from somewhere nearby. "There'll be hell to pay for that, Pinot. And I can smell that blue collar rogue, too. My goodness Skye, don't you know that brewers have to bathe twice as frequently as winemakers? Jack, there's still time to join civilization. You don't have to perish with your Oregon comrades! We know you've got class." Richard laughed like a madman as he finished his speech, circled the barrels, and rolled into their path like a commando. He rolled up onto one knee with a bazooka type water cannon pointed directly at the three Oregon boys. His face was heinously contorted; it looked like it was controlled by pure evil. His pupils were full of poison. "Surrender?" he asked calmly, sounding like a librarian.

"Damn veterans," said Anthony, raising his hands above his head in unison with Jack and Skye. "Nice move, Zinny." For some strange reason he decided to call Richard "Zinny" instead of Blushman. [Apparently, there's something about looking down the barrel of a weapon that increases a person's I.Q.]

Henry began his descent from the loft with a boisterous victory cheer, razzing his descendants like they had just lost a serious military exercise. "You mess with the bull . . . you get the horns!" He had his hands raised above his head, fingers forming antlers as he slowly walked down the stairway. Richard hadn't taken them out of his sights yet. The barrel of the gun was slowly panning left and then right, exposing both sides of his sinister smile to his captives.

"California · one, Oregon zero," said Henry, smiling warmly at his boys. "Truce?"

The Beaver Boys looked at each other and nodded their heads in appreciation, acknowledging the strategic superiority of their conquerors.

"We are merely humble farmers from the great Beaver State," Anthony said, locking his hands together in prayer. "We plead for your mercy and ask that you dine with us. Please, enjoy our bounty!"

Richard slowly let the barrel of the cannon sink to the floor when he felt Henry's hand touch his shoulder. A truce had been reached in Round One.

"That's one hell of a mural out front there, Pinot," said Henry. "Have you guys thought about sending Sunflower to rehab or anything?" He laughed and gestured for everyone to follow him over to the guardrail overlooking the next level. Located on the other side of the bottling line below, a huge buffet table (usually assembled only during crush) was overflowing with food and wine. "The girls have been working very hard. Cherise would be proud."

"Cherise would be drunk," laughed Richard.

"Good one, Blushman," said Skye, sensing a window.

"Ohh, the blue collar man not only smells like rancid barley, but he speaks, too?" Richard asked, pointing the gun at Skye's face again.

"Blue is better than chartreuse," said Skye, winking at Richard while blowing him a kiss.

"Now, now, girls," said Henry. "Let's save it until later."

For the last few years, there had been a moratorium on jokes about Richard's sexual orientation. His partner, lover, and best friend had been murdered on a lonely road in Guerneville, California almost five years ago. Joseph's car had broken down in the middle of the night in the wrong place at the wrong time. He was confronted by a drunken idiot who simply wanted the car, whether it ran or not. A fight ensued and Joseph was stabbed and left to die, alone in the middle of the road. No one knew at the time that Richard was gay. Joseph had been the plant manager and a good friend of the family for many years. It became clear to everyone following the funeral that their relationship had been more than professional. Richard was devastated. In less than three months he had joined a seminary and taken up chain-smoking. Henry was horrified. Sadly, Anthony felt ashamed. Not that Joseph had been murdered or that his brother was gay, but that after years of living in the shadow of the massive football star and war hero, Anthony felt vindicated. It turned out that there was a chink in Richard's impenetrable armor after all. According to Henry's sophisticated point of view, the great hormone dealer in the sky had apparently hid a couple of testosterone cards up his sleeve while doling out Richard's hand, leaving his son's genetic sequence "cane pruned." After years of self-inflicted torture and denial, the great Zinfandel finally relented and became the light and fruity "Blushman" that the great Totem Bear had spoken of during Anthony's one and only vision quest.

Skye, using typical Miller humor, managed to make light of the situation and draw Richard back into the family during crush a few years later, breaking the ice at the dinner table by bestowing the title of Blushman on his gay uncle. From that moment on, they would be the best of friends. Skye and Richard were both tall, thin, and laconic. They were also practical jokers who shared a preoccupation with witty insults and gardening. Usually, after a few rounds of banter, they would ease up on each other and talk about their roses and let the wine smooth away the wounds left behind from their confrontations. It was great entertainment for everyone except Rose, who managed to absorb every acidic remark as if they were intended for her as only a mother can.

"Stinker! Aunty Petal is a stinker!" screamed Halle. The Hops busted through the lower door of the winery in hot pursuit of Sunflower who was laughing and choking from fatigue. She looked up at the men in desperation, hoping for some cover.

"Save me, Richard, please," she said, still laughing.

Richard's years of military service and field training paid off quickly for Sunflower. Without a moment's hesitation, he had the Hops ducking for cover. A steady stream of water was cascading down from the gun above, soaking them instantly. His aim was perfect, easily picking them off one by one as they tried to hide under the table while giggling and screaming like they were in Sunday school detention. When he was sure they weren't going to escape, he threw the gun to Sunflower. "Here ya go, Petal," said Richard. "Give them a real bath. And get behind their ears. I think I saw some potatoes growing back there. They look like they haven't had a bath in weeks."

He looked at Skye and smiled. "Gee, Swiss Mister, you'd think with all the water you use in your business, you could find the time to give your kids a bath now and then." Richard was teasing Skye about the brewing business being similar to making instant cocoa "Just add warm water and stir vigorously," as Richard so aptly put it. This jab had very little impact on Skye because he knew deep down inside that all of the winemakers were just jealous.

"Yeah sure, Blushman," said Skye, "Don't give me that crap. Each one of you would give your left arm to be able to recreate a vintage by just adding water and stirring vigorously. No such luck, amigos. So sorry."

"You Hops are gonna get it now," said Sunflower, lifting the table cloth slowly.

Henry looked at Skye with a puzzled look on his face. "Did she say hops?"

"Yeah, Gramps," said Skye. "They're named after hops. Hallertauer, Cascade, and Kent I thought it was time to graft a few new varieties into the family bloodline. What do ya think? Like it?"

"Oh, isn't that precious?" said Richard, faking a lisp.

Skye shot a look at his uncle that said, "Shut the hell up."

Henry laughed as he watched his great-grandchildren run out from under the table while pointing at Sunflower's empty cannon as they charged at her. "Get her. Get the awful painter! She's a stinker!" said Halle, Cassy, and Kent.

"Well," said Henry, "I thought that since Cherise had taken care of Jack here, that I would just divide everything between you and Sunflower. But you can kiss your share goodbye now, Skye. You are officially out of my will." Henry's face was serious. He turned to watch the action below before he started to laugh, turning back to look at Skye with a smirk on his face. "Hops. That's a good one!"

The numerous mothers and sisters all filed into the cellar from the entrance below. They'd done their crying for the last couple of days and were now laughing, getting a little bit drunk, and being crude as only a group of women can. Sunflower had managed to escape through a freight door and was refilling the cannon in a secret place. The Hops could be heard searching for their aunt, laughing some but giggling more about their various plans for revenge. Jack was overwhelmed by the energy being exchanged as the controllers interrogated and the aloof ones shrugged. Each drama flowed through the barrels with the same intensity as a crush dinner. Jack wondered for a moment if it was such a good idea to hold the wake around the wine, thinking that perhaps the negativity and blame that was sure to surface might somehow affect its quality. He looked at his dad (who was blowing kisses to his mom) and relaxed, confident that this evening would generate more good thoughts than bad.

"Let's go, you Oregon platypuses!" shouted Henry. "Last one seated is spag," he said, referring to the baby diaper-type sediment found in the bottom of a wine barrel.

They joined the ladies at the table in an orderly (well, kind of) fashion. Skye and Richard nearly killed each other, and Henry had Jack in a headlock before he could pass him on the stairs. Anthony screamed like Tarzan and climbed over the railing, then dangled from Deck 3 before dropping to a table below, almost breaking his leg. Rose was the only one not laughing after the ruckus. Wearing a frown as they were seated, she surveyed the room for any sign of maturity among her boys. None could be found. Nowhere. Zip.

Henry winked at Lisa as he adjusted himself into his chair. She smiled quickly and thanked him with her eyes when she realized that he had caused such a commotion on purpose. He had called for the race to be seated in order to avoid the awkward moment of finding one's place at a large table. In the rush to not be spag, etiquette took over and the ladies automatically sat to the left of their husbands; even Rose did so, who was unknowingly eyeballing the chair to the left of the head chair that was now

Anthony's. It was the first time ever that Henry and Rose did not occupy seats 1 and 2.

Anthony approached his seat at the head of the table with a slight limp, smiling at Lisa. He looked at the bottles of wine that covered nearly every square inch of tablecloth. Some were short, some were tall, all were open. 60 bottles from around the world, all containing grapes related to their aunt's enigmatic totem. Anthony looked at Henry and shook his head. A small grin of delight was working its way through his beard. "Nice touch, Dad. Cherise would be proud." He shot a look at Richard before he could deliver his patented line about Cherise's fondness for alcohol. "Not now, Richard."

Richard swallowed a mouthful of air as he choked back the words he was about to say. He quietly cursed his brother for denying him such a perfect set-up. He smacked his lips and obviously said something different from what he was really thinking. "Cherise . . . would be glad, Dad. Nice job."

Skye looked at Richard and gave him a polite little golf clap. "Gosh Blushman that means a lot coming from a multi-tasker like you," he said. Richard had always said that a good winemaker had to be a master of multi-tasking. Skye had used that against him for years saying that multi-tasking to Richard meant smoking and talking on a cell-phone while driving a truckload of grapes in the fog.

A storm of children, water, and laughter ripped through the door like a tornado. Sunflower was stalking the Hops slowly, pointing the cannon first at the table and then back at the kids, suggesting with a great deal of success that they be seated and remain quiet. She was wearing a pair of welding goggles that transformed her from a harmless blonde to a ruthless exterminator. The Hops quickly found their appropriate seats in between Monica and Rose, and hushed each other while still laughing at Sunflower. She turned to Richard while slowly pulling down her shades.

[226]

"Thanks for letting me use your piece, Dick. I got behind their ears with no problem at all." She found her seat next to Jack and softly slapped the back of his head as she sat down. "Where's your friggin' manners? You don't pull out chairs no more, or what?"

Jack laughed as he reached for a bottle of wine. "Only for ladies," he said, getting slapped again.

"Okay, everyone relax," said Anthony, rising from his chair. "We're all here . . . strange as that may seem. And we all know why. Cherise is no longer with us. She apparently couldn't wait for the cigarettes to do the job, and decided to speed things up a bit. Oh, well. We all make decisions about our lives, no matter how painful they may be to the rest of us, and we all have to live with them. There's no way to understand what she was thinking or why she did what she did. So let's just try to enjoy each other's company this weekend and think good thoughts about her."

"Here, here," chimed Henry, raising a glass to his family. "This is a beautiful setting, kids. I'm sorry that we haven't been here before. Rose is just too damn stubborn!" Henry smiled at his wife and ducked away from her harmless jab.

The platters of food were passed around the table, and heaping portions piled up on the diners' plates. Small elegant carts containing various sauces, breads, and cheeses sat behind their chairs. A few servers from Char's restaurant were pouring wine and replacing the popular dishes as they were emptied, silently using the carts to perform their tasks.

Despite the laughter and the smiles on everyone's faces, the smell of burning vines was always present and a constant reminder of the reason for their assembly. As a casual joke or childhood anecdote about Cherise was told, the smell from the fires would register on their faces, causing their smiles to vanish. Thankfully, the awkward stares and guilty looks were washed away by the seafood course. The blackened salmon with dijonaise required large amounts of shiraz to cool it down. The rapid consumption of the Australian version of Cherise's totem eliminated any uncomfortable feelings left in the winery. Finally (thanks to the salmon), all was well with the world again.

The crush-like feast went on and on. Jack watched everyone eat while Sunflower cried. Monica and the Hops were treating Henry and Rose to a medley of familiar (but forgotten) nursery rhymes. Skye and Richard were calmly discussing the merits of barrel-fermented beer at the top of their lungs,. Anthony kept to himself while quietly digging for gold in his eye sockets, looking as if he'd learned to attack his allergies from watching the dogs. Char and Lisa were in the kitchen preparing dessert, discretely blowing the smoke from their cigarettes into the fan above the stove.

"Hey Halle," said Skye, "where's grandma?"

Halle looked around the winery for Lisa as she rubbed the back of her small hand into her hair. She got up from the table like a drunken sailor, climbed onto the seat of her chair, and then jumped off towards Henry with a giggle. She ran to the kitchen while shouting "Aunty Petal is a stinker, never been a thinker!" She disappeared through a door and after a few moments came out screaming. Bubbles of intoxicating laughter were popping out of her mouth as she ran to her father's side. "Nanna's in the kitchen, Daddy. She's seducing the sauce," she said, still giggling.

"Seducing the sauce, huh?" said Skye, smiling at his daughter. "I think they're REDUCING the sauce, Halle. What do ya think, Grandpa? Are they seducing the sauce in there, or what?"

"Well," said Henry, "if it's that damn zabaglione, then seducing just might be the most appropriate word for it. That stuff can be pretty lethal." Henry smiled inwardly for a moment, thinking about the first time he ever tasted the family's secret recipe. He looked at Rose and imagined her pouting at the dinner table back in Italy during the war. He remembered Corrina quickly handing her daughter a glass of pudding to stop her from crying about her brothers. He could still see the euphoria on Antonio Vessini's face as he sucked on his spoon, loudly cherishing every drop to lighten the mood during such hard times.

"I still can't get that stuff right," said Sunflower.

"That's okay, Petal," Skye said in a condescending voice. "Poached eggs are great with Port." He and Henry shared a laugh while Sunflower threw bread at them.

Rose tried not to laugh but finally gave up and joined in the chorus, offering Sunflower the same piece of advice for the ten-thousandth time. "Don't touch the bottom of the pan to the boiling water! How many times do I gotta tell you?"

"Yeah, Petal," said Jack, "don't touch the water to the bottom of the pan. You'll cook the eggs!"

Rose reached across the table and slapped the back of Jack's head at the same time as Sunflower. "Easy, paisano," Rose said to Jack, pointing her finger at him. "I'll give out the cooking advice around here, okay?"

Henry laughed and shouted at Anthony. "Hey Pinot, you're missing a good show down here!"

"Huh?" said Anthony, looking through his watery eyes at the rest of the table. It upset him to miss a stroke in his passionate scratching and he didn't wait for another word before returning to the orgasmic task at hand; he waved a gooey finger at his dad, and plunged his hands deep into his eye sockets with total dedication.

"Hey, Pinot," said Henry, "what's the single most important thing about a good bottle of wine?"

Anthony frowned at the easy question while water streamed from his infected eyes. "Who you drink it with, duh."

"And," said Henry, "what's the most important piece of equipment in a winery?"

"A mop," said Anthony.

"Besides that," said Henry.

"Your nose," snapped Anthony.

[229]

"Very good," said Henry. "And what should you always remember about a superior bottle of wine?"

"The color of your wife's dress."

Henry looked at everyone proudly. "I taught him well," he said, raising his glass.

The zabaglione was served and the table became silent as everyone experienced a unique memory related to the special dessert. They all thought it was strange to be seated in a winery and enjoying the classic crush pudding, but not being covered in grapes. The smell of burning vines was working its way through the winery, touching their hearts as well as their noses.

When they'd finished their meal and thanked the staff, they all filed through a door as if their exit had been rehearsed. Char produced the urn containing Cherise's ashes and smiled at everyone with tears in her eyes. Lisa gulped out loud and reached for Char's hand, offering support as the men lit cigars. The Hops chased Pino and Vino around the lawn; all five of their tongues were dangling with joy. Sunflower's sobs pierced their laughter as she wiped the tears from her beautiful face.

They walked as a group to the base of the mural, some holding hands and some holding cigars. The sun was still shining as a slight breeze blew across from the east. The smoke from the funeral pyres gave an illusion of fog dancing in the wind, and it made the Californians feel at home despite being in Oregon.

Char smiled at the mural and walked towards a burning pile of vines as she slowly opened the urn. Her hands were trembling as Cherise's ashes began to rise from the vase. They bounced on the currents of warm air from the fires, swirling first and then gently rising and gaining speed as they climbed into the sky. Everyone was crying as they watched the eerie scene. Jack couldn't help but think of a snow-globe as the ashes danced around Char like fairies in a jar. He watched quietly as Cherise continued her quest for the source of her happiness.

🍇 🍇 🍇

32

Jack smothered salsa on another bite of his taco as he watched the dogs wrestle on the lawn. He had about 20 hours of work to get done today and it was already late in the afternoon. He looked at the winery and moaned, thinking about the bottling truck that was due to arrive any minute. The next few hours were definitely going to be hell on earth. That's all there was to it. It would be six consecutive hours of frustration as another vintage found a new home one that would, hopefully, be comfortable and accommodating for many years to come. He laughed to himself for a moment, thinking about Sunflower. Are the bottles round because of an engineering coincidence, or is it because of some ancient Feng Shui master? "Hmmm," he said. "I'll have to write that one down."

Maria's car pulled up to the house just as he thought about calling her. He was pretty sure he'd left her two messages one on Tuesday and one on Thursday. He stressed-out for a moment, but then relaxed when he saw the smile on her face. She wasn't in a bad mood at all. Her long hair was bouncing as she walked up the driveway. His favorite flannel shirt wasn't quite clinging to her, but it was hanging very nicely. Apparently, she had gotten the message about helping out with the bottling run today. He was stunned at how good she looked in her work clothes. "How can I get anything done with her looking like that?" he said to himself, shaking his head. He wanted to go up and give her a hug, but he opted for the casual approach.

"You know you're probably gonna destroy those nice clothes,

don't you?" he said, watching her pet the dogs.

"I wasn't going to wear these, silly. I wanted to try out a pair of those coveralls I saw in the winery. You don't mind, do you?"

Jack blushed for a second. "Well, there's not a lot of room under a pair those things for clothes. You'll probably have to go naked underneath." He smiled and raised his eyebrows, not at all shy about his intentions.

"Oh, I planned on it," she said. "How did your weekend go, if you don't mind me asking?"

"Interesting. It was very interesting. I found out a lot about my family. How's school?"

"Almost done," she said. "How did Petal do?"

"That was the hardest part of the whole thing . . . watching her cry the whole time. She's gonna be alright, though. She can be pretty sensitive sometimes."

"Yeah, she seems like a real sweetheart."

Maria patted Vino's belly twice to signal the end of the rub, then climbed the porch steps and joined Jack at the table. She hadn't seen him in nearly a week and she wanted to tell him that she had missed him. She smiled as she sat down, flexing her lips a little to tell him how she felt but not wanting to rush things.

"I missed you," said Jack. He bent over to pet a jealous Pino, avoiding eye contact with Maria to lessen the impact of what he had said. He didn't want to seem too serious about missing her. "My Grandpa Henry could tell there was someone new in my life. He's an intuitive old fart. He called me a love-sick-puppy the first time he saw me."

"That's funny," she said. "My dad asked about you everyday." She picked up the spec sheet for the bottling run, looking for a distraction. Her palms were sweaty and her heart was beating faster. She actually felt giddy.

Jack looked at the winery in a moment of reflection, and then spoke absently. "Actually, you know what the hardest thing about this weekend was?"

"What's that?" she asked.

"Seeing my grandpa as an old man for the first time. Don't get me wrong, I know that sounds bad. But I used to see him all the time, you know, so I never noticed him getting older. He was just Grandpa. But now, after a couple of years without seeing him, well . . . I don't know. I can see it happening in my dad now and it's strange. These guys are like legends. I mean, Henry Mueller is practically a demigod in California he's always been bigger than life. And now he's just really old and slow and in pain."

Jack sighed heavily, watching with dread as the bottling truck turned into his facility. A flock of pigeons flew from the trail of dust from the truck, flapping their wings and cooing at Cornelius. Jack could hardly believe the old man's timing. He'd spent the entire weekend thinking about Cornelius every time he watched his grandpa move a little slower than he used to. He looked to see if Maria was watching as Cornelius shuffled his way up the driveway to his regular spot in the gravel. Cornelius's wrinkled hands were shaking and his blank face was pointed at the ground. He looked extremely tired. Some of the birds began to fly away as he patted at the empty pockets of his coat and wiped the imitation butter from his fingertips.

Jack and Maria were silent as they exchanged guilty glances and watched Cornelius's face as the birds flew away. Vino grew irritated and started to yap at the noisy birds. The sound of the dog's barking registered on the old man's face and he slowly looked up at the people on the porch. A spark of life flickered in his eyes and a smile crept across his face. He waved at them regally from his make-believe carriage, looking deep into their eyes. He suddenly looked young. The skin on his forehead tightened and his eyebrows became taunt. He looked like a proctor during a final exam. He slowly raised his hand and pointed at the two of them. The rhythmic spasms in his arm caused his finger to bounce back and forth between Jack and Maria. His eyes locked on the girl and his hand stopped shaking. He took a deep breath and smiled like a man who'd just found his car in a large parking lot after hours of searching. "Maria?" he

[233]

asked.

Maria's mouth dropped open as she jumped up from the table. "Grandpa!" she exclaimed, running towards Cornelius. Before she'd closed the gap between them, the emotions dropped from his face like a garage door closing unexpectedly. He made his familiar turn towards the tavern and cursed at the birds, forgetting the people behind him. "Grandpa, wait!" Maria stopped at his spot in the gravel and watched him walk away. She wanted to chase him but she knew it was useless. He was gone. She slowly turned towards Jack, looking at the ground. She knew she had a lot of explaining to do.

"I'm not a bad person, Jack. Really, I'm not. I know what you must be thinking. I'm sorry I didn't tell you he was my grandfather. It's just been so painful for so long."

Jack sat there quietly, feeling like a jerk for talking about his grandpa getting old. He watched Cornelius walk across the street. The old man's hand was shaking at the birds. "You're Cornelius's granddaughter?"

Maria nodded her head and sat down in the gravel. The dogs could tell she was sad and they joined her immediately, casually plopping their heads in her lap. "It's been so horrible, Jack. He forgets to eat. He's wasting away to nothing. I'm the one who puts the croutons in his pockets. They're not for the birds, they're for him."

They sat in silence for a long time. Jack thought about Henry while Maria scratched the dogs ears. Cornelius walked down the road. It took a horn blast from the bottling truck to shake them from their thoughts. "I have to go," said Jack. "Do you still want to work?"

"Yeah, that'll be a good distraction." She looked at Jack and smiled, thinking about the day they'd met here in the vineyard. "Hey, Jack, do you remember when these clowns trapped me in the creek?"

"Yeah," he said, laughing at the dogs. "Bad dogs!" He pointed at them and laughed. Neither one of them bothered to look up at

Jack from Maria's lap.

"Well," said Maria, "most of that creek is mine, not your's. Cornelius Mantel still owns most of the county. I've been studying the frogs to find out what I should do with that land."

Jack was stunned. He thought about her sitting in the creek cold, wet, and sexy. Then he smiled, realizing why she was so casual about his money and the land the whole time. Compared to her, he was a mere peasant. He imagined Sunflower twirling towards Maria's land across the creek, and thought about her constant nagging to plant grapes on the steep eastern slope next door. "What are you going to do with the land?" he asked, cringing as the truck's horn sounded again.

"I don't know yet," she said. She climbed to her feet, wiping the dogs' drool from her pants. "Got any ideas?"

"Well," he chuckled, "let me tell you about Sunflower's daydream."

PETAL'S NOTES

Acid: The yang of wine. Absolutely fundamental. Must be balanced with fruit. Contributes more than anything else to the wine's finish.

Acidic: Excessive yang. Too heavy on the testosterone:-)

Aeration: Casual introduction of air during processing. Doesn't hurt a thing, actually helps. Splash racking through a spaghetti strainer is another thing, however.

Aging: Duh. Even if you know the alcohol, pH, and free sulfur you still don't know a thing. High amounts of tannin and astringency will indicate some aging potential, but I like to drink 'em young anyway - yum. Every young wine has the perfect cheese just waiting out there somewhere: Go find it!

Alcohol: Directly related to the sugar level at harvest. Usually, 55% of the sugar in the grapes will be converted to booze by those little horndogs we call yeast.

Alcohol by volume: Keep it around twelve to thirteen and everything tastes fine around here. I like some of the rieslings at about ten, though. Who needs to get drunk off of one glass of wine (Jack).

Alter wine: Saved the grape and wine industry during Prohibition. Religious freedom for all - I'll have a scotch, thank you.

Amelioration: Addition of extra stuff during processing, including sugar, acid, sulfur, or whatever.

Amino acids: The stuff. None of this could happen without these proteins. They provide the nutrients for the yeasts during the orgy.

Anthocyanins: The red coloring agent or pigment found in the grape skins.

Aperitif: The starter beverage. In Oregon, try a dry riesling instead of a sparkling wine. Works for me - try it with wasabi.

Appearance: The visual indicator of a wines quality. Clarity, brilliance, deposits or sediment (except in wasabi riesling).

Appellation d'origine contrôlée (AOC): Snob wine usually says this on the label. Their expensive and worth every penny.

Appellation of origin: Means from HERE. The growing

[237]

region.

Aroma: Used to describe the fruity smell of young wines.

Aromatic: Use this term if there is a lot of something, like spice or berry.

Astringent: The dryness felt on the top of the palate caused by tannin. Youthful wines worth a darn.

Attack: The initial hit on the palate. The start v.s. the finish.

Baked: The wine smells cooked or hot. Sometimes from a warmer region. Sherries or Port can smell baked too.

Balance: A very serious term.   Should be used very carefully because so many people are comfortable with it. Color, body, acid, fruit, and sweetness are all implied when it is used. Should really just refer to sugar/acid ratio, though.

Balling: The sugar level or brix.

Barrel-fermented: There are many places to ferment wine. Tanks and vessels can be plastic, steel, ceramic, or whatever is available.   They should, however, always be round to maintain a positive energy flow through the wine. Certain types of wood can enhance or destroy a wines

[238]

personality or terroir.

Beaujolais: A region in France known for its light and fruity wines.

Beerenauslese: Selected grapes. A German term.

Bench-grafted: Attaching vines to rootstock.

Bentonite: A clay used to clarify wines.

Berries: Very common aroma in pinot noir.

Big: Refers to the weight of the wine on the palate. Related to alcohol.

Bitter: Can be a good quality when balanced with fruit. Usually caused by the stems and the seeds.

Blend: Mixing varieties and vintages to achieve a better overall product. Includes mixing vineyards or regions of the same grapes, too.

Body: Another reference to alcohol. More booze more body.

Bone dry: Fermented all the way down - barely a trace of fermentable sugars remain.

Bordeaux: Home to cabernet, merlot, cabernet franc, and many other of the world's finest grapes. Sauvignon blanc, too; if you're into whites.

Botrytis: The god of rot. Mold that can mean money or trouble depending on your marketing department. This critter drinks the water in the grapes and leaves a high sugar content behind.

Bottle sickness: Some wines will change dramatically after being bottled. They usually return to normal after a few weeks, but the psychological damage to the winemaker may already be done.

Bouquet: Applies to older wines only. If you use this term for a wine that's under ten years old you're an idiot. (Unless it's a Northwest wine:-o)

Boutique wineries: Perhaps the best place to have a picnic on the planet   try it sometime.

Brandy: Distilled white wine. Requires high acid grapes. Oregon's future?

Bright: Very clear wine.

VARIETAL TENDENCIES

Brilliant: Hidden power source. Vibrant clarity with no floaties.

Brix: Sugar level in the grape. Determines the final alcohol level and thus body, depth, and size of wine.

Browning: Literal. The wine is perhaps reaching the end. Some old reds can appear brown and lifeless but still be really amazing and enjoyable.

Brut: Very dry.

Bulk process: A method of producing affordable sparkling wine. The bubbles are artificially injected into a still wine.

Bulk wine: Huh?

Bung: Shut up, Beavis. A wood or synthetic stopper used to seal a tank or barrel.

Bung hole: Knock it off! It's the opening in a wine barrel and that's all.

Burgundy: An actual place - not just supermarket swill. The former home of the world's finest pinot noirs.

Buttery: Literal. Mostly California chards, so far.

Candle: A procedure used in decanting. Slowly pour the wine into the flask over the candle so you can see the sediment work its way up the bottle and into your glass. Whoa! stop pouring you slob.

Cane: Sturdy new wood growing from the original vine.

Canopy: Describes the row of vines. The leaves, grapes, shoots, and vines.

Cap: A seal that forms on top of fermenting red wine comprised of skins, stems, and grapes.. It needs to be punched down with a stick or tapeball bat to allow the yeasts to breathe and release excessive heat.

Caramel: Can be caused by too much heat or sometimes the barrel. In small amounts it can be very nice.

Carbon dioxide: A by-product of fermentation. Yeasts consume sugar and create carbon dioxide and ethanol.

Carbonic maceration: A method of fermenting grapes. The grapes are sealed in a container (like an incubator) and their own weight, and gasses (carbon dioxide) create pressure and break them down. The resulting wines are light and fruity with low tannin. Also a very short life span and distinctive nose.

[242]

VARIETAL TENDENCIES

Chablis: Yes, an actual place not a generic term for cheap white wine. Some of the white wines from Chablis are the most expensive, wonderful wines on the planet. (Chardonnay, most often)

Chromo: A type of paper used to test a wine's acids.

Claret: The reds from Bordeaux like Jack, Skye, Merle, and others.

Complex: All my grapes yield complex wines if they're handled correctly. Dad's winery is a complex, too.

Cooper: A barrel dude.

Estate Bottled: Using only our grapes.

Firm: Putting the ball nine feet on a two footer.

Generic: Don't go there.

Legs: A moronic term to describe the alcohol sliding down the sides of a glass. Give me a break.

Médoc: The sexiest wine region in France. It just sounds yummy.

VARIETAL TENDENCIES

Meritage: The real up-and-comers of American wine. Bordeaux meets Napa.

Must: All the goo in the tank before it's been fermented.

pH: Acid measurement. A serious guideline throughout the production process. A lot of things do or do not happen based on the pH. Should always be between 3.0 and 3.7 (max).

Racking: The dirtiest job around. That's why it's Jacks:-) Moving wine off its sediment from one container to another to help clarification, leaving an incredibly dirty tank behind that needs to be cleaned immediately.

Spag: The gooey purple stuff left in the tank after racking. Dead yeast, skins, seeds, ect.

Tannin Ink: The paint made by Shawna Caldwell from the spag after racking. It was used to make the lithograph of the fish and wine bottle on the cover of this book.

Titratable Acidity: A measure of tartaric acid. The other goal of a good grapegrower. Needs to be in a certain range (6.0 - 9.0 g/l) for Dad to make a quality wine.

•Juanita's Carnitas•

CARNITAS:

1 teaspoon salt

2 teaspoons ground cumin

2 teaspoons chili powder

2 teaspoons oregano

2 teaspoons garlic powder

2 teaspoons onion powder

2 pounds boneless pork roast,
   cut into 6-8 chunks

2 tablespoons olive oil

1 onion, quartered

2 cloves garlic, crushed

3 tablespoons orange juice

2 tablespoons tequila

SALSA VERDE:

2 pounds tomatillas

2 Vidalia onions

3 cloves garlic, minced

1/2 teaspoon salt

2 jalepeño peppers, veins and
seeds removed

3 tablespoons fresh lime juice

4 tablespoons fresh cilantro,
packed

Combine the salt and spices in a small bowl. Rub the spice mix into all sides of the meat. Let the meat sit for 1 hour and absorb the spices.

Heat the oil in a large, Dutch oven. Brown the meat in the oil, turning until lightly browned on all sides but not cooked through. Add the onion, garlic, and enough water to cover the meat. Bring water to a boil, reduce heat and simmer, covered, 1 1/2 hours.

Preheat oven to 350°F. Drain all but about 1/2 cup broth. Put the pork, the reserved 1/2 cup of broth, orange juice and tequila in the oven. Bake for 45 minutes. Remove from the oven and let cool slightly. Shred meat with a fork. Serve with warm tortillas, Salsa Verde, radishes, cabbage, and wedges of lime.

•Anthony's Salmon•

Blackened Salmon with Honey Mustard Sauce

2 tablespoons chili powder

1 tablespoon salt

1 tablespoon sugar

1 tablespoon onion powder

1 tablespoon garlic powder

2 teaspoons ground cumin

1/8 teaspoon cayenne

1/4 teaspoon fresh ground pepper

4 6-ounce salmon fillets, pinbones removed

2 tablespoons olive oil

3 tablespoons Dijon mustard

1 tablespoon honey

1 tablespoon mayonnaise

Mix first eight ingredients together. Rub dry spice mixture into salmon and allow to stand at room temperature for 1 hour to absorb flavors.

Heat oil in skillet over medium-high heat. Sear salmon fillets on all sides until well browned. Reduce heat to medium and continue cooking until salmon is slightly firm to the touch, about 7 to 15 minutes, depending on the thickness of the fillets and the desired doneness. Do not overcook. Transfer salmon to plates and let stand for 5 minutes.

Meanwhile, blend the mustard, honey and mayonnaise. Garnish the salmon with the sauce and serve.

Serves 4.

•Bennett's Bouillabaisse•

3 leeks, white and pale green
    parts only, sliced
3 celery ribs, chopped
2 fennel bulbs (1 1/2 pounds), sliced
1 large sweet onion, chopped
3/4 cup olive oil
8 cups fish stock,
    available at specialty stores
1 cup dry white wine
6 garlic cloves, minced
4 bay leaves
2 28-ounce cans stewed tomatoes,
    drained and coarsely chopped

3 tablespoons tomato paste
3/4 cup chopped fresh parsley leaves
1 teaspoon salt, or to taste
1 teaspoon freshly ground pepper,
    or to taste
1 1/2 pounds firm white fish fillets
    (halibut, cod or orange roughy)
two 1 1/2 pound lobsters, live
1 1/2 pounds mussels, debearded and
    scrubbed well
1 1/2 pounds littleneck clams

In a large, heavy-duty kettle, heat olive oil over medium heat. Add leeks, celery, fennel, and onion and saute until softened, about 10 minutes. Add fish stock, wine, garlic, bay leaves, stewed tomatoes, tomato paste, parsley, salt and pepper. Bring to a boil, then reduce heat, cover, and allow mixture to simmer for 45 minutes. Pour mixture through a strainer into a large bowl. Discard vegetables.

Return liquid to the kettle and bring to a simmer. Add white fish and simmer until opaque in appearance and cooked through, about 10-12 minutes. Remove fish from liquid with a slotted spoon and place in serving platter. Cover platter with foil to keep warm. Add lobsters to broth, cover and cook for 10-12 minutes. Transfer lobsters to serving platter and recover with foil. Place mussels and clams in broth, cover and simmer for 4 minutes, or until most of the shells have opened. Remove with a slotted spoon and place on serving platter, discarding any that did not open. Pour broth over seafood and serve with baguettes and crostinis.

Serves 4.

•Sunflower's Skewers•

Bay Scallops and Mandarin Orange Skewers

1/4 cup dry Riesling

1/4 cup orange juice

2 teaspoons grated orange rind

2 teaspoons soy sauce

1 garlic clove, minced

1/2 teaspoon fresh ginger, minced

1 teaspoon honey, divided

1 teaspoon Dijon mustard, divided

1 pound bay scallops

2 teaspoons sesame oil or peanut oil

1/4 cup mayonnaise

• Juice from 1/4 lime

• Horseradish, to taste

1 can (11 oz.) mandarin oranges, drained

In a medium-sized bowl, combine the dry Riesling, orange juice, orange rind, soy sauce, garlic, ginger, 1/2 teaspoon honey and 1/2 teaspoon of the mustard. Add the scallops and toss to coat. Refrigerate, covered, for 2 hours or overnight.

Preheat the barbecue. Drain the scallops, reserving some of the liquid for basting. In a small bowl, toss the scallops with the oil. Place the scallops in a small boat made out of heavy-duty aluminum foil. Add a small amount of the reserved liquid and place foil packet on grill. Cook for 6 to 8 minutes or until scallops are firm. Drain.

Meanwhile, in a small bowl, whisk the mayonnaise with the remaining 1/2 teaspoons each of honey and mustard, lime juice and a touch of horseradish; transfer to a serving dish.

Arrange 2 bay scallops alternately with 2 mandarin orange segments on wooden skewers until all the scallops and orange segments are used. Arrange the skewers around a platter and serve with the seasoned mayonnaise in the center for dipping.

Serves 4.

•Corrina's Gnocchi•

Baked Potato Gnocchi with Fontina Cheese

2 pounds baking potatoes

1 teaspoon salt

1/4 teaspoon nutmeg

2 eggs, lightly beaten

2 cups all-purpose flour

1/2 cup butter, melted

6 ounces Fontina cheese, thinly sliced

Steam potatoes over simmering water until very tender, about 35-40 minutes. Let potatoes cool.

Peel the potatoes and press through a food mill, or use the small grate blade of a food processor. Transfer to a large bowl and let cool completely. Stir in the salt and nutmeg. Add the eggs. Stir until combined. Gradually stir in about half of the flour, or until the mixture becomes stiff. Transfer the mixture to a lightly floured pastry board. Knead in the remaining flour, or until the dour is no longer sticky.

Line baking sheet with wax paper and lightly dust with flour. Working in batches with floured hands, roll about 1/4 cup of dough into a 12-inch long rope. Cut rope into 3/4 inch pieces. Roll each piece of dough down the tines of a floured fork, pressing lightly so the tines leave ridges. Set the gnocchi on the prepared baking sheets and continue with the rest of the dough.

Preheat of oven to 400°F. Butter a 13- x 9-inch baking dish.

Bring a pot of salted water to a boil. Add part of the gnocchi, several at a time, and simmer until they float to the surface. Using a slotted spoon, transfer floating gnocchi to prepared baking dish. Repeat until all gnocchi has been cooked.

Drizzle melted butter over gnocchi and toss to coat. Top with slices of Fontina cheese. Bake in preheated oven until cheese is bubbly and golden, and the gnocchi is hot, about 10 minutes.

Serves 4 .

•Rose's Zabaglione•

8 egg yolks
1/2 cup sugar
1 cup Marsala or white wine
1/2 teaspoon nutmeg

Combine all ingredients in top of a double broiler; whisk until well blended. Continue to beat over boiling water, being careful that the water does not touch the bottom of the top pan. Continue beating until the pudding is thick and light.

Serves 4.

• Antonio's Bagna Cauda •

Garlic and Anchovy Dipping Sauce

1 cup butter

1/3 cup olive oil

6 cloves garlic, minced

7 anchovy fillets, minced

• salt

1 white truffle, thinly sliced

Accompaniments: red bell peppers, artichokes, celery and assorted bread

Heat the butter in heavy pan. Saute the garlic, being careful not to let the garlic brown. Reduce the heat to low and add the anchovies. Continue to cook, stirring continually, until the anchovies turn into a paste. Season with salt, and add the white truffle.

Serve sauce hot with assorted vegetables and bread.

Serves 4 to 6 as an appetizer.

•Cherise's Chocolate•

Mocha Mousse on Marbleized Chocolate Wafers

CHOCOLATE WAFERS:

12 ounces white chocolate

12 ounces bittersweet or semi-sweet chocolate

MOCHA MOUSSE:

12 ounces bittersweet or semi-sweet chocolate

2 cups heavy whipping cream

1 tablespoons instant espresso powder

1 1/2 tablespoons Dutch processed cocoa, sifted

For the wafers, line the back of a 12- by 16-inch baking sheet with foil. Set aside. Prepare two double boilers,being careful that simmering water does not touch the bottom of the top pan. Alternately, place two bowls on top of two pans of simmering water. Melt the white chocolate and the dark chocolate separately, stirring constantly. Remove from heat. Beginning with the white chocolate, spread around the foil as if it were an abstract painting. (Jackson Pollack comes to mind.) Repeat with dark chocolate. Using the back of a spatula, level the chocolates, being sure to fill any holes. Allow to set up, but not become too hard. Using a long knife, cut into 2-inch squares. Allow chocolate to harden completely before removing from foil. The side next to the foil will be shiny and beautifully marbleized.

For the mousse, place chocolate in a large bowl. Bring 3/4 cup heavy whipping cream to a boil; pour over chocolate and whisk until all the chocolate is melted. Add espresso powder and blend. Set aside to cool.

Using an electric mixer, beat the remaining 1 1/4 cup cream in a chilled bowl until it forms stiff peaks. Fold into chocolate mixture. Add cocoa and stir until thoroughly blended. Chill until ready to assemble. Mousse can be made a day ahead.

To assemble, fit a #32 star tip into a decorator's bag a secure with coupler. Fill bag with mousse and pipe onto the marbleized side of the wafers. Garnish with fresh mint, if desired.

Makes 48 bite-sized desserts.

•Jack's Rack•

Dijon Crusted Rack of Lamb with Cabernet Reduction

CABERNET REDUCTION (not seduction):

2 tablespoons olive oil

1 medium-sized onion, chopped

1 carrot, chopped

1 stalk celery, chopped

4 garlic cloves, minced

2 teaspoons whole black peppercorn

2 tablespoons chopped fresh rosemary

1 tablespoon fresh thyme

2 cups cabernet sauvignon

2 cups beef stock

2 tablespoons tomato paste

1 tablespoon Dijon mustard

• salt and fresh ground pepper, to taste

LAMB:

2 tablespoons olive oil

2 frenched racks of lamb, each
   about 1 1/2 pounds
   (available by request
   from butcher)

1/2 cup Dijon mustard

3 tablespoons honey

3 garlic cloves, minced

For the sauce, heat olive oil in a large, heavy pan over medium heat. Saute the onion, carrot and celery until soft, about 5 minutes. Add the garlic, peppercorn, rosemary and thyme and continue to saute for another 5 minutes. Add the wine and simmer until reduced by about about half, about 35 minutes. Add beef stock, tomato paste, and 1 tablespoon mustard and continue simmering until reduced by about two-thirds. Pour sauce through a sieve into a bowl, pressing on solids, and season with salt and pepper. Keep warm.

Preheat oven to 400° F.

Heat olive oil in heavy pan over medium-high heat. Sear racks of lamb on all sides, about 2 minutes on each side. Transfer racks, meat sides up, to a shallow baking pan. Roast in middle of oven for 10 minutes. Meanwhile, blend together 1/2 cup Dijon mustard, honey and garlic cloves. Brush generous amount on lamb and continue roasting for 5 to 10 minutes, or until meat thermometer registers 130°F for medium rare. Transfer lamb to cutting board and let stand for 10 minutes. (This is crucial!).

Cut lamb racks in half or into individual chops; serve with warm Cabernet Reduction Sauce.

Serves 4.

VARIETAL TENDENCIES

Need some more copies of Varietal Tendencies?

Please send_____copy/copies at $19.95 each

Name_____

Address_____

City_____State_____Zip_____

Phone_____

email_____
Shipping
Book Rate: $3.00 first book, and $1.00 for each additional.

(allow 4 weeks for delivery at book shipping rate)

Please make checks payable to:

Tannin Ink

and mail to 2375 Montello, Hood River, Or 97031

Book total: $_____

Shipping: $_____

Total enclosed $_____

or call
(541) 386-7050
and order by credit card

[254]

WINE NOTES

WINE NOTES

WINE NOTES

WINE NOTES

WINE NOTES

WINE NOTES

WINE NOTES

WINE NOTES

WINE NOTES

WINE NOTES